YNDRASTA
THE CELESTIAL SPEAR

Other great stories from Warhammer Age of Sigmar

HAMMERS OF SIGMAR: FIRST FORGED
A novel by Richard Strachan

WAR FOR THE MORTAL REALMS
Various authors
An omnibus edition of the novels
The Gates of Azyr, Soul Wars and *Dominion*

CALLIS & TOLL
A novel by David Annandale

• VEN DENST •
HALLOWED GROUND
TEMPLE OF SILENCE
Richard Strachan

THE HOLLOW KING
A Cado Ezechiar novel by John French

THE LAST VOLARI
A Nyssa Volari novel by Gary Kloster

BLACKTALON
A Neave Blacktalon novel by Liane Merciel

• DREKKI FLYNT •
THE ARKANAUT'S OATH
THE GHOSTS OF BARAK-MINOZ
Guy Haley

• GOTREK GURNISSON •
GHOULSLAYER
GITSLAYER
SOULSLAYER
Darius Hinks

BLIGHTSLAYER
Richard Strachan

REALMSLAYER: LEGEND OF THE DOOMSEEKER
David Guymer

GODEATER'S SON
A Heldanarr Godeater novel by Noah Van Nguyen

BAD LOON RISING
A Zograt & Skrog novel by Andy Clark

YNDRASTA
THE CELESTIAL SPEAR

NOAH VAN NGUYEN

BLACK LIBRARY

A BLACK LIBRARY PUBLICATION

First published in 2023.
This edition published in Great Britain in 2024 by
Black Library, Games Workshop Ltd., Willow Road,
Nottingham, NG7 2WS, UK.

Represented by: Games Workshop Limited – Irish branch,
Unit 3, Lower Liffey Street, Dublin 1,
D01 K199, Ireland.

10 9 8 7 6 5 4 3 2 1

Produced by Games Workshop in Nottingham.
Cover illustration by Robson Michel.

A CIP record for this book is available from the British Library.

ISBN 13: 978-1-80407-944-7

See Black Library on the internet at

blacklibrary.com

Find out more about Games Workshop
and the worlds of Warhammer at

games-workshop.com

Printed and bound in the UK.

To my mother, Suzanne, who taught me what it means to be good.

The Mortal Realms have been despoiled. Ravaged by the followers of the Chaos Gods, they stand on the brink of utter destruction.

The fortress-cities of Sigmar are islands of light in a sea of darkness. Constantly besieged, their walls are assailed by maniacal hordes and monstrous beasts. The bones of good men are littered thick outside the gates. These bulwarks of Order are embattled within as well as without, for the lure of Chaos beguiles the citizens with promises of power.

Still the champions of Order fight on. At the break of dawn, the Crusader's Bell rings and a new expedition departs. Storm-forged knights march shoulder to shoulder with resolute militia, stoic duardin and slender aelves. Bedecked in the splendour of war, the Dawnbringer Crusades venture out to found civilisations anew. These grim pioneers take with them the fires of hope. Yet they go forth into a hellish wasteland.

Out in the wilds, hardy colonists restore order to a crumbling world. Haunted eyes scan the horizon for tyrannical reavers as they build upon the bones of ancient empires, eking out a meagre existence from cursed soil and ice-cold seas. By their valour, the fate of the Mortal Realms will be decided.

The ravening terrors that prey upon these settlers take a thousand forms. Cannibal barbarians and deranged murderers crawl from hidden lairs. Martial hosts clad in black steel march from skull-strewn castles. The savage hordes of Destruction batter the frontier towns until no stone stands atop another. In the dead of night come howling throngs of the undead, hungry to feast upon the living.

Against such foes, courage is the truest defence and the most effective weapon. It is something that Sigmar's chosen do not lack. But they are not always strong enough to prevail, and even in victory, each new battle saps their souls a little more.

This is the time of turmoil. This is the era of war.

This is the Age of Sigmar.

SLAYER

I am incapable of failure. I knew it from the moment of my great awakening, when the basso thunder of my maker-father's voice rumbled in my ears.

As the fires of Sigmar's forge cooled, the God-King breathed new life into my tempered flesh. For twelve seconds – a span of time which felt as long as the eternity I have come to know – Sigmar told me who I was, and who I would become.

You are my perfect daughter. You, who united the free peoples of Ghur against Chaos…

When the daemon hordes marched to destroy you, you resisted…

You struck at Doombreed, the king of daemons, and I heard you call my name…

That you, my perfect daughter, may hear me call yours…

Yndrasta. My Celestial Spear.

Light became my world, and Sigmar bestowed to me Thengavar. The cold spear's hungering metal pulsed with the power of Azyr.

Then Sigmar gifted me a more poignant token – a simple charm, a hunter's totem. It was a shard of chitin wrapped in cord, and its purpose was beyond my ken.

I accepted my maker-father's gifts with a lowered head. Eager to please my God-King, I uttered my first words. 'Father. What must I do?'

Sigmar's answer was lightning in my heart, an earthquake in my soul.

KILL.

In the woe-times, mortals look to their stories for solace.

I am not mortal, and I have no stories. My only solace is my maker-father's satisfaction, the fulfilment of my purpose. Not the myths of shamans, nor the chanted invocations of my name as Sigmaron's armies prepare for war. Not the perked ears and whimpered trepidations of beasts which have sensed the dreaded omens of my hunt.

Only the kill soothes the storm in my soul. Only the kill proves I am the daughter Sigmar made me to be. Where Sigmar's enemies roam, I hunt, then annihilate. This quest serves Sigmar's sacred ends. The God-King protects those mortals who whisper his name at darkened altars in the scattered realms.

In the palace-city of Sigmaron, beneath mighty towers and ivory walls, a blessed chamber lies in an ancient keep. Timeless power and the whispering of stars fill this hall. Here the God-King holds his holy court. He reigns over worlds from a sublime throne on a dais of ageless marble. This immutable stone shelf is a perfect metaphor, for Sigmar's kingdom is the foundation of order in the realms. His court has only ever known the tread of the worthy.

In the woe-times, as mortals look to their legends for comfort, I prove my worth. I frequent my maker-father's court, and upon the blessed dais at his feet, I lay the conquered crowns of my vanquished prey. Crowns not of gems and radiant metal, but skull and bleeding flesh torn from the necks of my quarry: Sigmar's foes.

These trophies are my tribute to Sigmar's glory. But too, I carry them with me. No mark in creation is more indelible than that of another being's extinction upon one's soul.

None understand me better than the creatures I have destroyed. The transcendent moment of their evisceration joins us in the perfection of my purpose. Through them – however briefly – I am no longer alone.

I am Yndrasta. In the woe-times, I bring the woe.

My wings carry me soundlessly to the rolling deck of a carrack. The sunless sky and oceanic horizon reflect the emptiness in my heart, a blank space that expands across my universe. Only the kill can fill it, yet this rootless feeling will not end soon. The quarry I have long sought – the kraken-god of Izalend – has escaped once again.

'Lord-Celestant,' I say. 'Send word to your fleet captains. Old Jasper May has slipped away, the coward. We resume pursuit.'

Arktaris Soul-Tithed, the Knight Excelsior to whom I speak, regards me in cold silence. The ship's planks creak beneath his motionless mass. He is an armoured titan, like all Stormcast Eternals, yet his breath of thoughtful hesitation ambushes me. Other Stormcasts would answer my command with all the flash of faith's fire. Arktaris burns his like a candle, as if he can carry it farther that way.

Behind the flawless white war-mask of his helmet, his eyes travel to Thengavar's humming blade. 'You are late, my lady huntress. Much has occurred in your absence.'

The carrack's mortals avert their gazes and make the sign of the hammer. Arktaris' Stormcasts – giants hailing from the Ruthless Tithe Chamber of the Knights Excelsior Stormhost – meet my edged glare, then look away. The Vigilors' emptied quivers catch my eyes. Dents and scratches mar the Stormcasts' snow-white battle armour. In the sea, pillars of smoke rise from other vessels in Arktaris' squadron. The gutted wreckage of six ruined ships founders in the rippling waves. In those glacial waters, mortal mariners flail and wail for rescue, struggling not to drown.

I return my empty gaze to Arktaris. 'Send word. We resume pursuit.'

When Arktaris finally answers, his inflection is not that of the Reforged killer I have come to respect, but that of an apostate, a penitent – of one who doubts.

'Yndrasta,' he says, as if wary of supplying my name. 'We have assisted your hunt for this mythic kraken for one reason alone – to see evil eradicated from the realm of Ghur. My chamber did not embark upon this quest for...' He casts out his armoured hand to the bloodied deck. 'For this.'

I face him fully. 'For what?'

'Pride.' He spits out the word. 'But you knew that. You abandoned our fleet as soon as we sighted your quarry. Just as the orruk junk-fleet closed in.'

'Do not offend your own chamber's honour. Last I checked, a rabble of scurvy orruks on metal rafts were no match for the Knights Excelsior.'

'You speak true. Those scurvy orruks and their metal rafts outnumbered my White Omen Fleet six to one, but they were no match. We bled to make it so, my lady huntress. All as you pursued your prize. For your obsession, half of the White Omen now lies vanquished beneath the waves of Glacier's End.'

I slam Thengavar into the carrack's deck. Loose timbers rattle in the ship. The force of the blow ripples through the ocean, and the splintered topsail of a damaged mast cracks and gives. Sailors dive for cover as it falls like a branch from a tree and smashes into the waves.

'Perhaps you would prefer I hold your hand,' I say. 'If the lives of your Stormcasts are the price I must pay for the kraken's death, that is Sigmar's will. Their time on the Anvil shall come.'

Arktaris' heavy sigh rattles the stern Mask Impassive of his metal helm. 'You speak as if you have never been Reforged. As if you have never endured the hammer's strike.'

'Spare me your quibbles. If you require mariners or ships, send word to Izalend. Surely their whalers and corsairs will eagerly join your White Omen. But if you require heart, Arktaris – look within.' I gesture. 'Is this not the White Omen Fleet?'

'It is.'

'Are you not Knights Excelsior?'

'We are.'

'And are you not inured to the terrible cost of your duty?'

'We are.'

'Then look the part. I have come to expect such putrid protestations from the Hallowed Knights, Arktaris, but not from you.'

He lifts his dark gaze. 'And what of the Astral Templars?'

I wince. 'What of them?'

'Even your favoured beast-hunters abandoned this quest. Three weeks ago they saw what I see now. Your fixation on the kraken defies reason. This is madness. This is obsession.'

In the insolence of Arktaris' words, I detect a changing wind. I cast my glance about the rocking carracks. Broken harpoons lie scattered on the deck. Bent cutlasses are stuck in blood-spattered masts. Wounded mariners shiver in damp blankets, and vapour billows from their blue lips and chattering teeth. What few able-bodied sailors remain mend damaged sails or patch the hull with tar and timber. The ship's wounded bosun helps a pair of cabin children roll a stinking orruk carcass over a broken gunwale, into the sea.

'You will quit my quest. You will abandon my hunt.' My eyes rise. 'You came to this decision in my absence?'

Arktaris nods the way another might give the order to hang a man. His knights' silence tells me he is not alone in his objections.

I scoff. 'Thus is revealed the true quality of the Knights Excelsior.'

'Do not doubt our quality. All our means serve Sigmar's ends. I know the duty of which you speak, Yndrasta. And we do not doubt.' He calms. 'But we are unlike you. We are pieces of one whole. One chamber, and one Stormhost. You are not, huntress. You were forged alone. I know in the furnace of my soul, even the Shining Lord would not have sacrificed so many of our brethren for the vanity you now–'

'*Vanity?*' I lurch forward. Lightning arcs along Thengavar's blessed length. 'Vanity, Arktaris?'

Alarm flashes through the other Stormcasts. One reaches for her weapons. This is a well-honed reaction, more instinctive than deliberate. Stormcast Eternals are children of Sigmar one and all. We would never draw our blades against our own.

But perhaps, deep in their bellies, Arktaris' words strike a chord. I am nothing like them.

'Vanity.' I sigh through gritted teeth. 'I thought you knew better. You are as blind as Joras and his Astral Templars were.'

Arktaris' gaze retreats to the restless waves. Rescue pinnaces carve through the sea to save the living and recover the dead. On another carrack, insurgent flames finally reach the masts. They devour the sails and rigging with Ghur's own hunger.

'I remember the first time a mortal called me heartless,' Arktaris intones. 'I thought she was blind not to understand the terrible necessity of our duty, our ruthlessness.' The doomed vessel's mariners leap into frigid waters, screaming as they abandon ship. Another rescue pinnace carves towards them.

Arktaris looks at me. 'But I think I know what she meant, now. You, my lady huntress, are colder than the void.'

Arktaris' words echo through me. There is nothing they can catch onto. Only the murder of monsters has ever stirred me – only the *justice* of ending their existence. The kill is a sacred act, a meditation on my faith in Sigmar. More than that, it is a moment and place forever fixed in the rootless temple of my mind. To live forever is to see one's memories eroded by the passage of aeons. With one's memories go the sediments of their personality, until nothing remains.

But in my heart, the glorious moments of my kills are ineradicable, firmer than the foundations of the realms. I will never forget them. Alone they ground me. They remind me I am anyone at all.

I pay Arktaris a disconsolate frown. 'I will speak to Sigmar of this.'

For all his stoicism, Arktaris seems relieved. 'If my decision dismays the God-King, I will make my case to him. I will pray for mercy in his judgement. But you, my lady huntress, are not him.'

A league above the ocean's glassy blue, I hover in the sky. My wings flex to dominate the cold air currents, to make them serve me.

The wind-filled sails of Arktaris' White Omen Fleet shrink into the soft line where the sea joins the sky. From here Excelsis' decimated armada resembles a shoal of icebergs prowling the frigid oceans of Ghur. The day we departed Excelsis, the White Omen's majesty was inarguable. Now, with its quest unfinished and its vessels entombed beneath Glacier's End, the fleet limps home in disgrace.

I am the most capable tracker in the Mortal Realms. I am a stalker, a hunter, a killer without equal. Yet the quarry which eludes me now – the so-called kraken-god of Izalend – defies the subtlest exercise of my skill. When word first reached me that Old Jasper May had reawakened from her slumber, I knew I would require help. I have tried to slay the leviathan alone before, so many times. And so many times, I have failed. Her feasting cycle, known in these parts as the Drownharrow, is brief. If she retreats into the depths of this ice-capped ocean, she will evade me for another hundred years.

I cannot fail again. I am Sigmar's perfect daughter, incapable of failure. I need this victory more than air in my wings or viscera on my blades. I *want* it, with all the fire in my soul.

A ghastly wind cuts through the gaps in my armour and chills my flesh. Every inch of me sags beneath the enervating weight of my mood. How long have I sought the kraken's death? How many times has she eluded Thengavar's steel? How many ages have I spent in this fruitless pursuit, repeated many times over?

My bleak gaze falls to the worn cord bound around my vambrace. An amber chitin charm hangs from the braided hair. Of the gifts Sigmar bestowed me, Thengavar's purpose was never subtle. This ancient totem could not be more mysterious. It is an unenchanted trinket, the merest of charms. I know not its purpose, nor origin.

In one way, it feels more powerful than Thengavar. When I behold it, the aerial frisk of young gulls over the sea cracks my lips into a smile. The salty spray of foaming waves makes me breathe deeper and close my eyes. I look upon this totem, and no matter what the awe-stricken hearts of mortals might show them when their primitive eyes behold me, I almost feel... whole.

I enclose the chitin totem in my grip. My existence exceeds mortal reckoning. I am more than human, more than even Stormcast. I am the hateful union of Sigmar's benevolence and barbarity, remade on the burning metal of his anvil. He claimed I was once a leader. But as Arktaris' wounded ships limp towards the horizon, I cannot understand how. I have never inspired others – I have only ever done as bidden. Now, against all odds, I must do it again. *Kill...*

I tarry no more, swooping towards the sea. Once I was slain; now *I* am the slayer.

Now I am alone.

CHAPTER ONE

'Sick Gumper was causing stillborns once.' Njda yanked her knife, and hot blood spurted into snow. 'Didn't know until Bavval brought the givers with torches. They found flies in his sled – three of them, fat and buzzing. I don't know how, but they'd rusted Gumper's iron. Bavval crossed his arms, said Gumper had insulted Brother. The sick man cried pus when Bavval killed those flies. That's the first time I felt the amber wind.'

More blood spattered the snow, and Njda lifted her foot. The black bilge's stink wrinkled her nose. She brushed sweat from her brow. Spruces and bare birches guarded the hill like soldiers on silent patrol. Snow stole through their branches as if the grey bands in the sky were a prison's walls to be escaped and hidden from on the earth.

Njda had bound her captive to a tree. Once the marauder quit moaning, Njda brandished her knife. 'The *noajdi* taught me to bleed the corruption before setting cultists free. That way your souls find their way where they should.'

'You dispense sweet pain.' Four iridescent eyes gleamed beneath the stitched leather of the marauder's brow. 'Join me. The Prince has need of pleasure-wrights as skilled as you. No more hurt. No more hunger. Only... *joy.*'

Njda made another cut and ignored the caterwauling that followed. 'I'm a finder. And I'm not hurt or hungry. I'm just bleeding you before you kill more of Riika-Min's herd. Then I'll set you free.'

She surveyed her handiwork. The marauder bled from two dozen wounds. Her blemished magenta flesh had paled to light violet. The erect horn that stood where her left ear might have been now sagged. But the sick grin on the cultist's lips made Njda wonder if she was doing this right.

A forked tongue flitted from the marauder's mouth. Tiny teeth lined its worm-like length. 'Not joy... You crave... *love.*'

Njda cleaned the blood from her mitten, then wiped her knife in the crook of her arm.

The cultist's ghoulish lips split her cheeks. Her crescent mouth cracked, too wide. 'You love your *family.* Your people. Your lands. Strangers you just met. You love your delicious reindeer, too. Taste their pain with me. The Prince will gift you a love you could never imagine. He will protect you from the bogcallers, as Sigmar-Stormcaller cannot.'

Crow's feet cracked the corners of Njda's eyes. She had never heard of bogcallers, and slaves to darkness didn't scare her, but the cultist's wily promise still found purchase. Njda imagined Riika-Min's *boazu* herds as they spiralled in the Sukuat's tundra. She thought of her people, the Suku, and their Izalender neighbours and their marvellous metalworks, and all the brutal wonders in the realm. She thought of her former betrothed and realised she longed for what the cultist offered.

Njda turned her knife in her hands. 'What kind of love?'

'*Glory. Lust–*'

Njda wrenched the marauder's tongue out, then severed it. She dodged a spurt of blood and tossed the flapping muscle to the snow. 'This isn't for Sigramalles Apmil,' she said. 'It's for you.'

Njda cut again and ignored the braying that followed.

After cleaning herself up, Njda waited. Corrupt blood attracted Ghur's predators the same as any other. She couldn't leave the cultist to them. If beasts devoured the marauder before the last black corruption had oozed from her veins, she'd die a damned woman. Like the cultist had said, Njda loved her lands, their purity. And abandoning anyone to Ghur didn't seem a kindness.

Wind knifed through the forest. Then the murmuring of spruce branches quietened and timber creaked. A birch with parchment bark uprooted, then wobbled uphill in a crashing path. Insects and grubs pushed from the hard humus, then squirmed and skittered through the snow. Even the wind was afraid.

Njda eased herself to the ground. Her hand clawed out and grasped her bow. She dragged it closer and stabbed her eyes at the cultist, but dread had peeled back the marauder's lids. The gelid air hadn't bothered the marauder before. Now she was shaking. She gurgled a warning from her tongueless mouth, but Njda already knew. This wasn't the so-called Prince. Fouler threats than the vague spectre of damnation haunted the coasts of Glacier's End.

Njda exhaled and slid an arrow from her quiver. Whatever was coming, it was from the sea. And Brother Bear hadn't scared it away, so it was powerful. During the Drownharrow, that could only mean one thing.

She had come.

Paralysed, Njda considered her options. She was safe here in the highlands. Ten thousand sledcrofts lay camped on the black sand shores between the wooded hills and the heady seas. They would be easier prey than her. Her *siida* numbered among them, though. Her family.

By her next breath she hurtled through the forest. She remembered the cultist and skidded to a halt, then circled back and slit her throat. As the marauder drowned in her own blood, Njda knew she had done her a kindness. In a realm as cruel as Ghur, people had nothing else.

Njda tumbled through the palisade sleds onto packed snow and plankwalks. Quiet crowds of Suku limped in the opposite direction, eerily focused in the way they got when screams and panic would attract deadlier predators. Their blue eyes met Njda's. Those who recognised her hissed for her to come with them, then fell silent as she ran on.

A hoary giver, Hari, guided a clutch of elders over smooth rocks bulging from the ground. Njda scurried beside him and jerked at the thick sleeve of his fur coat. Beads and bartered metal charms clinked on his indigo tunic as he spun.

Hari relaxed and lowered his baleen sword. 'Njda.'

'Have you seen my pa?' she asked.

'No. But your ma's looking for you.'

He nudged Njda with the elders, but she shook him off. Hari clucked and gestured to armed givers trotting up on their reindeer mounts. As Njda raced onward, she couldn't shake the thought they were forming a battle-line.

Sledcrofts creaked into glacial motion on both sides of the path. They resembled beached ships on timber skids, with scuppers for windows and canvas roofs. Suku herdsteaders goaded draught boazu from the sledcrofts' holds, then harnessed the reindeer to drag the sleds away like Izalender carriages. Others kicked out the pegs holding their homes upright. The timber landships groaned with hostility as they accepted the burden of their weight.

Snow fell in drifts and darkened the day. A team of lumbering boazu dragged a towering longsled from its lot. Njda bounded across the frozen ruts it left behind. In the blue bay, the air was still. Breakers pawed at a corpse, then seeped into coarse black sands. The sight of Gramb sprawled out dead hit Njda hard, then drifted off like a feather. Her feeble grandmother had wanted to join Gramp a long time.

Close by, her clan's sledcroft sat. Njda went inside and picked her way through. Brine dripped from shelves, and slush covered the deck. At dawn her pa had prepared for a journey to Suodji for the trade season. Where he was now – where any of her family was – she couldn't tell. But someone had come through in a rush. Their weapons were gone. The hold was empty, too.

Njda crouched through the pantry into the mudroom. She gathered a handful of scattered arrows into her quiver, then stalked back down the ramp onto the sands. She rubbed her hands and glanced at the driver's bench. She couldn't move the sled without their draught boazu. Hopefully her family had taken the reindeer, along with their weapons and metal tools. If they hadn't, that didn't matter. All they needed was each other.

The hair on Njda's neck stiffened. In the corner of her eye, Gramb had risen. The crone sipped tea from a chipped teacup. Frigid brine lapped at her gnarled feet. Despite a lifetime of Njda's knitted blankets never being warm enough – Njda *still* couldn't knit, and didn't care – Gramb seemed content. A pang of guilt rocked Njda. She'd assumed Gramb was dead. Her eye dropped to a splintered bone jutting from a bloodless break in her knobby knee. A thick, glistening rope ran from Gramb's damp white frizzle of hair to her heels. Gore and pink jelly dribbled down its length.

'I was so alone,' Gramb croaked.

Njda's stomach turned. She followed Gramb's gaze out into the surf. A dozen more Suku stood in the waist-deep waters, their hands joined. Eels teemed in the waves around them.

Njda reached out, but then her shivering hand fell back to her side. 'Gramb. We should–'

Gramb wobbled around. Fleshy orchids pulsed like anemones in her eyes. They had pushed through the back of her skull, from the rope – the *tentacle* – buried in her neck. She sipped at her broken teacup. Briny foam dribbled from her toothless gums.

'But then... you found me.'

Njda steeled her eyes. This was the Drownharrow. She drew her stubby knife, but Gramb had no blood to bleed. What would Bavval have done? This wasn't Chaos. This was worse.

The call of gulls over the surf drew Njda's gaze back to the enthralled Suku. Swaying, they staggered into the hazy bay like captive swine, and the teeming tendrils around them disappeared. It hurt to let fellow Suku be taken, but Njda could not resist the resistless. This was the Harmony of Ghur. As the Suku fed, so must others feed. Tjatsår Mai deserved to eat as much as any other.

Njda shoved her knife into its hide scabbard. She clasped her hands and bowed, then hurried the way she'd come. Gramb was good as dead. But she'd been dying twenty years, since Njda's birth to her betrothal and after. As long as Njda had lived, it had always been too late for Gramb. For the rest of Njda's family, there was still time.

The misshapen blobs of overturned longsleds resolved through the wall of falling snow. A hanging sign squealed on a broken chain. A frenzy of boazu tracks lay written in the morning powder, frozen into crust where blood had forged mud. In the whiteout, jagged, alien hills rose over a spruce glade. Njda couldn't remember them, but Riika-Min's ten thousand clans moved so often Njda couldn't recall half their grazing sites.

A handful of silhouettes prowled ahead, weapons drawn. Hari and the givers. They must have fought a hard fight, because their reindeer were all lumps in the snow, heat steaming from their massive carcasses. Hari's moan sailed from the haze. Njda could see him lying catatonic in the mud, a rangy giver crouched over him.

Njda rubbed her raw cheeks and jogged closer. She tore her pointed hood from her plaited queue. She scratched away the tingle her hood had spawned in her scalp. She didn't need the hood to tell her predators were near. Only Hari mattered – he'd taught Njda how to track as a girl.

Njda opened her mouth to speak when she realised Hari had been stripped. The warrior crouching over the naked giver dragged a wicked knife through his belly. Hari gargled as the rangy fighter ripped out a handful of ropy entrails. A scar-pocked hand with thick, yellow nails dug into his belly and cupped Hari's puddling gore. The warrior slurped. Hot crimson gruel dribbled down his jaws and dripped onto Hari's blue flesh.

Njda's gorge rose. More warriors stalked through the whiteout. Tattered furs soiled in mud draped them from their hunched heads to their ape arms. Rusted piercings studded their olive skin, which began to look less and less like war-paint. They peeled the planks off a nearby longsled. Two givers, both wounded, bellowed and sailed from the hold. The laughing raiders parried the givers' desperate blows. Four of them scampered up behind the Suku and, sniggering, chopped them down with chipped cleavers.

Njda stifled a whimper. She couldn't scour the butchery from her eyes. Hari grimaced at her, pleading and paralysed, until another foe-warrior waddled up and pulled out his arm, then lopped it off.

The hooded butcher's red eyes shot to Njda. It wasn't a *he* – it wasn't even human. Gristle hung from its jaws. Tusks stained with verdigris jutted from its greasy lips. An oily topknot dangled down its scarred porcine face onto its rusted iron gorget. The ugly cliffs of its caveman brow arched, and a panther's growl clicked in its chest.

The foe-warrior's face warped into a perfect parody of human horror. '*Hari!*' it parroted, mocking Njda. She had been screaming.

More hooded killers loped in. Heinous children scampered at their feet. No, not children – long-nosed devils with outsize heads and stringy arms that scraped the snow. Njda nocked an arrow and swivelled from foe to foe. They feigned fear, then snorted like pigs and cackled. She bellowed and loosed. Her arrow thumped into Hari's eye and erased the agony from his face.

Beyond Hari's body, the alien hills slid into the sky and toppled the nearest spruces. A storm of displaced air whipped the blizzard into a stinging gale. As the moving mountain undulated like a serpent, nests of eels erupted from blurred slits in its side. This was no wyrm. It was a tentacle, and it belonged to a kraken older than the world.

The green-skinned killers barked and snarled. Tendrils like those Njda had glimpsed teeming in the surf lanced through the snowstorm. They tore headlong into the blood-drinking raiders, hauling them from their colossal feet. Others were severed and left wriggling where the foe-warriors moved faster.

The twisted scar-face with the topknot turned its lifeless leer back on Njda. A sick promise poisoned its warped grin. It muttered a curse and green motes of magic smothered the red in its gaze.

Njda ran. The whiteout blinded her as she careened into its teeth. She smashed into the wreckage of another longsled and tripped onto a headless elder. She yawped and barrelled away. Abandoned treasures and provisions and fresh corpses littered the trampled snow. She'd wanted to help Hari. She'd done it. She was his murderer. He'd been her friend.

Breathless, Njda took cover in a shattered sledcroft. Wind blasted through the gashed timber. The calamity of the kraken's strike still shook the ground. When that calmed, they would come for her. The storm's howl suffocated the din of slaughter, and she closed her eyes and counted to six. She imagined the green gore-eaters slinking through the snowstorm, rusted blades raised, human meat stinking in their craws. They would do to her what they'd done to the givers. If not them, then the kraken.

Njda roared from the splintered sledcroft. Her taut bowstring creaked and her shoulder muscles screamed, but nothing was there.

The tension eased from her bow, and Njda vomited in the snow. She wiped the dribble from her lips and looked up to find a man looming behind her. Grey clouds filled his eyes. Blue paint striped his face. Pathetic wisps of beard covered his neck. Liver spots and blood marred the rest of him.

Njda inhaled and gripped her knife. He'd given it to her years ago after putting old Gumper from his misery.

'Njda,' the ancient shaman rasped.

'Bavval.' Njda squashed him in her arms and cried.

CHAPTER TWO

The whiff of pestled greens, plucked moss and burnt sage wafted behind Bavval. The blizzard howled through the sledcroft's hull. Njda could see her breath, but Bavval's presence warmed her. It was more than just the lambent vapour swirling in his tensed fingers. The noajdi had taught Njda everything she knew of the Suku's ways.

Rabbits' nails tapped the floor as they hopped at their feet. Their glowing eyes painted the room amber. Threads of magic connected the rodents to the fog in Bavval's hand.

Njda stalked behind the shaman and stared dully at the carcass on the deck. 'It's one of them.'

Bavval harrumphed. 'An orruk. I don't know this breed. They're often thicker, more heavy-set. Come, now. Our help is needed.'

The rabbits diligently made way as Njda crouched. She stared in fascination, then slid an arrow from her quiver and prodded the carcass. 'Someone did it clean. Why mutilate it?'

Bavval breathed deep. 'Anger. And pain.'

The greenskin's mouldy tongue lolled from its slack jaws. Its dead, red eyes reminded Njda of a shark's. The smell was unbearable.

She stood. 'Good enough reason for any of us.'

Bavval ducked beneath a doorsill. As Njda followed him, the golden aura danced in his gnarled hands. She had begged him to teach her to bind lesser creatures to her will, but after today's tragedy, mastering the amber winds would have to wait. She didn't want to be close to Ghur. Not now.

The stink of a bad wound sank like a hook into Njda's nostrils. She paused to listen to her pointed hood, but if the hunger winds blew, she couldn't sense them here. She vaguely recognised the clan carvings on the hull.

'Who is it we're helping?' she asked.

Shadows and the amber glimmer of six beady eyes aged the geography of Bavval's face. He cleared his throat and tugged his ear. 'Friends.'

Beneath jagged timber, a young man gripped the greying hand of his wife. Her side had been wounded by a grazing blow from a notched blade. To judge from the stink, the blade had been poisoned. The man was battered and bleeding but strong. Dried orruk gore encrusted his hands.

Njda clenched her fists. 'You didn't say it was them.'

'Is that an obstacle?' Amulets clinked on Bavval's wrist as his hand fell. 'You were this tall when you amputated Wulf's foot after his accident. But you can't help them?'

'Wulf's my brother. And he was climbing. They...' Njda *tsked*. 'He's Heigen. You know what they did.'

Bavval's brow wrinkled. He set his lips and eased beside the stiff woman. Tortured eyes flickered beneath her clammy brow.

Tears streaked Heigen's face. He'd clipped his hair after marriage, as was customary, but even with a flood in his eyes and fire in his cheeks, he looked the same as the day Njda first met him. As he wept, that old soaring joy in her fell.

Heigen peered up, through Njda, like she wasn't there. He bent until his lips touched his wife's ear. 'You'll be okay.'

Njda's anger fermented into a smoother vintage of grief. She crossed her arms. 'I saw a wound like this. Hari, out there. Fighting the orruks.'

'They envenom their blades.' A sigh rustled from Bavval's thin lips. 'This is beyond my ability to heal.'

Njda stroked her shaved temples. 'A herbalist lives in the Izalenders' court. I've seen her treat flogflower poisoning and worse.'

'No herbs can cure this.'

Njda bit her lip. 'Doesn't the red house keep an alchemancer on retainer?'

Heigen's eyes shot up. 'I don't have the furs to pay for a visit to the red house.'

Njda's heart raced. She fingered the mittens on her hands. 'We're not going to the red house,' she said. 'The alchemancer's sleigh is next door. He takes odd jobs.'

An age of silence passed before Bavval dispelled the aurora in his fingers. The amber glow in the rabbits' eyes faded. Awoken from a dream, they thumped through the dark ruins of Heigen's halls to the perilous snows.

Bavval clasped his hands, bent his head. 'Thank you, little friends. When your time comes. No sooner.'

Njda crouched opposite the shaman and ignored Heigen. 'To the alchemancer.'

All the vast tundra filled Bavval's grey eyes. 'On three.'

Njda counted. They lifted. They left.

Black sand ground timidly beneath their soft-soled boots. The banded clouds in the sky had dissolved into a grey wall of snow.

Banks of Suku sledcrofts stretched from the shore into the snowy murk. In sparse bivouacs, crumpled sleeping skins lay ominously strewn around longsleds and stamped-out campfires. Yesterday this had all been empty coastline and wooded highland. Today it was the carcass of Riika-Min.

Njda gestured for the others to wait behind a stony outcropping. They regained their breath. The sea whispered on their left, and on their right tired spruces stood sentinel around tidal shallows. For a heartbeat, the blizzard relented, and sunlight smouldered through the morbid veil of snowfall over the bay.

Flotsam and dead bodies bobbed in the surf. Beyond, walls of fog wreathed a titanic shadow.

Njda had cleaned fresh squid from her mother's by-catch before. The kraken looked nothing like that. Bug-shell as thick as castle walls encrusted Mai's fat mantle and fins. Curtains of brine cascaded from her mountainous mass. Kelp hung from spidery, jointed legs that stabbed into the headlands. Around them, spewing from the kraken's impossible bulk, the shadows of wyrms – enslaver tendrils – snake-danced in the sky. One suckered tentacle crushed the nearby shore in its grip; its oily mass had demolished a ridgeline. Tjatsår Mai was greater than icebergs, bigger than fortresses.

The blizzard blew hard, and a whiteout edged in on the nightmare. Njda squinted as Tjatsår Mai's tentacle slid into the sea. Stone tumbled into the fault-line it left behind. The realm trembled, and the kraken's plaintive groan echoed the way mountains did when they got angry. Salty foam lapped at their hide boots, then drenched the hems of their trousers.

Heigen lifted his leg. Njda gripped him and raised a finger to her lips. When the water receded, she stood. The subtle movements of her pointed hood and plaited queue tingled in her scalp. The hunger winds whispered to her.

A wave of icy slush rinsed spilt gore from the sands ahead. The bodies that had bled there were gone, and the tide devoured the imprints of their thrashing. A blazing sledcroft painted the white-out bronze.

Njda's gaze shot to Heigen, then his wife. Her brow smoothed. His wife's white hands quivered; the tips were going black. Njda fumbled her mittens from her hands to the stricken woman's. When her bare fingers brushed the cold wedding bracer on the woman's arm, Njda blinked, then swallowed. 'Quiet, now,' she told him.

Heigen nodded, and Njda stood. The serrated noise of a vicious tongue sawed at her ears. The sledcroft's grisly flames silhouetted a pack of hunched orruks and their gibbering minions. The foe-warriors dragged a rotted rope from the herdstead's yard. Tethered to it, Suku – dead *and* alive – smeared the snow-streaked sands.

'You'll live,' Heigen whispered. 'We'll live together.' His wife croaked, and his sobs loudened.

Njda's mother flashed across her mind. Then she blinked, and the gleaming snakes of Hari's entrails hanging from an orruk's jaws tattooed the backs of her eyelids. She glared at Bavval. 'Shut him up.'

Amidst the smoke and crackling flames ahead, an orruk growled and barked, then sniffed at the air. Njda held her breath until it snorted and lowered its head.

When the creatures left, Njda exhaled and gripped Heigen's shoulder. 'Get her off the beach. We're here.'

The wealthiest herdsteads of Riika-Min always bought bivouac rights to the high ground in the city's centre. Those sledmanses scraped the sky, but by the time Njda jogged to the lifeless copper pump at the court's wood-framed well, the greatest of them were gone.

Foetid fog choked the Izalenders' court. Trees loomed in the snow like cold strangers. In the sledmanses still here, doors swung on broken hinges, and frost-encrusted entrails festooned a sledge where they'd been tossed. Beneath a high balcony with shattered banisters, desecrated corpses on the plankwalk told a grim tale. The orruks had been here.

A shingle slid from a roof and crashed. Njda swivelled, then eased the tension from her bowstring. 'They were here,' she said. 'I swear. They always camp in the Izalender Quarter.'

Bitterness bent Heigen's plump lips. 'They left. Like herd animals abandoning their own to the wolves. That's why they stay here. They have the most time when the outskirts are attacked.'

Bavval wheezed. 'The herbalist was Suku. If Yan and that alchemancer left, so be it. We live in our kindred, and they in us. As long as any soul of Riika-Min survives, we all do.'

Heigen stared. 'Old man, if we are dead, we have not survived. We are *dead*.'

Heigen's wife moaned, and his ire melted. He swept to her side.

'This attack…' Njda examined the spoor on the ground. To leave tracks that deep, the orruks had to be all sinew and iron. 'Bavval, where's Brother?'

Bavval pulled in the hems of his fur coat. 'I do not know. He should have come.'

'You're really *not* as skilled as they say.'

Njda spun and loosed an arrow. The dart thumped into the wood-framed well. A woman with a lantern stared at the quivering shaft, then snorted. Wild russet shag tumbled to her shoulders, twisted into braids on her temples. With more fat in her chiselled cheeks and a softer complexion, she could have passed for Njda's sister. She was as lean as a wolf.

Njda lowered her bow. 'Magga.'

Magga lifted her chin. 'You're not dead. That's good.'

The faded dye and bare collar of Magga's tunic made Njda squirm. The baleen sword in her hand and bloodied rondel dagger in her belt were even worse. Magga stood as Fatebutcher must have when that mythic devil swept into the blessed *vargr*'s den in Druichan Forest. *The Wolf's Slaughter* had always been Magga's favourite tale. As a child she used to bind conifer branches to her back and pretend they were leather wings, then chase Njda through the winding plankwalks of Riika-Min.

'Magga.' Bavval wobbled forward. 'Does Master Valter still stock queencure from the apothecary?'

Magga shrugged. 'The *byrkaller* doesn't give me glimmerings to do his shopping. I guard his red house.'

Njda helped Heigen lug his wife up. She shouldered past Magga. 'You threaten Valter's rivals to fill your purse,' she said. 'Shaking thugs down isn't business. It's crime.'

Magga followed them with her eyes, then trailed after them. 'On your tall tower again, as usual. But you didn't see me. What's the difference between givers and takers when you get down to it? We all kill when we must. Not like you finders.'

Njda clenched her teeth. 'Givers give to the community. I guard the herds. You? You take. You'd be better off in exile with the rest of your kind.'

Magga jiggled the red dagger in her belt. 'Nope. Did good today.'

Bavval pinched his temples. 'Sisters, please—'

'Are we going to the red house?' Heigen's eyes flickered between them. 'I can't pay for the merchant's help.'

Bavval placed his hand on Heigen's wife's brow. 'It is that or let her die. Master Valter keeps queencure. It will heal her wounds.'

Magga whipped her baleen sword through the air. The great feather's sharpened fronds whooshed. 'You know what I do to people who break into Valt's sled?' she asked.

Njda's cheeks burned. 'I should put an arrow down your throat.'

'Please, Njda, just *try*.'

* * *

The red house rose into the snowy haze and cloudy twilight. Fog choked the gold finials rising from the spine of its arched timber roof. Sigmar's scarlet blanketed the panelled walls, and enormous balconies wrapped around its uppermost storey. On the roof, a colonnaded terrace cleft the sled's profile. The red sledmanse was a moving palace.

A dozen dead greenskins surrounded the double doors. Magga fixed her boot on one and chopped at its barrel chest. 'Hobgrots. Met a taker chief who'd killed them before. I think they came for loot.' Magga's grin died as Njda and Heigen carried his wife past her. Inside, a candlelit gallery brimmed with upholstered furniture. How Valter's draught aurochs could drag it all during migrations was a mystery. But then again, the merchant-lord owned two hundred of them.

Njda left Heigen and his wife beside the hearth. 'She looks highly awful,' Magga said as she emerged. 'Dead in a few minutes, I reckon.'

On the porch, twilight twinkled off pillaged metal tools heaped over bundled reindeer furs. Markings from a dozen clans decorated them. Njda pointed. 'What's this?'

'*Damn* you, Magga! Who have you let into my house?'

Footsteps pounded from the sledmanse. Valter dost Riika stormed from the double doors. Gilded pistols clanged against an ornate chestplate beneath his trimmed overcoat. Long sideburns and a cavalier's moustache covered his tanned leather face. A hideous scar encrusted his left eye. His lacquered boots were no good for the Sukuat's snows, but they matched the gold spurs at his heels, for the horses he didn't ride.

Valter scowled. 'Magga, a woman's dying in my foyer.'

Bavval had paced around the porch. As he crunched through the snow back to the entrance, Valter's rugged brow smoothed.

'Master Valter.' Steam billowed from Bavval's nostrils. 'Your skids are frozen. Where are your infamous aurochs?'

Valter stammered. Magga scoffed. 'Noajdi, if you think we're leaving in this, think again. Valter's sled can't take us anywhere. And his draught animals are gone.'

Valter frowned. 'What do you mean, gone?'

'Neighbours cut them loose. *Something-something,* didn't want them to die.'

Valter burned red. 'What do I pay you for, Mag?'

From the sledmanse, Heigen cried.

'Bavval,' Njda said. 'The queencure.'

Magga ignored the storm-swell of Valter's curses and pointed up. 'Check the terrace.'

As Njda ascended the red house, Magga's and Valter's bickering echoed through its storeys. Fine curtains and painted shutters adorned the inner floors. A dumb-waiter hung halfway from the ceiling at the end of the dim gallery. Ottomans and couches and empty shelves crowded the portico on the rooftop terrace.

Njda rifled through the apothecary's cabinet, then smashed open a locked drawer. Her eyes wrinkled as she deciphered the drunken scrawl on a creased sheet of wine-blotched vellum.

Dear Sick-Valter. Circumstance has compelled me to liquidate our supply of queencure to make this year's payment to the vultures. I know you will understand, for while your sickness is only yours, our debts belong to us both. What is good for me is good for you. Yours, Valter-In-Good-Health. P.S. – May this bottle of 4th Quarter improve your humours in these trying times.

An empty bottle of wine rolled in the drawer. Njda slammed it shut. The city's talk had it wrong. *Greedy* wasn't the word for men like Valter.

Wood clattered. A grinning hobgrot leered from the shingled roof beside the terrace. Mouldering tatters warmed the stringy neck beneath its poxy, dagger-like chin. Disgusting red eyes blinked over a pair of cracked lips, which peeled back to reveal two crooked banks of yellow needles.

Njda snapped an arrow out. A swipe of the hobgrot's curved knife deflected it. Her second arrow thudded into the shingles where it had been. By the time she nocked her third arrow, the hobgrot had closed the gap. It tackled her to the deck and screeched. Blood boiled from its jagged teeth into Njda's face. She grunted and rolled it aside, then twisted her arrow from its chest and slashed its throat.

She limped to the terrace balustrade with her salvaged arrow clutched in her fist. Orruks loped between the abandoned sled-manses towards the Izalenders' court. Greasy laughter oozed through the fog. The flats of the orruks' toothed blades drummed the trees they passed. Hobgrots waddled at their feet dragging serrated hooks for snagging captives.

One foe-raider dragged a Suku woman by her ankles. She gagged, and metal clanged as the orruk dashed the woman against the copper pump. The foe-warrior's distorted pink face rose towards Njda, and it grinned. An oily topknot dangled in its eerie visage.

Heinous giggles drew closer. Njda ran back and slammed the terrace door, then barred it. On the mid storeys of Valter's sled she passed Bavval as he raced to bar the window shutters and balcony doors. Downstairs, Valter and Magga had made temporary peace. Magga refreshed her blade grip and paced between the double doors and the hearth. 'Njda. Note again we didn't need you to find them.'

The orruks' leader lurched through the square. Clotting blood dripped from the mask of distorted flesh plastered on its face. The face was Hari's; the red eyes glowing in its gashed sockets were not. An arrow flitted from Njda's bow. The orruk grunted as the dart thumped into its shoulder. Hari's face slopped from the creature's piggish mug, then caught on a tusk. It spat his face into the snow and ground it into the frosty mud.

'What do you *want?*' Njda loosed another arrow; it sailed over the orruk's head. 'Is this not enough?'

The orruk's lifeless eyes pawed at Njda. It dragged a pitted yellow nail across its belly. '*Guts.*' Its poxy lips contorted into an atrocious smile. The others hooted like apes.

The beast stepped onto the balcony. Njda craned her head up at it and inched back. Valter slid through the portal and tossed an armful of junk to the deck. He slammed and barred the doors, locking the orruk behind them.

Panting, the merchant slid a pistol from his belt. 'I think we can bargain with them.'

Magga dragged him away. Njda moistened her lips and drew an arrow. At the hearth, Heigen murmured obliviously to his gurgling wife. Njda fixed her eye on the seam between the doors. Above, shadows flickered across the shuttered windows. The sledmanse's roof thumped. Muted sniggers echoed through the ceiling. Boots and blades' hilts slammed the terrace door against its frame.

'*Chum,*' the orruk outside growled. Its minions squelched with laughter as buckets sloshed closer. Fluid splashed the door, and pulverised human meat trickled through the wooden frame. The double doors slammed against their hinges.

Njda's sweaty fingers slipped, and an arrow thudded into the threshold. She screamed and nocked another. Death didn't scare her – the living and the dead were one family. Together they watched over their people and the lands they loved. That was the Suku's Harmony. Life, death and the bitter balance between them. Still, she wanted to live. Let her siida barge in now. Let her mother and father sweep in with bows drawn and all the storied Stormcasts of the Izalenders. Let anything happen, so long as this was not the end.

'We could use an amber breeze!' Magga shouted. But Bavval was guarding the roof terrace; magic swirled around him higher in the gallery.

Njda steadied her breathing as the world shrank around her. The confines of Valter's sled halls became all the expanse of the universe. An icon rattling on the wall caught her eye. Sigramalles Apmil – the Izalenders' bearded thunder god.

The God-King had never been to the Sukuat. He had never seen its mountains rise and stride across the horizon with the waking of the sun. He'd never heard a Suku prayer drum or read its portents, never sung a Suku fairing or been faired to. Njda had always prayed to the spirits of the tundras and seas instead of the Izalenders' God-King. Right now, Sigramalles Apmil would do.

Njda's lips cracked to shape the first syllables of her fairing. She hummed the tone of her song.

Wind sliced through cracks in the sledmanse. The candles in the great hall guttered. The sled's timber beams shook until Njda's ears tickled, and dust rained from the rafters. For a breath, loaded silence replaced the thumping of hobgrots' feet on the roof. The hunger winds had grown scared, even submissive.

The doors flew from their hinges. The hunched orruk frowned. Drool roped from its cocked jaws. Snow swirled in and whipped at the Suku, and a pair of disgusting eyes leered out from beneath its cowl. It crouched under the threshold.

Valter's pistol barked, and smoke stung Njda's nose. She loosed her arrow.

The orruk grunted twice, then chuckled. 'Gruelbags. I'll give you sumfin' for that.'

Valter raised his second pistol. Njda nocked again. Magga whipped her baleen sword and screamed. 'Come on! *Biro jeknja* die!'

A shadow fell over the court. A meteor crashed into the snow. The realm rocked, and Njda staggered as an icy shockwave blasted through the portal. The clash of iron followed, punctuated by the wet champ of jaws on sinew and bones popping from sockets. Bestial roars decomposed into porcine squeals, then ceased.

In the doorway, the orruk's vile grin fell from its lips. It spun and raised its chipped sword. A lance of bitter steel shot out and skewered its shoulder, pinning it to the ceiling. Purple blood oozed to the plank floor.

Beside the hearth, Heigen whimpered and smacked his wife's cheeks. At the threshold the orruk's muscled legs thrashed and rocked one of the doors against its frame. A darker giant blocked the light outside beyond it.

'The kraken,' the shadow growled. 'Where?'

'Mork's teef, 'ow would I know?' A crunch followed and the orruk's head rocked. 'Awright,' it slurred. 'Fought about it. Fink I know.'

Njda let her string slip. Her arrow slapped into the back of the orruk's skull and it fell still.

The steel lance slid away. Its wielder tossed the dead foe-warrior aside. She pounded before the threshold, and spines rattled in a mantle of bristly granite fur on her shoulders. A monster's slack-jawed head hung from one end of the fur. Fossilised gore caked the roots of its fangs.

Njda gasped. The vargr. But nothing like Suku myth had described it. Yet the slayer who had taken its flayed pelt as a trophy was just as Njda had always envisioned. Acting on raw instinct, she loosed another arrow. It stuck in the giant's armour like clay. The shrouded figure slid the dart from her breast. She didn't snap the shaft. The length which had penetrated her frosted warplate had simply smouldered away.

'The kraken,' she snarled again. 'Where?'

Njda lowered her bow. No matter how many furs she wrapped herself in or how close she lay to the hearthfire, *The Wolf's Slaughter* had always made her gut roil and chilled her fingers and toes. The Harmony required a delicate balance between life and death, but the sole purpose of this mythic monster's existence was to kill.

'Fatebutcher,' Magga breathed.

CHAPTER THREE

Behind the interloper, stars twinkled in a black sky. A shifting gold-green aurora shimmered in the void between them. The clouds had fled, and the sun and the stars painted the Izalenders' court into a mural of moony white and stark shadows. Even the air had sucked itself from Njda's lungs. Her shallow breaths spawned futile wisps of vapour in the manse's vacuum.

The timber porch creaked beneath Fatebutcher as she spoke. 'The kraken. *Where?*'

Magga's baleen sword rattled. Valter's second pistol shook in his hands. Njda had always thought herself calm, in control. It wasn't true. Everything about this devil-huntress thawed her courage and liquefied her bowels. Njda should have cowered, but she'd spent a lifetime not doing the things she should have done. Not staying in Riika-Min like her father had said, not helping her mother with the morning catch. Not saving her clan.

She crept forward, hands raised. 'Mai's gone. During Drown-harrow she comes and goes, then sleeps a hundred years.' Slowly,

Njda clasped her hands and bowed her head. 'Mai's had her fill. Only us left.'

The huntress' icy eyes flickered. They shone like a snow-panther's at night. Besides that merciless silver, the only light in the sled twinkled from the stars. The slain vargr's fur mantle dripped blood, as if the huntress had skinned it mere moments ago. Ichor froze into a hundred black mirrors at her muddied feet.

Her hand parted from her silhouette. A long spear thudded to the deck. 'So you know of the beast.'

Njda battled to steady her legs. Beaten metal armour rimed with winter and dried sea salt encrusted the giant in the threshold. She almost glimpsed a woman's face in the shadows beneath the vargr's mantle. The dead wolf's six eyes blinked at her.

Instinct told Njda to run. She planted her feet and shook. 'Are you...?'

'Where does she slumber between Drownharrows?'

Fatebutcher's voice rumbled in Njda's belly as much as it echoed in her ears. What that earthquake told her defied belief.

'Forgive me,' she whispered. 'Tjatsår Mai... She is like a god. If you hunt her, you hunt Ghur's own daughter. Who are you?'

A breath of bleeding silence followed. Fatebutcher sighed, and a chill moved through Njda's bones. The barred shutters in the red house's upper storeys bumped against their window frames. The icon of Sigramalles Apmil shook and smashed to the floor. Down the gallery, the dumb-waiter squealed on oiled rope.

'Yndrasta.'

The porch planks creaked as the huntress departed. The crunch of snow and chink of armour faded. Another shockwave gusted through the house, and Njda shielded her face before the snow blinded her.

Bavval had crept downstairs. He wavered before the hearth. 'Njda, don't.'

Njda spat ice and grit from her teeth. She huffed. 'Please, we need help. Our people–'

Lazy motes of snow floated in the barren court. Coagulated blood and eviscerated entrails gleamed in scattered mounds. The stars were gone, smothered by a white sheet in the sky. Vultures orbited overhead. Njda craned her head at naked birches and snow-dusted spruces, splintered sledcrofts and the bent copper pump. Like the blizzard that had besieged them, the devil-huntress was gone.

From Valter's sledmanse, a low wail rose, first faint like the fog-horn of passing airships, then loud and close. Njda's shoulders fell. She brushed the wet from her nose. Heigen's cries filled her lungs; his tears brimmed in her eyes. So much time had passed, but she hadn't buried her feelings as deep as she'd thought. If she didn't try harder, her old hurt would come up from beneath the snows with spring's thaw.

Her eyes gathered her wasted city, or what was visible of it beneath the heaping snowdrifts. Heigen need not suffer for long. Soon they would all join his wife.

CHAPTER FOUR

Njda stumbled through the wreckage. Torn canvas awnings flapped in the wind. Fires crackled in the snow-piled ruins of burnt-down sledcrofts. The aroma of grilled meat wafted to her, strong enough that if she closed her eyes, she could pretend the Crown Day feast had come. Soon the ten thousand herdsteads of Riika-Min would awaken from last night's drunken reverie and dispel the eerie calm. Her father, eyes red with worry, would curse as he found Njda laughing with her neighbours around a split boazu carcass, then take up the spit and join them.

Two plumed jackals fought over the entrails of a grey-eyed maiden. A third chewed on a boy's bones. Njda chased them off and wounded one with an arrow when it tried to defend its scavenge. As the curs' yelps faded into the ruins, Njda doubled over and retched. She fell and dragged her fur sleeve across her mouth. She knew these corpses, just as she had known all the others.

Njda hadn't been able to remain in the Izalenders' court. Not with Heigen clawing handfuls of mud from the ground and weeping, and Magga and Valter bickering about how or if they should drive him away. After the blizzard and the departure of the malevolence that had saved them, the morning's horrors felt like the memories of a dark dream. But the storm had ended and the nightmare remained. Njda picked herself up and resumed her search for survivors.

The dead had taken up residence in Riika-Min. As Njda searched, a distant wail filled her with hope. She followed a fury of boazu tracks and a sledcroft's skid trail back to an empty bivouac. She turned the corner and froze, then crept back.

A legless woman levitated over the abandoned site. Diaphanous rags draped her emaciated form and swayed in a breeze that wasn't there. She sobbed, and a rictus gleamed on her bare skull beneath wisps of damp hair. A butcher's knife and chains hung locked within her skeletal hands.

The haunt ceased wailing. Its eyeless sockets shot towards Njda, who hugged the cold ground. While defending the herd or tracking lost calves she'd fought her share of wights and skeletons, but Hari had always told her never to battle ghosts. Haunts were grief incarnate – no mortal could win that war. Njda crawled into a smashed sledcroft, rose, bowed her head and left.

No more than a handful of herdsteads must have escaped. Njda racked her head trying to recall another attack this devastating. Her ma had told her of a mad moon that once gambolled through the southern skies. It had sucked the shimmering night aurora through the craters of its nostrils like drug vapour as a horde of maddened greenskins cavorted over the hills. Then the givers had fought them off and the noajdi had dispelled their mushroom plagues. When Njda was a girl, a pair of giant *stallo* had thundered in from the hills to take their pick of meat from the outer bivouacs. Brother had killed one gargant and scared the other away. In each attack, no more than a thousand lives were lost – a fraction of Riika-Min's population, not difficult to recover from.

But those foe-raiders and Tjatsår Mai… together they had slain Riika-Min.

Njda buried her hands in her pockets and closed her eyes. She hummed an old fairing, but it didn't calm her. In Valter's sled-manse, standing against the orruk, she'd started to sing a fairing for Sigmar's salvation. In Njda's mind, there had been no equivocation, no ambiguity. She had prayed to *Sigmar,* the saviour-god, not the spirits, nor the ancestors.

Had he sent Fatebutcher? Did Fatebutcher serve Sigmar? It would have made sense. The gargant vargr of the dark Druichan Forest had once terrorised Izalend. Who would the Izalenders have appealed to but Sigmar to slay it? The Suku may have revered the vargr, but that had been out of awe, not love. The Endwolf had been a child of Ghur and its Harmony, but Harmony was no saintly divine. Harmony was the realm's harsh balance, the tendency of life and death towards natural equivalence.

Fatebutcher had been harmonious in her wicked way. She had come and killed that the Suku could live, then left. Maybe Njda's sullied faith had complicated the God-King's intercession. Maybe Sigmar had dispatched a tarnished reflection of the Suku's tarnished beliefs to save them, then let them die. With the rest of the sled-city gone, their chances of survival were fading. Like a herd, Riika-Min's strength had been in numbers as much as mobility.

Bavval's hoarse roar perked Njda's ears. Back at the red house, Magga shouted. Njda only made out two words.

'*Magga…! Stop…!*'

She raced back the way she'd come. In the Izalenders' court, a mound of freshly turned dirt rose beneath a bent birch. Valter leaned on a shovel. His trimmed coat hung from a branch and his pistols were crossed at his back. He picked his nose as Bavval helplessly tried to part Magga and Heigen. They wrestled in the snow, their tunics stretching as they yanked on the rondel dagger that quivered between them.

Magga wanted to kill Heigen. In big, practised movements, Njda loosed an arrow. The dart clanged against the dagger's round blade and it flew. Magga shook the shock from her hand and glared at Njda. 'Are you stupid?'

Njda drew another arrow and marched up. 'Lay a hand on him and I'll–'

Heigen bucked Magga and scrambled for the dagger. He raised it to his throat.

'*Magga!*' Bavval barked. 'Stop him!'

Magga swept forward, too fast for Njda to follow. She booted the rondel blade from Heigen's hands, then kicked his face. Red-eyed and dazed, Heigen crumpled.

Magga belted her dagger and collected her baleen sword. She seized Njda's wrist and twisted the arrow from it. 'You're really *not* as good as they–'

A shot thundered through the court. A tendril of smoke curled from the barrel of Valter's upraised pistol. He shoved it into his belt beside a hatchet and threw his coat on and smiled. Beneath his greasy moustache, his gold teeth were hard to pick out from the yellow. 'I've decided you lot can stay,' he said.

He shook out his coat's trimmed hems, perhaps awaiting some display of gratitude, then jutted his chin out. 'What?'

Bavval wetted his hands in a barrel and pulled his fingers through his beard. He hunched like a man drunk on thrill, sickened by it. 'What will we owe you, Master Valter?'

Valter shrugged. 'A small fee. On revolving credit, if you like. I'm sympathetic to your plight.'

Bavval grunted and ladled water into a pail. He kicked ice from his boots against the porch and drifted through the red house's smashed doors. Valter rubbed his burly hands across his face and inhaled sharply, then followed the shaman in.

Magga propped her feather-like sword on her shoulder and twisted a braid behind her ears. 'We buried his wife right.'

Njda threw her bow across her shoulder. Heigen's shallow breaths stabbed out, as if all he had wanted was the bliss of sleep. 'Help me move him.'

Magga tossed her sword to the porch. She shifted her dagger in her belt and crouched. 'I've a clean tunic. Your size.'

They heaved Heigen up, and Njda shook her head. 'I need a hood. And I don't wear faded dye.'

'It's either faded dye or fresh blood. And this one has a hood. You should know. Your folks gave it to me.'

The survivors sat at trestle tables around Valter's snapping fire. His hearth stretched towards the dim ceiling. Flames roared in the brick surround beneath a heavy mantel. Earlier, Magga had grumbled as she heeded Valter's order to close the shutters in the higher storeys to preserve heat. The gallery resembled a candlelit ravine of planks, curtains and painted pictures.

The red house was the most spacious sledcroft Njda had ever seen, and the most luxurious. That Valter's neighbours had cut his draught aurochs free didn't surprise her – he'd left them in the cold to make room for his opulent furniture. Even the most incompetent Suku herdsteader knew to stable their reindeer in their sledcroft's hold.

Fire crackled as Valter stuffed jellied meat into his mouth. He rinsed a mouthful down with spiced mead. 'You're all welcome to more.'

'In exchange for letters of debt.' Njda's mind drifted to the drunken scrawl in the apothecary's drawer. She nibbled at a morsel of dried fish. A full belly wouldn't fix the ache in her heart. The thought of her family made her sick. So did the vision of that girl's grey face as jackals gnawed at her toes.

By the hearth, Bavval dispelled the magic fog from his hands. He blinked blur from his eyes, then reached into his pail and splashed his face. After he rinsed off his blue face paint, his flesh seemed tougher, his wrinkles deeper. 'No good.'

Magga brushed down her baleen sword's fronds, then paused to remove a tin from her coat. She pinched glowing metal dust and rubbed it into the corners of her eyes and stared wistfully at the ceiling. She gazed at Heigen, who was tied up and sleeping by the fireplace. 'That man's so highly pathetic.'

'Valter,' Njda said. 'Thank you for burying his wife.'

Valter pursed his lips. His grey eye made her wince. 'I recognise we have bigger problems to tend to. I won't bill him for it just yet. Maybe next year.'

Bavval folded his arms into his sleeves. The hearth's flames danced in his eyes, as if they showed him their secrets. 'We must face the facts. Riika-Min is dead.'

Magga stiffened. Her hazel eyes searched him. 'Your soul-slaves couldn't find a single survivor?'

'No. And they are friends, not slaves.' He nodded to the wall. 'Something out there is killing them. Many things, I might reckon. The city's givers are all dead or taken. Toothed hunters roam the ruins at will. A pack of cave squigs killed my only fox. I've only crows and rabbits left.'

'We don't know all the givers are dead,' Njda said.

Bavval's rheumy eyes glistened. 'I know they are gone. Everyone is.'

Valter snorted. He ripped salted meat from bone. 'The real question's why you aren't possessing creatures that can defend us. Or calling Brother.'

Bavval's eyes wrinkled. 'You know better. I'm a shaman, not a wilding druid. The soul call is difficult for deadlier beasts. And despite our offerings, none can summon Brother. He serves the Harmony alone.'

'You mean his belly.' Valter slurped from a clay cup. 'If you're all staying tonight, we'll have to draft contracts. Magga, don't look at me that way. Go get the quill and paper.'

Magga laughed and leaned against the trestle table.

'We must discuss our next move,' Bavval said, turning to Njda. 'We must reach this decision carefully, or it will be our last.'

Valter clapped his cup down. 'I'll tell you lot what I'm doing. It's snow season. When the blizzards come, we'll want cover. So long as you can afford the provisions you use, you're welcome here.' He gestured at his sledmanse in a way that told Njda he was used to bragging about it.

Bavval's eyes narrowed. 'And then what?'

'We weather the snows. Wait for the wilderness siida. Other Suku have got to be near the coast. They must've heard the old lady come and go by sea. When the wild ones come, we ask for safe passage. Then we won't have to leave alone in the heavy snows.'

'The snows aren't the problem,' Njda said. 'The wilds are. But Riika-Min's no safer. We're five of us in a stranded sled.'

Valter burped. 'More reason to stay.'

Njda loomed over Valter and gazed at his food. She sauntered to the dumb-waiter and marched back. 'I saw your pantry. It's full. But even if we were safe here – and we're not – we'd need more than that to outlast the snows. The herds are gone. There'll be no forage for weeks. Even if we ate each other, we'd starve.'

Magga cackled. 'Valt's expert at eating others alive. Did it to our folk all the time.'

'Only their coffers.' Valter spoke through a mouthful. He pointed his knife. 'Where's that quill and paper?'

'I'll get right on it. *Boss*.' Magga's sneer fell from her lips. 'You happen to find any food in the others' homes during your pillaging?'

'It wasn't pillaging. And no.' Valter picked at his teeth with his tongue. 'Most folk lived day-to-day. Some pickled vegetables, a few butts of bread. Maybe there's more in the outer sleds.'

'Why were you pillaging the homes of the dead?' Bavval asked.

Valter swigged mead. 'I wasn't pillaging. I was collecting old debts.'

'Like I said, shaman.' Magga rubbed her eyes. 'Valt owned the debt on half the city's herds. If Izalend's monks ever make a bestiary of the Sukuat's greatest predators, Valter dost Riika would be entry number… two.'

'You wouldn't be able to read it.' Valter gave a greasy chuckle. 'Collecting from debtors after they die isn't a sin. Half this city owed me up to their roofs. I've my own debt to liquidate, mind you. That's debt with real vultures, the kind of folk who wouldn't lift a finger when you're dying in the street. The kind who drink from golden chalices filled with herdsteaders' blood.'

Njda furrowed her brow. 'Soulblights? In the Sukuat?'

'Worse.' Valter shuddered. 'Bankers.'

Magga looked at Bavval. 'If you have a plan, I'm all ears. I'd love to get away from this reindeer chip.'

Valter chortled. 'You'd come crawling back the minute you craved your glimmerings.'

As Magga glowered, Njda looked between them. So *that* was what Magga had taken from her tin. Shavings from minted glimmerings of Excelsis. Njda had met addicts to the currency before, but Magga was nothing like them. She wasn't raving about her prophetic visions; her pupils weren't spinning like tops. But then Magga twitched and sighed, and Njda gave her a long stare and a second thought.

They stewed, and Njda paced. Riika-Min spent most of the year in the inland taiga following Brother Bear's migrations. Once a season, Brother stirred from hibernation to hunt. He chased the Suku's herds across the lands and fed on reindeer, then slumbered when he had sated his hunger. The Suku followed their herds and great Brother, trusting the mythic beast would rise to protect its territory if other predators approached. Why Brother hadn't intervened against Tjatsår Mai or the orruks was a mystery, but the real question was what to do now.

Njda stopped. 'This is Glacier's End. Izalend's fleets don't patrol this side of the continent. The coast is dangerous. We're easy pickings for predators and scavengers. The foe-raiders might still be out there, too. They could return. All that and worse will fall on us in days, or less.'

Valter's good eye glittered. 'How do you know all that about the fleets?'

'Njda hears and sees things which escape us,' Bavval said. 'She spends as much time beyond the palisade sleds as you once did, and she's found more lost calves than any other finder I've ever known. As for the wilderness siida, do not assume they will help us. Don't forget I come from the wilds. Out there, the clans see things differently. They would gladly let us die for a chance to do to us what you've done to your neighbours.'

'Liquidate old debt?' Valter grinned. 'My kind of people. I still say we stay. We'll awaken Brother. He can protect us.'

Magga scoffed. 'Like he protected us from the kraken? Or the hobgrots and orruks? You blind fool.'

Valter's forehead creased. 'Which of us can read again?'

Magga cackled and shot to her feet. Her sword whooshed as she fenced with shadows.

Valter kicked his leather boots up. The wooden legs of his chair creaked. 'Suppose all that's right,' he said. 'What do you propose, shaman? We get out there and salvage the longsleds? Rebuild Riika-Min? Walk the palisade with torches and pokey sticks? Mind you all, I wouldn't repopulate the Ten Thousand Sleds with a one of you.'

Magga circled back to the fireplace and leaned against the ornate mantel, then pushed a red ember from Heigen with the toe of her boot. Heigen – still swathed in blankets and tied with cord – dozed fitfully.

Valter chuckled, pleased by their silence. 'You all agree with me.'

Njda thought of her pa. 'What about Suodji?'

'That must be fifty leagues out,' Valter said. 'None of the Suku and Izalenders going to the trade fair will find us. We're too far out of their way.'

'We could find them. We could go to Suodji. Ask for sanctuary.'

'They wouldn't help. Suodji's not Riika-Min. You all think me an Izalender, but only because you've never seen Suodji. The year-rounders there are hardly even Suku. The city's all grey stone and turf roofs, workshops on every corner. They don't even tend the standing stones in their mountains. The itinerants do it as a toll.'

Njda chewed her tongue. 'But you are byrkaller. A middleman between our people and the Izalenders. You have accounts with the Izalender and Suku merchants there, don't you?'

'That won't help as much as you think. And I don't see what it has–'

Njda planted her knuckles on his table. 'The time will come when Riika-Min rebuilds. Imagine your reputation when we speak of how you gave us sanctuary and supplies, then led us to safety. Word will spread across the siida – maybe even to Izalend. You'd be a hero.'

'I'm not a hero.'

'Your business would boom.'

Valter fell silent. Bavval's eyes narrowed. He fought the wry smile brewing beneath his lips and nodded.

'That's assuming anyone escaped from Riika-Min *to* rebuild,' Magga muttered. 'You said yourself, the wilds are no place for lone mortals.'

Njda shook her head. 'There have to be survivors. I walked the city and its outskirts. Sledcrofts are missing, and the dead reindeer don't account for all our herds. Some must have escaped. The wilds couldn't claim them all. Where else would they go but Suodji?'

'Izalend, if they had sense,' Valter said.

Magga gave Njda a sideways look. 'Even if we wanted to get there, we have no draught elk and no sled that actually moves.'

Valter grumbled.

'What I mean,' Magga said, 'is we have no sled with skids that aren't frozen to the earth, that isn't too heavy to be useful, with a master who cares enough for his draught team to keep them warm and notice when they're gone.'

Valter cocked his bad eye. 'I noticed when you told me.'

Bavval cleared his throat. 'Magga's right. This is a palace, not a sledcroft. Even with two hundred aurochs we would move at a crawl. The orruks would find us and flay us alive.'

Valter craned his head around. 'It is a palace, isn't it?'

'What if we move on foot?' Njda asked. 'We're Suku. We've our tunics and furs. Even Magga's dyes should be bright enough to scare predators. We can pick more chamonite charms from the dead to sew in. What those don't scare, we hide from. Our furs carry the boazu's magic. They'll hide us in the taiga like they hide them.'

'And we have a finder,' Bavval said. 'Your snares should prove as useful as your bow.'

'And a taker.' Njda peered at Magga, who tried hard to look unmoved. 'With you we need no givers.'

'Don't inflate her ego,' Valter said. 'Those war-braids and that baleen sword don't make her a taker. She hasn't exiled herself yet.'

'But you count on her to keep your home safe, and she has. She killed biro jeknja and kept you alive. On foot, whatever we can't flee or hide from, maybe we'll kill. And this is all to say nothing of the amber wind.'

All eyes turned to Bavval. He met their gazes and grunted. 'It is decided. We move on foot.'

'I don't remember deciding anything,' Valter growled. 'I still feel like staying put.'

'Then do so alone. You are no longer a boy, Master Valter. I will no longer pity you your circumstances. The rest of you, eventide is long. Gather what provisions you can while we have daylight. Salted meat, fatty cuts if you can, but black bread, too. We leave in the night, after the dusk predators have gone to hunt.'

Magga stood and checked her tin. Njda collected her bow and arrows. 'Bavval is noajdi,' she murmured in a tone she hoped was gracious. 'He's the only one suited to lead us.'

Magga clucked. 'Forget Valt, Njda. I guarantee he'll come. He can't stand being alone. And he's a coward.'

Valter crossed his arms. 'Mag. You're fired.'

'Enough.' Bavval glanced between them. 'This is where we are now. Like it or not, we are kindred. We stay together, through good and bad. Agreed?'

Magga nodded, but the words caught like knots in Njda's ears. Her kindred were her siida, not these companions in misery. She wouldn't forget her true family just when they needed her most.

Valter slid his legs from the table and heaved himself to his feet. He stomped to the hearth and kicked Heigen. 'Still got a death wish?'

Heigen's bleary eyes slid open, then stared at the fire.

Valter stooped and cut his bindings. 'Find him a better coat while you're out. He'll help clear my pantry. Oh, yes, stop look-ing at me. Magga's right – of course I'm coming.'

Magga threw a waterskin on her shoulder and stalked to the door. Valter brandished a thick finger at Njda. 'You better be good to your word. Tell the world what Uncle Valt did for you. And if you find any reindeer pelts in the wreckage, I'll pay a penny glimmering per pound. Those go well in Skythane and better in Excelsis. If we're going to Suodji, I'm taking them to sell. I've debts to clear, mind you.'

Njda blinked as Valter started upstairs. Together, they actually had a chance. She draped Heigen's old fur coat over his shoul-ders. He hung his head low and buried his face in his hands. At the door, Magga tested a bent harpoon, then flung it down. Valter returned and piled crockery from his table into a wooden basin. He gnashed his teeth and let it slam. 'Leaving it all behind any-ways,' he mumbled.

Njda took Bavval aside. 'Tjatsår Mai and the orruks may still prowl the coast. Let's move inland.'

Bavval glanced over her shoulder at the others, then met her eyes. 'Speed is imperative. Something tells me they have done their worst. Another peril concerns me.'

'The huntress. Fatebut–'

'That is not her name.'

Njda's brow rose. 'Should we worry about her?'

Fear glinted in Bavval's foggy eyes. He knew something about Fatebutcher – *Yndrasta* – he wasn't sharing.

'Bavval.' Njda stepped closer. 'Should we worry?'

Magga dragged Njda to the door. 'Everyone brags you're our people's greatest finder, but I'm always the one finding you. When will folk speak of what I've killed? Hurry up.'

Bavval averted his gaze, and Njda shouldered her bow. When she closed her eyes, behind her lids were branded the vargr's bloody fur, its dead gaze, the rime of frost and sea salt on beaten armour, the piercing starlight of a snow-panther's glare.

Njda's legs wobbled and her fingers sweated. She sucked in a last lungful of warmth, then prowled with Magga into the cold. Bavval wouldn't lie to her. He never had before.

CHAPTER FIVE

Hysh's stubborn rays raked the sky over the sea. The dying sun painted the clouds crimson and gold. Njda and Magga tossed stiff, ropey entrails from the dog sledge in the Izalenders' court, its front curled up like a shoe's toe. They found rope to drag it, then pulled it downhill to the nearest bivouac.

In the pantry of a desolate sledcroft, Njda dusted ash from a hardened hunk of bread and tossed it on a fur. She stepped over a shattered door and returned to the sledge. Snow crunched and glittered as the last dregs of the day's warmth refroze the thaw. Njda tossed her take into the sledge, where a pair of mittens caught her eye. She tried them on and smiled. Hers had been buried with Heigen's wife. Had Magga noticed?

Njda picked up a decorative shield in the sledge. 'Why do we need this?'

Magga rattled a box of pepper. 'Why do we need *this*?'

'To eat.' Njda tossed the shield into the wreckage. A great bladed feather lay beneath – a second baleen sword. Magga's scowl dared her to say something. Njda tromped to the next sledcroft for more provisions.

Besides meat, they took paper-wrapped blocks of cheese, butter and lard. The goods were stamped in Izalend. Magga made a point of reading the labels aloud, glancing at Njda to make sure she was watching.

Later, Magga hefted an armful of arrows to the sledge. 'For your quiver,' she said. 'Are those my spare mittens?'

'No. And I'm full up.'

'I'll pack them in my quiver.' She showed Njda the leather case strapped to her back.

'That's how takers fight,' Njda said. 'In threes, all with quivers.'

'Archer, swordsman, spearman. Yes.'

'I'm not a taker.' The dagger in Magga's belt drew Njda's eye. Forged steel was a fine prize indeed, for a nation that considered metalwork to be magic. A shame to see it in the service of pointless bloodshed. 'Why is it you want to go to war?'

'Honour and glory.'

Magga's answer was so flat, so immediate, Njda laughed. 'I'm sorry. I thought you were kidding.'

'I'm not. Honour and glory.' She reached into her pocket and tossed a flint into the sledge. 'At least I actually find things we need.'

They picked their way through the hollowed-out ruins of Riika-Min. The slow sunset teased mile-long shadows from the trees and savaged sledcrofts. When they came across the dead – the gruesome fragments of them – they piled their remains on the scrap timber and shredded canvas of their homes, then set fire to them with the flint and Magga's steel. They could not dig birch graves for the dead and taken of Riika-Min. There were too many, and they were only two.

Soon the city smouldered, and fire stained the sky redder than the sunset. The piney aroma of smoke singed Njda's nostrils but soothed the turmoil in her gut. Riika-Min felt cleansed, in a way. Flames cauterised the pain, and even the haunts began to flee. Pillars of snaking smoke comforted Njda. Empty expanses made her head spin. The open sky reminded her of the sea that had brought Tjatsår Mai – the sea that had taken Gramb and hopefully no one else. And that was to say nothing of the tundra.

'Why honour and glory before home?' Njda's abrupt question surprised even her, but she committed to it.

'I've nothing else here.'

'You have us. Your people.'

'Like I said. Nothing.'

Magga stalked to another bivouac and toed through a pile of debris. Njda juggled her words in her head. She was a white elk, an oddity. Magga was Riika-Min's most capable warrior, but she'd always refused Hari's invitation to join the givers, who were more honoured than anyone. She hadn't exiled herself to find a warband of takers, either. And whether or not Valter employed her, he had never respected her.

Magga raised a picture frame. '*Camera obscura!*' she called. 'Never thought I'd see one. It's their child, feeding their lead draught reindeer from his little hand. You can see the rough on the reindeer's tongue.' The frame crashed where she tossed it. 'Must have cost them a fortune. Should have bought steel instead. We'll burn it with their bodies.'

By the time they returned to Valter's sledmanse, Hysh's long farewell had ended and dusk lay on its deathbed. Flickering stars punctured the black welkin. Auroral bands of light shimmered overhead. All the untold centuries of Riika-Min's history felt written in those miraculous bands, as if their ancestors watched over them from the aether. Riika-Min had survived calamities before. This, too, it would survive. Njda pulled her eyes from the entrancing heavens back to the ravaged earth. The jagged shadows of razed sledcrofts and frozen mirrors of blood on the ground banished her hope.

'There's no room for furs!' Valter whined when he saw the sledge. 'Or my... things!'

'You are young, Master Valter. Carry your plunder.' Bavval dropped an armful of ice-picks and skis. 'Heigen, take this end of the tarpaulin. Take this – no, Heigen – wait.'

Bavval's gravelly voice ground to a stop as Heigen snatched the waxy tarpaulin from him. Heigen shook it out, brushed past Njda and repacked the sledge. He applied pelican fat to the tarpaulin and bound snow-shoes to the outside, then rubbed his hooded eyes and trudged away.

Bavval muttered and ambled off. Valter stooped and prised at the sledge bindings, then disappeared. He returned with a packed rucksack.

'Magga pack that for you?' Njda asked.

'You're not the only one who can dress a ruck, finder.' Valter threw the sack by the sledge and tightened the straps.

'You're carrying that? To Suodji?'

'Old man won't let me load it on the sledge, and boy-widower didn't leave room for it. So yes.' He patted his ruck. 'We'll need this if we don't want to be treated as paupers in Suodji. And I've glimmerings for Magga's pay.'

'You fired her.'

Valter treated Njda to a thoroughly patronising grin. 'Mag's a mercenary soul. She'll ask for her old job back, like she always does. Feed her dreams of a better life and a future that doesn't exist, and you have her in your pocket. Everyone's in this for something, finder. It's only you I haven't figured out.' He winked his dead eye and left. Njda shuddered and searched for a pail to wash herself.

Irritating though Valter was, he was right. Everyone was in this for something. They worked together, but only in a jaundiced, toothless sense of the word. Even so, Njda's chances of reaching Suodji were better with them. If her pa and siblings left for the trade fair before Mai's attack, Njda might find them there. They could help her locate the rest of their siida. Like her ma.

Njda squeezed her eyes shut and shook her head. She cleared her breath and entered the red house. Her ma was gone. Thinking of her did no good. She slid her stockings off by the hearth, then stared at the fire.

Yndrasta was in the doorway again. Whenever Njda looked, every time she closed her eyes, the shadow of the huntress filled the portal, her eyes aglow like a wolf's. The devil's hunt for the kraken had driven her to them, then away. She might as well have written it on the wall. But who hunted a kraken? Perhaps the Stormcast Eternals, wherever those legends roamed. For a devil like Yndrasta, there had to be another reason, something more than honour and glory. Or perhaps Yndrasta was no better than Suku takers. Perhaps she had served Sigmar, then abandoned him. Perhaps she preferred to slaughter Ghur's wonders and monsters for frozen shards of Ghyran water and the ground-up dust of penny glimmerings. Perhaps one day she would hunt *them*.

Njda ran her palms along her shaved temples, then undid her queue. A possibility haunted her, a concept she dared not voice. Yndrasta had come too late to save Riika-Min. Unhappy coincidence, perhaps. That, or she'd arrived precisely when she–

'When are we leaving?'

Njda blinked. Heigen loomed before her. 'Did you ask Bavval? Starlight hunters prowl after sunset. The dead of night, probably.'

Heigen's freckles sat like dead stars in his ruddy cheeks. He rolled up in a fur by the fire and lay as still as a dead man.

* * *

Njda's ma stood on the shores. White foam seeped into black sands, then bubbled. She smiled the way she always did, with her dimples as deep as graves and laughter lines like the slashes the orruks had carved into the dead. Rather than sending Njda away as she had yesterday morning, to tend to her duties as finder instead of helping with the dawn catch, Njda's ma beckoned for her to join her. She sank into the waves.

Njda's lungs locked up. She wrestled her coat off and kicked her boots from her feet. She thrashed through the breakers and gasped, then dived into the surf.

'*Wake, Njda. I need your help. It's Brother.*'

Njda's groggy eyes slid open. Bavval had tucked his beard into his deep blue tunic. Shadows cast by the hearth fire wreathed his ancient face.

'You smell like urine,' Njda said as she stirred, careful not to wake the others. The survivors lay in a pile by Valter's hearth. Someone had fed the flames. 'Is it time?'

'We have a few hours. Here. To cover your scent.'

Njda gazed at the bowl of crusty golden paste in his hand. 'Maybe in a few hours, Bavval.'

'I need your help,' he told her. 'I need to go to Brother's lair.'

Njda propped herself up. 'You told me he couldn't be summoned.'

'And he cannot. But he did not come yesterday. Something is wrong, and Brother is… He is our brother. I fear for him.' Bavval glanced at the yellow paste in the wooden bowl. 'Please. I would go myself, but I am older than I was. Before the kraken came, rare was the daylight which saw me brave the outskirts beyond the ring. Now is night. I cannot wander the wilds alone. You know these lands. You hunt the outer snows for the pleasure of it. I have seen the trophies you take from the rightly dead. You will protect me.'

Njda crept from her nook beside Magga and, apparently, Valter.

The evening before, the byrkaller had risen higher into his movable fortress to sleep on his notorious four-poster, which had been delivered from Izalend in pieces over the course of a season. The Suku kin had all placed bets on which shipment would be the last. In the end no one had won the pot.

Njda gathered her bow and arrows. 'Who'll take the watch?'

'I will.' Heigen sat perched on Valter's feasting table, his arms wrapped around his legs, a quilt draped over his shoulders. 'Can't sleep.'

Njda frowned and leaned in. 'Can we trust him not to–'

'I'll watch him,' Magga said, staring at the hearth flames. 'Valter's the only one asleep. I don't trust any of you to hold a watch.'

Bavval and Njda traded a look.

Magga craned her head around. 'I won't let him swallow my dagger. Trust me.'

'I didn't mean to.' Heigen's throat bobbed. 'I don't know what I was thinking. I just… I couldn't. I won't harm myself.'

'Good.' Magga rolled back towards the fire. 'You didn't have a good reason, anyway. All you are is alone.'

Night cursed the sprucelands around Riika-Min with unsettling quiet. Moonglow and starlight streamed through haggard trees, and the death-cold touch of air tensed Njda's skin. Here and there, emberflies glowed and faded like Yndrasta's eyes in the portal. Suku legend held the burning spirits' forebears first taught them their *fairings,* the songs of Ghur's own tongue. That was before the first age of darkness, when the fey beings of this world faded into wisps of magic and never sang again for fear of what might hear them.

Njda broke the snow before Bavval. As she crunched through the knee-deep drifts, her head swivelled, alert. Even in the woods, they were exposed, practically naked. Njda scanned bare tree trunks and snowy brush for subtle movement, then paused and glimpsed a rocky outcropping.

She raised her bow. 'Brother's in the gulley past those rocks. A cave below the bluffs.'

Bavval shuffled closer. Despite his years, he moved like a man who climbed mountains. And he *had* climbed mountains, when Njda got lost as a girl chasing rams up the foothills. Bavval had bargained with the ravenous peaks for four hours. The tectonic noise of their language had avalanched from his throat until he'd finally threatened them with amber fire. The summits let Njda go with a warning not to break their fast with the temptation of her meat again.

Bavval had scolded Njda, but afterwards they'd laughed all the way to Riika-Min. A lifetime had passed, and now the carrion timber of their home burned on the shores and drifted in the bay. All Bavval's good nature had bled away from him like the face paint he had rinsed off the evening before. Beneath the foetid paste they'd used to cover their scent, Bavval smelt as he always had – like freshly pestled balms and burnt incense. But he had changed.

Once Bavval caught up, Njda pressed ahead. 'If Brother's not here he'll be hunting,' she said.

'Or gone.'

Njda's hairs stood on end. 'You think so?'

Bavval's eyes travelled the dark. His face reminded Njda of the corpses she had burned last night. She'd grown so used to the blue paint caking his face that his wrinkles scared her.

'I do not know,' Bavval said, in a silvery moan that betrayed sadness instead of wisdom. 'I know yesterday should not have happened. Not with Brother. And if Brother was hungry, why hunt the wilds? Why not come for our herds? They graze around his lairs for a reason. But did you see him? Feel him?'

'No.'

Bavval harrumphed. 'The herdsteaders raised no alarm before Tjatsår Mai's attack, either.' He tugged at Njda's long hood, and she started. 'Calm, Njda. You listen to the hunger winds, as I taught you. We feel how they blow, sense the predators breathing the air. Did you feel them at all yesterday?'

Njda remembered the cultist tied to the tree, black blood oozing from her veins. The marauder's offer still stewed in the cauldron of her mind. 'I did. But that was Tjatsår Mai, not Brother Bear.'

'No, dear Njda. My grandfather survived the last Drownharrow. When I was a child, he told me Tjatsår Mai could pass through the seas without shifting the hunger winds. I know too little of biro jeknja to know what they are capable of, but I suspect you sensed them. But Brother Bear? I have never heard of a Suku guardian-beast coming and going unnoticed. So if he did not emerge to help us, and he did not leave, then the question remains. Where is he?'

They scaled the outcropping, then descended into the gulley. Climbing the granite jags should have been easy, but ice and scree complicated their descent. Whenever Njda heard rocks trickle or branches rustle she gripped Bavval's wrist, then scanned the darkness and sniffed the air. Once she was certain they were alone they moved again, two arrows and her bow clutched in her hand.

At the gulley's base, in the rocks beyond a bone-strewn clearing, a cave as dark as the void loomed. The murmuring shadows reeked of carrion.

Njda gripped a ledge and peered out. 'If we come any closer he'll take us as an offering.'

'I know. Forward, Njda.'

Njda skirted the gulley towards the cave. The hair on her neck rose at the sight of more bones scattered in the half-thawed mud. The stars and auroral shimmer overhead illuminated the clearing.

Few were the predators of Ghur which would dare approach Brother Bear on such a night. Those that could were powerful enough to defy the guardians. But two humans? Njda bit her lip and willed herself forward. It felt like stepping off a cliff.

She froze and squinted. Just beneath the slope leading into the cave lay a hill of white fur. The motionless mound filled the darkness, vague, almost invisible. She had mistaken it for snow at first, but snow did not sway in a breeze.

'That's him.' Her eyes remained locked ahead. 'Asleep. I think I hear him breathing.'

Bavval was quiet a long time. 'Loose an arrow,' he said finally. Njda turned. 'What?'

'Loose an arrow at him. See if he stirs.'

Her breath quickened. 'You cannot be serious.'

Bavval clenched his frail jaw. Wind tousled the wisps of his beard. 'If he wakes, leave him to me. I will calm him, if I can. But you will live.'

'Bavval – the Harmony. We put an arrow at him, he'll take our lives. Let's turn back, leave him behind us. We've learned what we came to learn. He slept through the attacks.' The words soured Njda's tongue.

Bavval's gaze held her still. 'Beasts are territorial. Brother should have sensed Tjatsår Mai's approach. And if he did not, he still should have roused himself to repel her attack. We belong to Brother Bear far more than he ever belonged to us. He herds us, jealously, as we herd our reindeer.'

'But Harmony–'

'–is made to be broken. Harmony is Ghur's way. Ours is Harmony's defiance.'

Njda bit her lip again. The hill in the cave hadn't stirred. 'I don't understand.'

'No. But you shall. The customs of Izalend tamed us in a way that centuries of Ghur's horrors could not. But I hail from the wilds. There the truth is remembered. That is why we shamans come to you, dear. That you do not forget.'

Njda nocked an arrow. Its shaft rattled against her bow.

'Fear' – Bavval raised a finger – 'is a very good thing. Do you trust me?'

Njda swallowed. 'I do.'

'Loose the arrow. If my suspicions are correct, Brother will not hurt you.'

Njda's thumb stroked her arrow's fletching. She imagined the dart whistling through the air and thudding into Brother Bear's hide like a splinter. In her mind, he rose like a titan from myth and roared until her ears bled. His six black eyes crushed her, and he reared up and staggered out into the muddy boneyard and dragged boulders from the bluffs. He made paste of them with his six colossal paws, then shoved them into his stinking maw.

Once, Njda's mother had taken her and her sisters to watch the white bear feed. He'd shambled from his lair like a gargant, then devoured a live reindeer whole. The bull's rack of antlers had cracked like twigs in his jaws. Njda had been sickened and angry and scared. Her ma had forced her to see.

Smiling, her ma had smoothed her hair. 'Close your eyes and count your breaths. When you open them again, Brother'll be back in his lair, asleep. But he'll be listening. And when something comes for us, he'll awake.'

Njda's eyes clamped shut and she counted her breaths. When her eyes opened again, Brother was still there. Only her ma was gone.

Njda's bowstring snapped. The dart flitted into Brother's fur like a needle into a mountain. Njda held her breath, but nothing happened. The white hill in the cave didn't budge.

'*Ha!*' She stood and expelled her pent fear. Her smile fell from her lips. 'Oh no. No, *no.* Brother.'

Bavval patted her back and trudged ahead. 'Njda. It is as I thought.'

The shaggy mountain of Brother Bear's corpse loomed. Njda had lost track of how long she'd been sitting on the damp cave floor and gazing at his clouded eyes. Trapped in its own pelt, the dead vargr had blinked at Njda in the red house. The sight of that slain myth's helpless imprisonment on Yndrasta's shoulders had emptied Njda's stomach. If only Brother would do the same... But he was gone, and he was not coming back.

She wobbled to her feet and dried her cheeks, then joined Bavval. She had seen enough weaklings to know she didn't want Bavval to think her one. Bloody mud and snow gripped the soles of her hide boots and squelched with each step.

'He's pitiful,' Bavval whispered, his voice like a sack of gravel. 'Look at him.'

'I saw him feed as a girl. I didn't forgive my ma for that. Now I wish I could see it again.'

'We teach our children to respect Ghur's might. That is the source of our strength – respect.'

'You're right. She was right. I didn't see. I do now.'

Bavval finished his prayer to the spirits and returned his amulet to his wrist. He tugged a mitten from his wrinkled hands. With white fingers the shaman stroked Brother Bear's outsized muzzle. He planted his forehead against Brother's black nose, once moist, now slick with frost.

Njda's face smoothed as her shaman began to sob. She teetered behind him and touched his back. 'There, Bavval. There.'

'I saw him as a cub.' Bavval blubbered like a child. 'Before he left Mother, before he found us when she died. I think he knew we needed him.'

Unassailable quiet followed, and an unease Njda couldn't break.

'Tjatsår Mai took Gramb. Maybe it's wrong, but this… makes me feel emptier. Like the wonder in the realm is gone with him.'

'Our people may soon follow.' Bavval paled, then dredged a wet laugh from his lungs. 'Forgive me. That is grim. As long as we live there is hope.'

'But maybe you're right. My family…' Njda shook her head and glared up. Brother was so massive. All the duardin shovel-engines in the realm couldn't bury the feelings his death had spawned in her.

Bavval donned his mitten. 'We all have our place in the Harmony,' he said. 'It does not end when we die. It only changes. We carry Brother with us now. And all Riika-Min.'

Njda circled the white mountain and bumped her bow along Brother's black claw. In warmer climes, she could have ploughed fields with that. 'What did it?'

Bavval bent his head. 'You need not ask.'

'Biro jeknja.'

Bavval smacked his lips as he moistened them with his dry tongue. 'An Izalender road marshal told me of these orruks. *Cruel-boys*, they call themselves. And cruel they are. Cunning, too, if they lost not even one of their own in the kill.'

Njda searched for spoor in the mud. The only tracks were theirs and the craters of Brother's paw prints. She shouldered her bow and scaled Brother Bear's arm. Using tufts of his shag as handholds, she reached the furry bulwark of the beast's breast. The blessed guardian's carcass was still warm.

Bavval paced below. 'What are you doing?' he asked.

'I found snares beyond our last bivouac. I thought more marauders were following us. But these were cruder than theirs, and poisoned. Always dead things nearby, but not sacrificed on stumps, and no eight-point stars. No – torn to shreds, gutted alive. I could see their thrash marks in the snow.'

'The road marshal said as much. They kill for pleasure.'

'This doesn't look like a joy-kill. Someone wounded Brother on a hunt. He came here and died. Could have been done cleaner, but still smooth. If I'd wanted to, I'd have done it like this.'

Bavval hesitated. 'To get to us, the orruks had to kill him.'

'But if Brother scared the orruks, Tjatsår Mai should've sent them running.' Njda peered down. 'What if something besides the orruks stirred the hunger winds yesterday?'

'Stop.' Bavval stared so hard Njda flinched. 'I fear her as much as you, but she is not a devil. The Izalenders tell different stories of Fatebutcher. To them, she is a saint of Sigmar. Sigmar's *saints* are righteous, the priests of the tall temples say. Like the *Bord-Uz-Avta*.'

'Those champions delay their enlightenment to protect their kin,' Njda said. 'This *Yndrasta* wanted to slay Tjatsår Mai.'

'Say no more, Njda. Do not invite this doom upon us.'

So, the devil-huntress *had* served Sigmar. Njda knelt by the red crater in Brother's chest. She removed her mitten and touched the bloody fur, still hot. She tasted it but sensed no poison and spat. 'I didn't know Sigramalles Apmil was a god of doom.'

Bavval cleared his throat. 'Perhaps the *cruel-boys* did not flee because they expected the kraken. Or perhaps they fear nothing. Come, we should return. If this cave runs deep, fouler things will emerge when they sense Brother's death. The herdsteaders found spider tracks and old webs in the sprucelands when the city encamped yesterday.'

'The madcaps.' Njda slid down from the great guardian's corpse. 'Fair enough.'

Bavval patted the bear's nose again and sighed. 'I feel terrible waking you for this. And with our journey tomorrow.'

Njda forced a smile to her lips. 'I was more worried about you,' she said.

'You have a kind heart. That is why you are the strongest of us.'

'What do you mean?'

Bavval gripped her shoulder. 'Do you remember when you dragged Wulf back to Riika after his fall? You were sick, blue from the cold. Truth be told, we were more worried about you than him. As much as Wulf cried, you had saved his life when you cut off his broken leg and stitched it closed. Blood fever would have killed him otherwise. As you still recovered, you only asked of him. You were the same with sick Gumper. It took all our strength to hold that poor man down. You were young, but we needed you, and you did not hesitate to lend your hand. I feared a darkness in you. That you wanted to bleed him in return for the tears he bled from your mother, and for the unborn sisters his blight-magic stole. Remember what you told me?'

'I wanted to help him.' They trudged towards the cave's mouth. 'What are you getting at?'

'Your father was always scared for you, and for good reason. But you have your mother's heart. She taught you to do good in the realm, even at risk to yourself. I never told you, but Gumper's fall put the fear of gods in me. Watching you then, Njda, I felt the full truth and power of our ways. You are strong. You always have been.'

Stars twinkled through the cave's mouth. Njda turned to commit the final sight of Brother to memory, to never let it go. 'Harmony is cruel, if it did this to Brother. He was ours. We were his. This will break the others' hearts.'

'We share nothing of this. Let us spare them this pain.'

'Magga will ask.'

'Then we shall tell her he abandoned us in search of other prey.'

That would have been no better, but Njda held her tongue. As Bavval tramped on, a thought curdled in her head. She circled back, gripped Brother's shag and scaled his mountainous back. Holding herself in place, she peeled back the wet mat of crimson fur surrounding his exit wound. It was clean. No broken barb from an orruk lance, no flesh sloughing from ravenous venoms. Njda peered into the cavity and saw through to the bear's chest.

She dropped down, surveyed the cave once more. Whoever killed Brother hadn't gutted the beast. They hadn't tracked him here for meat or trophies. They'd just run him through like a boar, then let him die. Behind Njda's eyelids, a spear haft thudded against the planks of the red house. The cold steel flared blue with smoking heat. Yndrasta's eyes still glowed like immortal stars; the spear glimmered and pulsed in her mailed fist.

Njda blinked away the shadow of the huntress in the threshold. She glanced once more at Brother's wound.

'Njda!' Bavval called.

'Coming.'

The biro jeknja had had little reason to pick a fight with Brother. Even if Bavval was right and they'd meant to kill Riika-Min's guardian to get at the sled-city, the idea they hadn't lost a single orruk in the killing seemed far-fetched. They were brutal and deadly, yes. But Brother had gutted gargants.

Yndrasta had slaughtered that final pack of orruks as a hound might kill mice. And she had come for the kraken. If one sought to kill Tjatsår Mai, luring her to Riika-Min by killing their great guardian was one place to start. It was exactly what Njda would have done. If she were a monster.

YNDRASTA

I lose the kraken's trail at sea, same as so many times before. Certain the beast has escaped Thengavar's silvered tip, I roar into the white skies. At this peal of thunder, clouds part and oceans ripple. A stunned flock of migrating pterosaurs plummet like arrows, then shake off their daze and recapture the air beneath their leather wings.

I alight on the first roost I find. A devourer iceberg, part of a shoal that prowls the seas of Glacier's End. For all the threat they might pose to hapless mortals, these nameless creatures are docile beings. They feed on ice and snow and the sea's bounty, only rarely infecting the land, where trapping more substantial prey or feeding on carrion is easier.

The icy mass creaks and groans but tolerates my presence, and its digestive frosts retreat. Had I sensed hostility, I would have sunk it then and there. Less discerning than the iceberg are the half-ogor scavengers populating its milky crags. They emerge in twos and threes, four dozen of them, then leer up at me. A moment's glance at their patchwork armour and scar-latticed bellies tells me they are outcasts from the Winterbite Mawtribe. Half-ogors are rarely tolerated among full-bloods. More often than not, they are devoured once they reach maturity. Most know better than to stay.

A scowling brute with an overbite and sallow cheeks raises its chipped cleaver at me. 'Oh, good. Meatsies. I was a-hungerin.'

Equally pleased, I let Thengavar hunt. In a heartbeat my spear stakes the vicious brute to the ice, and its flab jiggles from my throw's force. The half-ogor's dullard brethren blink at their gurgling brother, then lift their piggish eyes to me. Perhaps they hope I am disarmed, but when they glimpse Thengavar humming in my hands once more, they stand stupefied. Their dead leader topples, liberated from Thengavar's merciless metal after it rematerialises in my hand.

The iceberg tastes the coming glut. Insurgent frost creeps up the dead brute's sallow skin, snapping and cracking as it begins digestion. The half-ogors tumble over each other in their race to flee down the crags.

The hunt that follows hardly deserves the name. In Azyrheim, domesticated felids toy with mice they catch in their masters' pantries. In Glacier's End, pods of mega-orcas ram their bulbous snouts to spike mammoth seals from the waves and send them cartwheeling over the water. For these predators cruelty is play, a distraction. For me, such leisurely kills are a meditation.

As I butcher the half-ogors, an unbanishable thought scratches at my patience. These ogor-sons cannot hide from me. So how is it Tjatsår Mai, massive as she is, continually defies my pursuit? Long are the ages that have passed since the first time I exerted such effort to slay a foe. That was during my mortal life, against Doombreed, the daemon king of Khorne.

In the spray of a half-ogor's spilt vigour, an unbidden memory drifts before my eyes. A long chamber floored with round paving stones, each like the pebbly scales of a seraphon's saurian skin. Colonnades of carved timber flank the chamber's central aisle. Between each pair of columns, hay-scattered pegasus stalls invite the bold and reckless to leap through their doors and plunge into the heavens beyond.

Through those portals I spy the scarlet skies of my home. Aerial cavaliers soar and wheel through rose-tinted clouds, practising their dives.

The Deva's Eyrie, my people called this place. Our tribe's queen, Hyndaratha, ruled from this throne room, which doubled as stables. We were no effete Azyrite courtiers, with gilded halls and worked-stone keeps and fountains of ever-flowing wine. We were the Devadatta – the huntsmen-cavaliers of Ghur, lords of mountain and sky. At the dark dawn of the Age of Chaos, when all other kingdoms failed, we endured. We were Ghur's final hope, and our bloodstained ivory banners invoked not despair, but a dream of victory in the hearts of those we saved. As war vanquished Sigmar's peace and the cackling servants of the Chaos Gods besieged the Mortal Realms, rumours blazed that on every battlefield, Sigmar's faithful had fallen or retreated. All but we.

'Others fall. We ride,' my queen, Hyndaratha, told me once, long after I had earned my spurs. No myths of decorum divided the champions of the Devadatta from our supreme. The queen was friend to us all.

'We have learned to fear these lands,' she continued, tossing me an apple. 'To fear is to respect. To respect is to consider the strengths of one's quarry before exploiting its vulnerabilities. Look at Tarrabaster. He analyses before each strike, like a duardin logician.'

In the red clouds beyond the chamber, the master of the hunt dived in pursuit of a wounded chimaera. One of the beast's long necks ended in ragged flesh that spewed gore. Its remaining heads had decided they would be better served by flight. As their four dragon wings punished the skies in vain cowardice, Tarrabaster's ululations echoed through the mountains.

Tarrabaster's feat transfixed me, until the queen's elbow jarred me from my vicarious frisson. A wry grin graced her seasoned features.

'I taught him that,' she said. 'I picked it up from speaking in court. Before issuing decrees, I hold my breath and count to three.'

'Courage must be forged in the face of fear,' I replied, suddenly noticing the apple in my hands.

The queen clucked. 'Yes, but that is trite and not what I'm getting at. Court gives me diarrhoea. I count to three to force it down.'

I had dropped the apple and burst into laughter. Her eyes had glittered, and she'd quickly added: 'It helps!'

Knowing that Hyndaratha's royal station was a burden made her no less imposing. The queen was a legendary huntress. She had driven the monstrous hellicores to extinction. And the Three-Eyed King must have feared her, for not long after she had shared her wisdom with me, his false emissaries lamed her in an assassination attempt.

The ploy cost Tarrabaster's life. When I replaced him, the queen entrusted me to lead the Devadatta's grand alliance against Chaos in Sigmar's name.

For years I succeeded. We struck where the enemy expected us least, tearing out their throats and ripping off their heads. Word of our ferocity spread, and powerful allies joined our cause. The worm-folk of Shu'gohl, and their capricious rivals from the lesser worm cities and the nascent Vurm-tai steppe clans. The Askurga Renkai – Ghur's noblest vampire knights, led by Toura Vai and her daughter in darkness, if not blood, Lauka. Nameless aelf-wanderer beastriders, too, and the peerless swordmasters of their more elevated kin. Human nomads who fought in wyrm-scale armour with sharpened sabretooth war-picks. Aza-Karakier, duardin whose ancestral holds had long fallen. They carved runes of vengeance into their bare flesh, enshrining the fulfilment of their grudges in the notched kill-marks on their axes' hilts.

The day I learned of our doom, embassies from these mighty peoples crowded Deva's Eyrie. I was marshal of this host, but I still considered myself a huntress. I sat upon a simple wooden bench before my queen's dusty throne. Hyndaratha's hands had not gripped its eagles'-head armrests since her laming. The last of the hellicores' lifeless heads hung above her empty seat, testament to her faded might. Each morn I stared at that stuffed skull, dreaming blearily of how I might surpass my queen's glory. I never expected to. But the day comes for us all when we are transformed by that which we did not hope to achieve.

In my lamellar, with my pronged hunting lance leaning against my leg, I rose to brush the neck of my softly neighing steed. Ruladaha nickered, and I whispered into her ear. 'Soon, Rula. Soon.'

Lauka approached in rose-hued warplate, her flowing hair as pure and sable as the night. She still stood on two legs then, and bowed ten degrees, in the manner in which the Renkai greeted equals.

Then, she uttered the omen of my obliteration. 'Doombreed comes.'

From Lauka, I learned the daemon king was the greatest servant of Khorne, the Blood God, sent by his unholy patron to shatter the spine and will of our alliance. This daemon grew mightier with each mortal he slew. By now, he had broken eight empires. He was a titan whose tread shook the realm, whose shadow darkened horizons. Where he strode, his name was given bloody incarnation. For the far countries and kingdoms crossed by the daemon king's mile-wide footsteps were indeed the breeding grounds of doom.

Lauka's sylph-like neck straightened. 'The tyrant's tireless march leads him to here. The Askurga Renkai will stand beside the Devadatta, as ever. But the daemon means to carve out the heart of our resistance – the mountains of *your* people.'

Enthralled by the prospect of such ferocious prey, I gave my order without hesitation. 'Prepare for battle.' These words breathed belligerent animus into my hundred captains, whose bloodthirst rivalled my own.

Then three heartbeats passed, and a haggard voice uttered a single, shaking syllable. 'No.'

Hyndaratha had spoken. Bent with weakness, her face stroke-warped into a permanent grimace, the faded crone leaned on her throne. She had heard the tidings and my decision. She had counted three stabbing breaths, then issued her decree. Amongst the Devadatta, Hyndaratha's word was law.

I naysaid her. I argued what we all knew. Before the end, Chaos must be confronted. What did it matter if this occurred sooner rather than later, so long as we were ready? And we were ready. *I* was ready.

My queen did not repeat herself. The clouded gems of her eyes scorned my unruly youth. In bleak silence, she hobbled away.

'I will speak reason to her,' I promised my allies, careful to avoid their eyes.

Fierce Lauka, wizened by her years and her bond with her mother-in-night, bowed. 'Be wise, huntress.'

By evening our forces had organised despite my queen's will. I paced outside Hyndaratha's chambers and rehearsed the words I would say. She was weak; my argument must be forceful but elegant. The skaven poisons which had nearly robbed her of life had ravaged her vigour. Hyndaratha was not yet old, and yet all the ages of the universe were moulded in the ossified arc of her spine, the sag of her mouth.

For reasons I cannot explain, I hesitated. Three seconds became three minutes, then neared an hour. I paced with a semblance of courage but did not dare to act. In the end, I did not even rap upon her door.

Upon Ruladaha's winged back, I careened from Deva's Eyrie into the scarlet murk of dusk. That night the two million torches of our host blazed through the foothills towards Wrothquake Valley, where we would meet Doombreed's ruinous advance. My people and our allies had answered my call and taken up their spears. But ten million more champions and the promise of triumph could not have filled the gulf of my queen's absence.

Frost encrusts the eviscerated half-ogors at my boots. I should know better than to underestimate any prey. I should recognise when I require allies. Just as with Doombreed, I cannot slay Tjatsår Mai alone. The beast is too wily. Too cunning.

Arktaris' fleet will be too far gone to entice back into my hunt. Lauka Vai, were she here, is lost to me, lost to reason, lost to time. All my remaining allies are extinct save for those of Shu'gohl, who roams sands which might as well be as distant as Azyr.

But that girl and her kin in the despoiled sled-city, with their dyed-blue tunics and pointed hoods, remain. I had sensed the amber touch of Ghur in their wilding souls even as I had scorned their needs. The girl who stood before me had known of Tjatsår Mai and the Drownharrow. No matter her city's wretched fate, if her people could eke out an existence in this barren tundra, they had to have been canny.

I jet into the air. Wind currents settle beneath me, and my meteoric flight carries me back the way I came. I would seek out these survivors and demand their service. I would entice them into my hunt with the prospect of vengeance for the city Tjatsår Mai stole from them.

Arktaris' words reverberate in my skull, chipping at my glacial calm. *You, my lady huntress, are colder than the void...*

He was right. But that does not change what I must do, or who I will sacrifice to do it. I had nothing before Sigmar gave me my first and final task. At least, nothing worth remembering.

CHAPTER SIX

Njda's ma drifted in twilight. Gossamer strands of her hair spidered through black waters. A nest of eels writhed at her ankles, each fleshy vine splaying into a translucent anemone of grasping petals.

Njda's shoulders burned as she pumped herself through the gelid sea. Bubbles streamed from her mouth. The black crush trapped her voice and imprisoned her words. *Ma! I'm coming!*

Her ma's eyes snapped open. Glaucous light gleamed from within the laughter lines. Meeting that cold glare felt like staring at dead suns.

'*We wait, Njda. We swim.*'

Njda gasped. The others snoozed around her in a damp ditch. Fresh flakes of snow dusted their coats. The low fires of Riika-Min smouldered beyond the trees.

Bavval pulled his hood lower and buried his hands into his opposite sleeves. 'You said we could start moving again once the birds were quiet. Your snares are silent, too. Is it time?'

The night was coldest before dawn. Njda's furs sheathed her, but no part of her wanted to move. Cold air knifed into her lungs as she heeded the taiga's call.

Over dark junipers, the omen of sunlight tinted the horizon blue. Wind rustled through the woods, and treetops swayed to the music of the realm. Within the taiga's evergreen legions lay snow-carpeted glades and a hundred thousand promises and perils. Shelter, where it could be found. Game, running water, fresh greens. Marigolds and sundry marsh flowers that could cramp bellies or heal birth sickness. The Sukuat gripped it all jealously in its cold, earthen knuckles. Hidden amongst the treasure, death lurked, but so did life, for those strong enough to seize it.

Just as the seas of Glacier's End made Njda dizzy and filled her belly with ice, the vision of the taiga's bounty and Suodji's distant shield mountains promised... possibility. A chance to leave her pain behind, though she couldn't. An opportunity to love something wonderful and terrible that would never love her in return.

Njda had been born to these lands. The realm had always scorned the Suku, always tried them, always nourished them. In the end they could never leave, and Njda didn't want to. Spirit and blood bound her here.

Njda kicked the others awake as she checked her quiver. 'Let's go.'

The tops of taiga trees swallowed the last vision of Riika-Min's flames and the tomb-still seas of Glacier's End. The Suku marched in a file through the sprucelands, over the hills. They dragged their sledge over old stones and brittle brush and soft snow. Magga picked green cones from the low-hanging boughs of pines to chew on. Valter plucked marsh flowers, then pushed his heel into permafrost and turned over a wedge of rich earth. In pine glades, blinding white snow caught the sun's light, and Njda squinted. She could have led the others on a shorter path across the peninsula back to the shores that would bring them to Suodji, but the white desert lurked beyond the mossy trees. The fear Tjatsår Mai somehow drifted in the tundra, her ancient tentacles scouring the snows to strangle their necks and souls, haunted Njda. If only Sigramalles Apmil would put his heavy hand to the lands... But he would never come. The Sukuat's majesty was unbreakable, its wonder untameable. Ghur's dangers could not be vanquished.

After hours of hard trekking, Njda helped the others across a crest in the forest. Heigen pushed her hand away, and the sledge cracked over stone behind him. Bavval thanked her and wobbled down the other side.

Valter hiked up his pack. 'Where'd you get that?' he asked.

Njda peeled stringy flesh from a spoonpear, careful not to let the juice dampen her lips. 'I told you we passed three groves. You didn't fill your pockets?'

'Fill our pockets with what?' Magga balanced on a stone and waited to cross. Her chiselled features sharpened. 'Aren't those poisonous? And didn't you say we couldn't eat?'

'I wouldn't call this eating. And only the seeds and skin.' Njda passed two fruits from her coat. Magga dangled hers by its stem, as if letting it closer would kill her.

Valter stared at the fruit in his rough palm and snorted. 'Noajdi, you see this? Our guide says we can't eat until nightfall, then stuffs her face in secret.'

'Secret? No, I–' Njda's face flattened. 'We need to reach the shores again by night. After sunset the kings of the forest won't tolerate our presence. A rest will slow us down, and we're already behind. At nightfall we'll camp. Bavval, can you help explain?'

Below, in a stony glade, Bavval watched Heigen unpack their sledge. A fire already crackled in a hasty pit. Heigen shovelled snow in pots to melt, then began sawing through their reindeer meat and a sheaf of herbs he had plucked from the brush.

Njda tamped her toes on the hard loam. 'An hour, no longer. Don't go far.'

Valter tossed his spoonpear and clapped. Magga shoved her fruit back into Njda's hands and shoved past. They shared a curt exchange with Bavval before they stumbled into the treeline. Njda pinched stress from her temples. If they needed privacy to relieve themselves, at least Valter had pistols and Magga had her blades. Truthfully, a fire and a quick bite wouldn't hurt. As far and as fast as they'd moved today, the lands' freeze ached in Njda's bones.

She slumped against the sledge as Heigen cooked quickly and confidently, at a pace Njda hadn't thought possible. Soon the contents of the sledge were neatly packed again, the salted reindeer meat cut and stowed. Steaming portions of stew filled a row of crocks. Garnishes of redolent snow sage and ash's heather dusted the bowls. The empty cauldron hissed as snow melted in it, and the old iron soaked.

Njda closed her eyes and drank in the rich scent. She rocked up. 'Eat. I'll clean. Bavval, can you find Magga and–'

Bavval's head hung to his chest. He snored.

Heigen waved Njda off. 'I'll do it. You find them.'

'I'll take bowls to them,' she said. 'Let's be quick.'

Heigen grunted and dumped a pail of meltwater on the campfire. The pit smoked and snapped as he reversed the pail and sat on it, then swallowed a spoonful of stew. With a grimace and a sigh he lowered his crock, chewing slowly, eyes fixed on the forest. Then he leapt up and grabbed a cloth from the sledge and started scouring the cauldron.

Njda's jaw tensed. Hysh skirted below the treetops. Night was soon. She tried to ignore the expanses beyond the evergreens – all that sky, and all that tundra – but the emptiness crept in through her periphery. She drew her pointed hood in around her face and stepped closer.

'Heigen, I know you suffer. But we're kinfolk of Riika-Min. We were almost joined by siida.' She forced a smile to her lips. 'You'll always be my friend. If you wish to talk, *need* to talk, I'll listen.'

Heigen froze. Drifting snowflakes caught in his cropped hair. Frost coated his sleepy lashes. When Njda was younger, a forlorn fragment of her heart had hoped she'd painted her own fantastical man onto the blank canvas of Heigen and his hooded eyes – that no matter her childish feelings for him, she would be better off without him. But when Heigen had finally conquered his shyness and responded to Njda's gifts of venison, dried flowers and salted fish, he had revealed himself to her as every part the kind thinker she had seen in him.

She saw it again now, in the agony underlining his gaze. She heard it in his brutal silence. The cold didn't bother Heigen – he seemed to relish it.

'I don't want to talk.'

The spruces' shadows had darkened, as had Njda's impression of the taiga's menace. She took the crocks of stew to track the others down. She couldn't call for them, not from here. Let them eat as they walked. She began to crunch along Valter's trail of bootprints in the snow.

Behind her, a ladle clattered. 'Njda.'

Heigen gazed at her the way wights did before they struck. His hands had balled into shaking fists. 'You don't understand. You think you do. But I loved her more than anything. More than Riika-Min. More than you. You can't know. Not until you lose someone like that.'

Njda's brows arched. She wanted to shout, or strangle him. She wanted to weigh her siida against Heigen's wretched wife and shove those lopsided scales in his face. She wanted him to know where she had been that night, crying herself to sleep beneath the silent stars in the wilds beyond Riika-Min. The distant revelry of Heigen's wedding had echoed through the slate hills the way raucous marauders did as they hunted for spoils and slaughter.

Her breathing slowed, even as her heart raced. She sensed no malice in Heigen's words – only a reckless breed of truth, perhaps one which healed him to speak. That did not lessen their sting.

Njda trudged into the snowy pines and hissed her steaming anger into the wind. *I know, Heigen. More than you ever could.*

Njda's blood was up by the time she found Valter. He had gone too far. With no reason to ever leave Riika-min to tend his herds or stock his larders, perhaps the merchant thought Ghur's wilds a thrill. If he did, he was a fool.

Valter stooped by a stream and clutched a jewelled dagger. As Njda stormed closer, he tapped dirt from the knife into the water. 'Victuals! Excellent. Set it by the rocks. I'll have a taste when I've shaved.'

'You'll eat on the go.' Njda clapped a crock down, careful not to let its steam dampen her mitten. The spruces swayed. Wind tussled with frosted grasses and bent horsetails on the stream's edge. The breeze tickled Njda's scalp through her hood. 'Be quick,' she said. 'We need to leave.'

Valter's eyes followed hers. 'I used to hear them speak, too. Used to listen, like you. But I never wanted to be a finder. I just wanted to live. And live I did, as do we all. Until we die. And die we do.'

Njda's face smoothed. She saw Valter, then. A jaded man, but also a child to Riika, same as her. The wilds' peril and their beauty were a medicine for grief. After Heigen she had done the same. For all Njda knew, Valter had loved someone in Riika-Min. Or maybe he had loved his own wealth like a person. One way or the other, he hurt. They all did.

Njda lifted the remaining crock. 'Go back. I need to find Magga before this gets cold.'

'She likes it cold. Stay a breath.' Valter wetted his heavy

moustache and shaved stubble from his leather jaw. 'I know you think me a greedy man, collecting debts on the dead. But my debtors have kin in Suodji, and I won't collect against them. I'm doing what I can. What I must, as you did.' He tapped his knife. 'That was a brave thing you did in my halls, standing against the orruks. Against her.'

'We all stood against the orruks. And her...' Njda straightened a rebellious strand of hair. 'Have you heard the one about how Tjatsår Mai outfoxed Fatebutcher?'

Valter nodded.

'I never wanted to be part of that saga,' Njda said. 'Did Bavval tell you about saints?'

Valter cracked an ugly smile. 'During the trek. But he's wrong. Yesterday I knew, sure as Sigmar's fury, whoever of us stands against this shadow will die. But you didn't scare. You faced her like a true Ghurish woman. That takes steel.'

Njda's eyes narrowed. Valter didn't seem like a man generous with his words for nothing. She gathered up her coat hems and squatted, then watched.

Valter's blade scraped more stubble from the rocky leather of his cheeks. 'Judging from this meal, you've clever hands, too.'

'Heigen cooked this. What do you want?'

Valter rinsed his blade. 'Marriage, if you'll have me.'

Njda recoiled. 'Me?'

Valter frowned. 'Why not? You're smart and strong. Both qualities which would benefit me. You'd be an asset. And I'd be good to you and your siida. If... You know.'

'If I find them. When I find them.'

Valter shrugged. 'We all live, we all die. Wherever they are, I'd treat you well. You could go to salons in Izalend. Wear steel armour and fine boots.'

Njda's nose twitched. 'I don't want steel and fine boots.'

Valter's eyes shifted. One was good and green, like the forest after the thaw. But the dead eye, grey and scarred, unnerved Njda. Like it was enchanted, and through it Valter could see the prices of people and wares at market.

'Marriage would benefit us both,' he said. 'But we'd need to earn each other's trust. Show me I can count on you. That you have my back, so I can have yours.'

Njda bared her teeth. 'And how might I show my appreciation?'

Valter's eyes flitted to his pack. 'Good metal there, for the ones who carry it. You're generous, like me. The whole city speaks... *spoke* of it.'

'That you carried this ruck from the camp into the wilderness to keep your eye on its treasure says much of your generosity.'

'What I'm getting at' – Valter brandished his knife – 'is we'd have to show each other we could bear each other's burdens.'

Njda chortled and rose. 'You thought if you asked me to marry you, I'd carry that?'

'What? I never, I was–'

'You know it's a waste to even bring, yes? That it'll get you killed?'

'A waste? Do you even know its worth?' He threw his knife down and groaned. 'Help me convince the old man to let me toss it on the sledge. It's not heavy, I swear. And we took those pelts!'

'The furs aren't for selling. They're so we don't freeze to death while we sleep. And you've complained about the ruck's weight all day.'

Valter stooped and snapped his knife into its sheath. 'Consider my offer retracted.' He snatched up the crock Njda had brought. The way he ate, he looked as if he were chewing molten rubber.

Njda chuckled. Valter was a crooked, fragile little thing. 'Out here your life depends on us. Not wealth.'

Valter barked his harsh laughter. '*My* life depends on my wealth.

I've been here and there. Our only place in the realm is bought at market or settled at blade's edge, and that's the truth. Speak to a mariner in Izalend a day, they'll teach you the realm's ways.'

'I know the realm's ways. No one survives alone.' Those words settled in the base of Njda's skull. She liked them. 'Whether we like it or not, we need each other. Anyone who watches how you treat Magga for half a second can see you don't get that. Maybe you should speak to a herdsteader for a day. Might learn a thing or two.'

'I treat Mag well. Gave her a place to live, paid her her glimmerings.' Valter sneered, thumbed his breastplate. 'I'm a good man.'

'No one likes their food cold, Valter. Just like no one likes you. If you're late back to camp, we're leaving without you.'

Magga's trail snaked through the snow around their camp's outskirts, then returned to the fire and wound back through the treeline. Njda's scowl touched her eyes by the time she found Magga standing vigil in a meadow of heather. No doubt she had another barb nocked on her tongue about Njda not finding things – but no. Magga's hard, hazel eyes peered up the dig at the trees looming on a ridge.

'Quiet.' Magga gripped her rondel dagger. 'Ready your bow.'

Njda's skin tingled. She sniffed the upwind and prepped an arrow. She only smelt trees, but the woods' sound was wrong. Almost... backwards.

Magga's nose wrinkled. 'Oh!' She let her sword hang and bent to the crock Njda had set down. She gulped a mouthful without chewing. 'Aqshy-hot! My kind of stew!' She swallowed the rest and dropped the crock. As Njda frowned, Magga waggled her hand. 'Knife.'

Njda passed it. 'What's wrong with yours?'

'Daggers are for cutting throats and spiking skulls.' Magga

opened her tin wallet and shaved metal from a glowing coin. She licked her fingers and pushed a pinch of fuming dust into her eyes. Her eyelids clamped shut.

'Don't do that here,' Njda said. 'It's not safe.'

'A taste of the future never hurt anywhere. Especially in lands that want to kill you.' Magga's eyes snapped open. She seemed fully... functional. 'So what was your answer?'

'I... what?'

'Will you marry the stupid oaf? He must have asked by now.'

'Has he asked you?'

'Loads. But he stopped ages ago. Wanted me to guard the red house for free, I think. But I wouldn't. Not for free.' Magga pinched more dust from her tin and packed it into the corner of her eyes. She shivered and blinked the red away.

Njda pointed. 'Is that safe?'

'He wants a retainer. Likes the idea of it, I think. Valt wants a household like the nobles of Izalend. That's what Izalenders call their siida, he says. Households. It's all so foolish.'

'The households or the nobles? Magga, put that away.'

'All of it. Siida, too. You can't count on anybody or anything but yourself. Anyone with half a head knows that. Heigen cooks damn well. Have you heard of Aqshy? I heard food there makes your lips dance.'

Magga sighed and crumpled. She flattened a patch of heather and patted the ground. Njda stared, then swallowed the curse brewing in her throat. She hadn't realised she'd longed for this moment with Magga until it came. In their youth they had been friends – Magga had visited Njda's sledcroft for every other meal. Even as children, she had carried the false dream of freedom, to be bound to neither living nor dead.

Magga's blissfully blank expression told Njda she had got what she wanted. Her chiselled face was unburdened; her strong shoulders were slack. She leaned with the wind where she wanted but carried her freedom alone. Magga had nobody but Valter. Njda envied her utter independence even as she pitied her for it.

The glimmering dust had warped the bright of Magga's eyes. 'So?'

'I considered it.' Njda sat. 'Did you?'

Magga grimaced. Joy and bitter amusement wrestled in her puckered lips. 'Marrying him? Are you mad? Yes, of course I did. Look at his sled. But no, all the wilds no. It's not even his age. Be around him long enough, you see how he sees the world.'

'I've been around him a day and I see how he sees the world.'

Magga grunted. 'He loves his boots. Polishes those spurs at night, you know. People are things to Valt, too. I've known him years and that's how he sees me. I guard his longsled from crooks like him, so he pays me, keeps me up. But never once has he asked how I am. Never once has he asked me to sit at his table. He docks my pay if I eat from his stores. He'll write us all up a bill in Suodji. This I guarantee.'

Njda raised an eyebrow. Magga might not have counted on anybody but herself, but it sure seemed like she wanted to. 'Why was he so worried about crooks in Riika-Min?'

'Valt's head is stuck in Izalend. So is his heart. He sees the world like they do, with their Freeguilds and conclaves and their brotherhoods of larcenists. In his eyes, all herdsteaders are thugs like him. And anyone who's not wishes to be one.' She ripped heather from the jet earth. 'Maybe he's right.'

Njda chewed her tongue. 'Do you know about me and Heigen?'

'We all do. Heigen's highly witless. You're lucky you got away.'

Njda winced. 'Heigen's fine.'

'Maybe you're witless, too.'

'This isn't my point. Heigen would have been as useful to my siida as Valter, if not more. He's a good herdsteader. When we were children he trapped as fine as me. But what good is any husband or wife to my siida now? If they're out in the cold, then none. When I find them I'll sweat the little things.'

Magga's head rotated towards Njda as if on a track. 'You really are witless. I hope you're sharper with your bow than with your thoughts of family.'

Njda snatched her knife back. 'You don't get to say that.'

'Wilds, do you know how naive you sound? You know what my siida did for me? Nothing. My father loved Izalend's rotgut more than me. And for the icicles of Aqua Ghyranis to buy more of it, he let their endless wars take him from us.'

Njda's sneer fell away. 'Your father was a taker.'

Magga clambered up. Her gravity drew Njda with her.

'Why else would I have shared plates with your kin every other night?' she said. 'He was a taker all right. And that was what he did. He took. Nothing we gave him was enough. And when he died, he still kept taking. Took the childhood from my life, and my mother, who surrendered to despair without him.' Magga stamped. 'My siida left me alone in this realm. Tjatsår Mai didn't do that. The biro jeknja torture-rats didn't either. My kin did. You'd be fool to keep thinking of yours. Leave them with Riika-Min and the dead. Because one way or another, they left–'

Magga jolted into a stiff statue. The hazel rings of her eyes twisted and shifted like sand. Njda's rage drained, and Magga's horror drew their gaze up the dig across the heather.

Dusk light silhouetted two trees on the crest which had not been there before. They stood like skeletal soldiers, each ten feet tall, their knobbled trunks shaped into powerful legs. The spruces swayed with the wind, but the sentinel trees remained stock-still. Unnerving spirals were carved – *grown* – into the hard bark of what looked like… faces. Two knotholes in their trunks began to look more and more like jealous, watching eyes.

'They kill us at sunset,' Magga breathed. Her baleen sword's fronds rattled as she clutched its hilt. 'They hang our skins from the branches and dance.'

Panic cascaded through Njda's legs. Sunset would be within the hour. They needed at least that much time to break from the sprucelands to the relative safety of the coast. If they didn't make it…

Njda towed Magga back with her towards camp. From the darkening treeline, more skeletal trees loured, their trunks creaking as they shifted and watched. The kings of the forest had never been known for kindness.

CHAPTER SEVEN

A lance thudded into the loam, pinning Njda's trousers. She slammed down and stripped parchment bark as she yanked her leg against the wicked shaft until fabric tore. The ocean's crash was close. Even in the dusk light she could make out the ragged line of the shore's crags.

Valter hauled her up. 'That's for free!' His pack jostled as he bumbled ahead.

Magga stood at the crags. Her baleen sword whooshed and rattled as she hacked through a snowy hedge. Bavval was close behind her. A knot of magic sputtered in his gnarled hands, but the amber glow in his eyes fizzed and spat. The shaman's spell winds held no sway here. The forest and its magic belonged to its kings.

A hammer-shaped charm bounced around Heigen's neck as he dragged the sledge at a run. Their cargo jounced behind him, and Njda ripped their last pair of snow-shoes and skis from the sledge. Only food and furs remained.

'Dead weight's gone! I'll push!'

Heigen grunted. Njda threw a glance behind them. In the shadow-ridden woods, an icy gheist stared. Spectral hair billowed down its muscled torso, but its legs were gnarled roots that might have chopped themselves free from the earth. A hissing sickle curved from its white arm like a long talon.

Njda rubbed her eyes, but the mirage remained. An eerie hymnal drifted from its lips. The forest sang its fickle wrath in a haunting melody, like the kings' merest presence had driven the trees mad.

Njda threw her full weight behind the sledge. Ravens cawed and wheeled overhead. Bavval, eyes foggy, straddled the shredded brush between the forest and the shingly crags. 'Hurry! They are almost here!'

Njda and Heigen burst from the trees. Their sledge cracked into stone and overturned. Njda toppled and crawled from the vines writhing beneath the leaves. Bavval stumbled and snapped. A silver haze pulsed from his spindly fingers, and the ravens scattered. For half a heartbeat, the soft glow highlighted a shadow that reared to the canopy, a great goldwood covered in moss and ice, its knot-hole eyes nested in craggy bark. Njda jerked an arrow from her quiver, but by the time she nocked the titan was gone. A birch rose in its place like a ghost.

Below the crags, breakers rolled up frigid black beaches, and sand steamed with strange life. Njda eased her bow down. The kings of the forest were gone. The Suku had quit their intrusion by nightfall. Gramb had told Njda the old tales – they would not be harmed.

Valter bent over his knees and hacked for air. He spat a wad of sputum into the shingle. 'I need wine.'

Magga jumped on the crags and cackled out the last fumes of her high. Wet tree sap stained the shoulders of her fur coat and faded tunic. 'You all see that? I beat one!'

Njda shoved her arrow into her quiver. She blasted across the shingle and yanked Magga's coat hem. 'I told you not to use that filth.'

Magga shoved back. 'That *filth* saved our lives. I saw what was coming for us, didn't I? And when I fought that tree-spirit, I saw where each of its blows would land. *That's* how I bested it. With my filth.'

'You didn't best a tree-king in combat.' Njda snatched a green tree needle from Magga's braids. 'You got stuck in brush, you sick dimwit.'

Magga prowled from Njda's grip and glowered. Heigen righted their sledge with a bang and stroked his carved medallion. 'She didn't come.'

'Who?' Njda asked.

'Yndrasta. Bavval, you said she served Sigmar. She didn't come this time. Have we sinned?'

Bavval brushed sweat from his blotchy brow. Over the black seas of Glacier's End, hints of evening aurora shimmered. The sea horizon lit up like sunrise at night. 'I know none of her legends. I only know what the priests and missionaries in the Izalenders' court shared with me. Nothing else.'

Njda tidied her queue. 'I know something. Sigmar's hand is far from these lands.'

Valter mumbled and looked away. Bavval grew a shade paler. 'Careful with your words, my sister.'

'You think he'd send his cursed saint to kill us? He's not so generous with his attention. Look around you, all of you. This isn't Sigmar's realm. This is our Sukuat, our Ghur. So what if Fatebutcher slew the blessed vargr for Sigmar's Izalenders a century ago? She will not help us. Sigmar's favour means nothing here.'

'Njda.'

'What? Sigmar's cities are already mighty, and he is a god. Fate-butcher had her chance to spread his goodwill when we needed it. She left us. Like a snow-djinn freed from its cave after tricking a mortal to take its place.'

Silence dominated the rocks, broken only by the crash of waves. Njda reined in the pressure in her chest. Magga had been wrong about her family. The spirits and ancestors might have abandoned them, and maybe Sigmar and his wretched saint had, too. But her clan had not left her behind. The Suku had spent generations in unforgiving wilds. They had depended on each other and no one else. Njda's family would never have given up hope on her, just as she would not give up hope for them. Two years ago, on her deathbed for the fourth time, Gramb had made them promise to stick together. That had been a silly oath to swear, because where else would they go? All they'd had was each other.

Bavval cleared his throat. 'She is not Fatebutcher. She told us her name. Fatebutcher was a monster we named from Izalend's hearsay and rumours. A way of understanding the miracle they revered, the force we could not reckon. But we know who came to us in Riika-Min. I have told you before, and so I tell you again – do not invite doom upon us. Do not invoke the name of the God-King and his saint in anger.'

Njda hiked up her bow. She trudged to her place behind the sledge. 'You're so sure they'd be offended. But they're not listening. None of them.'

With no more headlands between them and Suodji, the city's shield mountains bulged on the horizon like the bellies of expecting mothers. Njda would have given anything to clutch her anger in her chest forever, but when her gaze travelled from the peaks to the star-swathed void, the rage slipped from her heart and her breath was stolen from her lungs. All the gods of all the realms had spilt all the colours of creation into the night. How natural and fair such beauty should stand vigil over lands as ruthless as theirs.

They lugged the sledge down the coastal bluffs, then moved slowly over slick rocks until they reached the coarse jet sands. As they took turns pulling, sparkling stars and auroral twilight brightened the black beach. Sand crunched beneath their boots and the sea sang.

Valter peppered the realm's music with endless complaints. 'Back's killing me. Can we sleep here? Or here?'

'I'll say where,' Njda said. As long and as far as they had moved, they couldn't strike camp in the open. Heigen wordlessly dragged the sledge onward. He seemed thankful, as if sleep and its omens only haunted him. Magga stumbled at their van and retched as she came down from her high. Njda fell in beside Bavval and turned every four steps to check their trail.

Bavval's hunched head hung. As Njda confided in him, he contorted his lips and blinked at the curled toes of his boots.

'I know Riika-Min is gone,' she said. 'But we're one people. One family, you said. Do you still see it? I don't. What Magga said to me at the camp… It was hateful, and pain's no excuse for it. We've all weathered our lives here. Not a single season was ever kind to us. People can be hard. I know I have been. But she spoke to me like I was a fool.'

Bavval's breathing jostled rocks in his lungs. He licked his lips. 'A lagoon ahead. Can we camp there?'

Njda stretched her neck up. 'Too open. We need trees or rocks.' Her feet flattened and her heart dropped. 'You're not listening.'

'You said something?'

Ahead, Valter's bootprints warped and dissolved as waves devoured the shores. 'You too,' Njda murmured. 'You've all forgotten.'

'I know just who we are.'

'Before the attacks, you listened to me. You were my friend.'

Understanding rose in Bavval's clouded eyes like a cold sun. He slowed. 'Is this the jest of a cruel woman? Or the complaint of a spoilt girl?'

Njda's cheeks warmed. 'What?'

Bavval pointed. 'Look.'

The others trudged, and their tired march kicked soggy sand up their backsides. Magga stared at her feet. Frost bejewelled Heigen's clipped scalp and ears. He tramped like a soulless machine, like the clockwork toys the Kharadron had once brought to Riika-Min when Njda was a girl.

Bavval's rugged voice became a low whisper. 'We are all that remains. Do you understand? Everything we knew is dead.'

Njda's stomach churned. 'You don't know that. Sleds got away.'

'Mute Gunvor. Do you remember her? You brought her meat on the feast solstices. Bancu and Nilpa – I taught them as I taught you at their age. Juho, Ruben, Ville, always getting into trouble. And Edel... dear Edel. She was my...' Bavval croaked. 'She was a good noajdi. They are dead, Njda. Gone to the far family. Those are only a handful I saw. Men, women, girls, boys. People we loved and laughed with as long as we have known these lands and their cruelty. They are dead.'

'I knew them too. You needn't remind me.'

'Then how can you be so childish as to think anything could occupy my mind right now other than what happened to them, or what could happen to us? The Sukuat is as treacherous as all the winds of Ghur. My task, my *duty*, Njda, is to keep us safe. You quibble to me of hurt feelings. I fair for the living and the dead. You ask me to care. Njda, I do not care.'

The others had halted. Magga's eyes were sunken pits. 'I'd love to sleep tonight,' she moaned. 'One day. When you two catch up. What, is here good enough?'

Njda shook her head. Magga groaned and resumed the trek. The haunting roar of waves pulled Njda's eyes out to sea like a riptide. This time she didn't fight the flies it spawned in her gut. She got the same feeling when she hunted, or slit the throats of animals trapped in her snares. Killing other living creatures had always felt like killing part of herself. It was necessary, of course, as death was. But Njda couldn't accept the deaths of her kindred Suku of Riika-Min.

Suffering was an old bedfellow to the Ten Thousand herdsteads. But no matter the hardships they faced – the poisonous pines that flayed healthy men, or the slinking marrfoxes that pilfered babes from their cribs – *life* had always bound the Suku. Survival had joined Njda with her city and her siida. Now Riika-Min was gone, and all that shared tribulation felt wasted. Njda's family and city were unwritten. So was she.

Njda's dreams swam back to her. She tried to imagine her ma's face, but then a pair of eyes glinted at her from the shadow in the threshold. The night aurora cast more shadows around the marching Suku, like ink spilt on oil. Gulls screamed on the horizon.

Bavval stroked frost from his white beard. 'Forgive me. Forgive my blunt words.'

Njda's shoulders slackened. 'Always. And forgive me. You're right, of course. As usual.'

'I am not. It is… You are young. You have not seen the realm as I have. You do not understand what is at stake. You are a finder. Bold, with nothing but hope for what can be gained. But you lack fear for what must be lost.'

Another breaker rolled far up the beach and forced Njda closer to Bavval. She gripped her chest and imagined brine in her ma's lungs. 'I fear, Bavval. I fear so much.'

'Valter was a child when I came to Riika-Min. I had been seeking out your city to offer my guidance as noajdi. Back then, he explored. He was a curious roamer with light in his eyes and the tundra in his heart. He loved more than any of us. Like you.'

Njda lifted her gaze. 'What changed?'

'Everything. One day, life was gorgeous and full. The next, we found our kin asleep outside their sledcrofts, or at market sprawled on the planks, unable to wake. Seaweed hung from the eaves of the highest sledcrofts, and water had fouled our trade pelts like the ocean came and went. We knew not what had happened, except the ocean must have risen. A ravener tsunami or worse. But a day's catch of fish had started to rot, and as we spoke we understood we had all lost a day. None remembered what had happened.'

'And then?'

'Days and nights passed. The slumberers never awoke. They died by slow starvation. Before Tjatsår Mai and Gumper, this was the most terrible thing I had ever seen. I thought nothing could be worse.'

'I've never heard of this.'

'We dared not speak of it lest we summon the horror again. Like Yndrasta, you see. If there is evil in her, I would not have that close to us. So I speak only of her good and pray that if Sigramalles listens, he hears.'

That seemed foolish, but Njda bit her tongue. 'What's this to do with Valter?'

Bavval's lips curled. 'His siida had lain among the afflicted. He had spent the night in the taiga with the herds, trapping for pelts and scaring off marauders. After he returned, he never left his family's side, but they never woke. He buried them by himself.'

Valter trudged like a stallo gargant. His ruck's bulk dragged him side to side. He was less clumsy in the damp sands than Njda had expected. And yes, he complained of his rucksack's weight, but were they truly complaints, or did he just enjoy it when others heard him? He'd moved easily through the bush yesterday, too.

Bavval's unruly eyebrows shook as he coughed. 'He stood vigil over them. Half-living, half-dead. He sold his bow for food. No one helped him, and for what? For Harmony they said, but they were scared. Times of plenty were rarer than they have been, Njda. Each siida looked to its own and no one else.'

'What'd he do?'

'Slept on the sterns of longsleds between migrations. In blizzards he watched the herds in exchange for food. When his boots fell apart, he warmed his bare feet in the reindeer's steaming stool. Have you not wondered where he gained the skill to become a byrkaller? He did not grow up in Izalend like most of them. No, he learned to peddle the dried reindeer chips back to herdsteaders after the snow season. They bought it and burned it for fuel in exchange for Izalend's currency, and so Valter mastered a new trade. Sixteen seasons ago Riika-Min crossed the Everflame to barter in Izalend. A visiting merchant saw his promise and offered her patronage. If you had seen how she treated him, you would think Magga and Valter have a far warmer friendship. He might as well have been a pelt to her, to be brushed and beaten until he was dustless and shining.'

'Greed helped him live.'

'Yes. Because we did not.' Amber flecks glistened in Bavval's grey eyes. 'Our people look to the noajdi to understand Harmony like it is a mystery. But never forget, Harmony exists in humans as much as Ghur. What happened to Valter was Harmony, too.'

Njda shook her head. 'Why tell me this?'

'We have nothing to offer each other but ourselves. That is not always warm, but it must be enough. Accept your kinfolk where they are at, Njda. Cherish them. For nothing lasts.'

Water lapped in the lagoon. Enormous toadstools of cleft, grass-clumped limestone jutted into the sky like tall strangers. Heigen's eyes bored through Njda as she banged another snare together.

Magga waggled her toes by the fire. Valter muttered as he counted out three glowing glimmerings from his purse.

Heigen sighed, jigged his feet. A chill knifed through the rocky columns, but sweat glistened on his brow. Njda lowered her snare. 'Can you set whiners?'

'I don't even know what that means.'

'Want to learn?'

He crossed his arms. His head rocked in a sharp nod, like he was parrying a knife with his chin.

Njda brushed her hands and ambled off. Valter, now repacking his ruck, glanced up. 'You say you're making wine?'

'Yes. Find grapes and join in.'

'You'll break his shrivelled heart, Njda.' Magga clapped her glimmerings into her tin wallet. After she stowed her azure pennies, the firelight painted her features gold. 'Where're you off to?'

'Looking for driftwood and washed-up sea-hair.' Njda brushed by Bavval, who snoozed against the sledge. She hobbled from their camp along the rock.

None of Riika-Min's finders had known so many types of snares as Njda. She favoured the whiner, which was simple to make as long as one could fashion cord and sense the wind's hunger. When properly placed, the snares warned of approaching danger after they were tripped. As long as Njda had a brace of whiners and her bow, the bush felt as safe as a second home.

Crystal shallows rippled under the beast moon. An eight-point starfish with uneven legs wriggled. Its movements were random, unnatural. Njda smiled and stooped to crush it in her fist. She paused, and ice coursed into her belly. Beside the pool, a rampage of fresh tracks marred the sand and shingle.

'What's wrong?' Magga leaned against a jagged column of rock and slid her boot on. Blue danced in her hazel eyes like candle-light on an oil slick.

Njda shifted her bow. 'You see this?'

'I see your nose in the dirt. What's wrong?'

Njda crouched and crawled. Clumped grass skittered from the limestone pillars, then sank its roots in new nooks. Njda pushed her knuckles into the sand. 'Reindeer tracks. Three toes. Boazu.' She sniffed, tasted, then spat grit. A storm swelled in her belly.

Magga sauntered closer. 'Wild reindeer. Impressive find. Next you'll tell me the ocean's near.'

Njda frowned. 'There a reason you're following me?'

'Yes. I wanted to apologise.'

'For what?'

'You know what.'

'I want to hear you say it.'

'For how I said what I said today. It's true, but I should have said it nicer. You're soft, Njda. Weak.'

Njda grunted. She would have rather smashed her fingers with stones than listen to another of Magga's apologies. 'Look. Skids, boot tracks. These are Suku.'

Magga's hands instinctively reached for her rondel dagger. 'Where?'

Njda interpreted the spoor in the sands. 'I can't tell. They came in a hurry. Left in a hurry.'

Buckles clinked and straps rustled as Valter staggered closer. A pistol dangled from one hand and his ruck hung hiked on his shoulder. 'Beginning to think you two had grapes after all. What's this?'

Magga plodded after Njda. 'Our finder thinks she's found her family.'

Valter toed at the sand. 'Are those orruk tracks?'

'Too light,' Njda said, blinking. 'Why would orruks even be here?'

'Orruk pirates aren't confined to the sea. If a junk catches sight of us, we might as well be dead. They'll send a skiff to come skin us. Doubt we'll even have time to hide.'

The thought of more foe-raiders made Njda as queasy as the ocean they prowled did. 'Quiet, both of you.'

Valter stuffed his hands in his breastplate. 'Truth be told, the pirates are worse than the breed that struck us. They don't just kill you. They take your things. And once they have you, they chain you in the bilges of their junks. Yank your arms off, then your legs. Their grots stitch up what's left to keep the meat fresh. But if they have enough prisoners in their bilges, once they eat your arms and legs, sometimes they throw what's left into the sea for a chuckle.'

Magga snorted with laughter, and Njda's cheeks burned. 'The orruks in Riika did that, too,' she said.

Valter's smile faded. 'They didn't take ours alive.'

'They did. I saw them. Their eyes moved when their bodies couldn't, like Heigen's wife. The orruks dragged them around like halved carcasses to toy with. Even after Fatebutcher saved us, those they left behind still lived. They froze to death in the snow.'

Magga's smirk slid from her lips. 'I walked the city's grounds. I didn't see that.'

'You didn't look. You were too busy lifting the hems of their tunics looking for knives. Too blinded with that metal you rub into your eyelids.' Njda clambered up and faced them. 'They did it to Hari. Gnawed on his guts while his eyes cried. I put him from his misery like a trapped fox.' Njda's finger thudded into Valter's breastplate. 'Maybe they did it to your debtors, too. That's what you called them, right? You remember their names?'

Valter's heavy brow bent.

Njda returned to the spoor. 'Maybe if the *cruel-boys* throw them into the sea like your junk pirates, they'll wash up here where we can find them. We'll ask their names then.'

Magga stormed before Njda and dragged her heel through the

tracks, as if it were a subtle trail to be lost rather than a mess that covered the entire lagoon. 'Stop. Just stop. You won't find them.'

Njda seized her heel. Caught off balance, Magga toppled. Njda stiffened and moved to help her, then snarled and shoved her back into the sand.

'I find the first clues someone besides us survived Riika-Min, and what do you do? You follow me! Mock me! You say sorry when you're not! Weren't you crying for sleep? So go! Sleep!'

Magga jolted up, her dagger reversed in her grip. 'Don't touch me.'

Njda slipped her knife from her belt. 'Or what?' Valter chuckled awkwardly and stepped between them, but Njda rammed him away. 'What, Mag? You think I haven't gutted bandits in the bush? You think I wouldn't gut you?'

A braid fell from Magga's mane into her face. 'I always knew you were soft. So high and mighty and perfect, but soft. "Our perfect finder," the city said. "She hears the fairings of Ghur!" Your clan's gone a day and you come apart like spoilt meat. How does it feel now that life's gone awry? Want to know what the rest of us don't do? We don't hold our breath and blubber in the sand at the tracks of wild reindeer. We don't pretend it means our siida are alive, or our city. No one came here. If they did, they–'

Njda tore off her pointed hood. Her scalp had been on fire with its movement, but she wasn't sure if it was the wind or Valter holding her back. 'Say it. Say it and I'll tie you to the rock and bleed the bad from you.'

Magga whipped around. A dark blob bobbed in the shallow pool. Worm-like lampreys slithered across the ragged flotsam, in and out. Bone and fresh entrails glistened by the light of the beast moon snarling in the sky.

A whiff of carrion wrinkled Njda's nose. Once upon a time, the waterlogged corpse had been a woman. Movement snapped her eyes to the top of the rocks. '*Magga!*'

The blue sands in Magga's hazel eyes turned. She swivelled as a shadow lunged from a limestone formation. She hadn't just reacted – she had anticipated. As a long-tongued jackal lay spitted at her feet, a second snapped its jaws. Thunder pealed as Valter emptied his pistol and slew it.

Magga crushed the throat of the first beneath her knee, then spiked her dagger through its skull. 'Scavengers.'

Magga squealed and staggered back. More lampreys squirmed from the sands and shallows towards the jackals' corpses. Magga's face went the shade of starlight. 'No. No, not this.'

'That's Jonne.' Heigen had crested the nearest rock. He stared at the gutted Suku corpse bobbing in the pool. The woman's fur coat and indigo tunic were in shreds, to say nothing of her flesh.

Njda met Jonne's grey gaze, then peeled her eyes away. Reading Jonne's grisly spoor felt like pulling her own teeth. 'She wasn't killed here. Look. Blood on the stone where she crawled. She came here to die. Still alive when we left the forest, I'd guess.'

Valter's eyes narrowed. He raised his burly arm to the sea. 'What's that?'

Njda scrambled higher up the rocks and gaped. With the aurora and stars blazing, it was easy to see. 'One of ours,' she said. 'A sledcroft.'

CHAPTER EIGHT

Growlers of snow-dusted ice thronged the dark waters of a frigid bay. There a sledcroft of Riika-Min foundered. Njda would have known it anywhere. Only the carpenters of the sled-city built rear lintels like that.

Magga wiped her dagger in the crook of her elbow. 'Njda, wait.'

As the beast moon's growls thundered through the sky, Njda scrambled to the sand. Her heart raced as the foundering sled-croft rotated in the icy bay. The drifting boulders and the sled reminded her of what a tinker had once told her of Izalend's celestial orreries, ornate realmspheres that rotated on metal stems in cloistered courtyards blanketed with snow.

The others gathered behind her. 'They rushed to cross the bay,' Njda said. 'But the ice was thin.'

Sand streamed like stardust from Magga's fist to the ground. 'There's white in the beach. Little flecks.'

'Old bone. Many things have died here.'

Magga tugged at her sleeve. Njda snarled, but gems glistened in the corners of Magga's sunken eyes. 'Don't go.' Her soft timbre reminded Njda of the tundra calm following a blizzard's passage. 'I've seen this place.'

'In your visions? In your high?'

Magga had never looked so small and cold. 'Heigen falls into a nest of monsters. Valter drowns, because he swims like a stone–'

Valter scoffed. 'Who says I'm going?'

'You do. All of you do. And Njda… Baby eels crawl through your eyes as you drift. The ones from the pool. They eat you inside out, like Jonne. I've seen it. It's all I see. How we die, a thousand times each night. Don't go.'

Ice bobbed by the shore. Njda's fingers brushed the boulder as it passed. In the dark waters, a distorted reflection of the moon snarled. 'You saw us killed in the forest, too. But that didn't happen.'

'Most of them don't. Most are lies, I know. But that doesn't mean they can't happen.'

'What do you care if we live or die?'

Magga pursed her lips. 'Your family fed me. Many nights, many cold nights. They wouldn't have you do this for them. They wouldn't have you die.'

Heigen trudged to the water's edge. His hooded eyes judged the distance to the first growler. He leapt, then steadied himself. As his feet scuffed over ice, he centred his weight, then bounded to the next growler.

Njda slid her bow from her shoulder. 'Look after it. I'll be back.'

'Wait.' Valter dropped his rucksack and unbuckled his breast-plate. Beneath, moonlight caught on a threadbare tunic. All that finery, and he couldn't afford fresh dyes or embroidery. 'Look after this. A penny in it for you.'

Magga backed away. Her eyes brightened. 'Bavval.' She turned and sprinted. '*Bavval, wake up!*'

Valter groaned. 'Come. Let's go before the noajdi boxes our ears.'

Njda stared. Heigen she understood – he'd hardly been able to sit still as it was – but she couldn't fathom what Valter wanted. The sledcroft's steel, maybe, or its pelts? A cheap thrill balancing on ice in waters so cold they would stop his heart? Maybe it didn't matter. He was here.

Njda leapt and grunted. She steadied herself, then offered her hand. 'Bavval doesn't box ears.'

'Not any more.' Valter rocked up behind Njda, who scrambled to the other side as the ice leaned. 'But you've never seen him angry.'

The sledmanse's timber creaked in the black waters. The landship spun in slow circles and broke up the sky's shimmer in the wake. Waves crashed, but not in the bay. They feared to come too close.

Heigen slipped. His hands went wild then clapped the ice. He regained his balance. 'Something's in the water,' he said.

Njda nodded. If she gazed long enough, she thought she could see a pit beneath the wake, between mountainous reefs. The sight of those jagged depths prickled her skin. A kraken could have hidden in there.

Valter cursed. His leather cheeks blushed as he fought for balance and a grip.

'Heigen.' Njda pointed. 'Don't stop. Keep going.'

'You needn't pretend any more,' Heigen said.

'What?'

'You should've let me do this alone. Without you we're dead. Without me, things would only be easier.'

'Things would be easier with more ice,' Valter said. 'But take your time.'

Njda pumped her fingers. 'You really think that, Heigen?'

'Njda. Ever since my marriage, life has been war. Riika's collectives might as well have exiled us. No one bought my herd's milk or pelts. No one forgave me for how we ended.' He turned, and his lips crinkled. 'No one forgave her. But she wasn't to blame. And now she's gone.'

Valter's nails scraped ice. 'Tilting here. But please, *take your time.*'

Njda's heart sank. Moments ago she had taunted Magga as she begged Njda to stay. Now Njda understood.

'No one wishes death on you,' she said. 'I prayed your sled would leak and your skids would crack. I hoped she hated your cooking and your ears fell off. But I never wished you death. I wished you life.'

Heigen's brow softened. Water splashed in the bay.

Valter yelled, eyes wide, as a black bulb broke the dark waters, then submerged. Its wake rippled closer. A shadow simmered beneath, long like a wingless wyrm, as wide as a sledmanse.

The growler rocked. Heigen's foot slipped. He slammed to the ice and gasped, then slid over the edge. His mittened hands scrabbled for a grip. '*Njda!*' he cried. A long scrape followed, and water splashed again below.

'Sigmar blind me.' Valter freed an arm and slid his hatchet from his belt. 'First he takes his time. Now I've got to save him.' He cannonballed into the water. Bubbles burbled where he disappeared, and Magga's words skimmed into Njda's head. *Valter drowns. He swims like a stone.*

She dived. Shadows swallowed the sky, and water murmured in her ears. Frigid knives stabbed her limbs. Njda seized up, then pumped herself towards Heigen. The seawater stung her eyes and blurred her vision, but she vaguely made out Valter, too, a thrashing patch in the grey.

In the depths, an indistinct silver saucer emerged. The captive glow of moonlight caught in the gigantic eye and revealed jagged reefs enclosing an ancient chasm. The serpent sliced through the reefs like a doomful ribbon.

CHAPTER NINE

Njda heaved up a lungful of water. A froth of brine and bile splashed onto ice-speckled sand. She straightened and wiped snot from her nose. A heavy fur mantled her shoulders. Beside her, Heigen shivered. Water dripped from his ears.

Bare-chested, Valter paced, massive and red like the home he'd abandoned. His teeth chattered like clinking crockery during a tremor. He chewed the ends of his moustache and rubbed his good eye, muttering. 'What've we done? Oh, what've we done?'

Magga hunched cross-legged before them. 'You're all so highly… stupid.'

Heigen shuddered. 'We almost died.'

'I couldn't let you idiots die.' Valter sniffled. 'But I didn't think anything would happen to him. Never him.'

Njda glanced at Heigen. He seemed fine. Nearby, the bay's waters churned. The sledge had been pulled up, and two boots with curled toes hung over the edge. Grit rattled in Bavval's ancient lungs as he wheezed and snored.

'Still asleep.' Njda threw her damp tunic on, careful not to stumble. Sensation prickled into her legs. 'What happened?'

'Bavval saved you,' Magga said. 'With them.'

A black dhow sculled through the inlet. Growlers dispersed around the oily hull. The titan submerged, and water rippled up the beach. Bloody bubbles foamed on the surface as the pod of the leviathan whales feasted below.

Njda wanted to thank Magga, but when she looked at her, the unspoken words stuck in her throat like treacle. 'You did better than I could have,' she finally said.

Magga gazed at the sledge. 'I only asked for help.'

Njda padded over. Bavval's skin was snow white, and sallow pits of bruised flesh encased his eyes. Each breath rattled in his lungs. She squeezed his hand. His bony fingers stung like icicles, and she lifted the furs covering him. 'Where are our stores?'

'He used the amber magic.' Magga's swords cracked in the sledge beside Njda's bow. 'He called the whales.'

'He's not a druid. How could he summon them? Where's our food?'

Magga's dead stare told her the truth.

Njda's brow smoothed. 'He sacrificed it to them. To the amber wind.'

Magga slouched against the sledge and her eyelids slid closed. 'Not just the food. He grew thinner, Njda, before my eyes. His flesh hung from him like a wight's, like the realm had sucked the fat from him. I think he's dying.'

Njda squatted. 'It never should have come to this. You were right. I didn't listen.'

Gulls screamed over the bay, or hopped between growlers waiting for scraps. Njda winced as she waited for an acid jibe, but Magga only patted her leg. 'I was wrong. You lived.'

Njda's spent smirk reached the edges of her eyes. 'Now you don't have to starve alone.' They traded a look and laughed.

'Are you stinking mad?' Valter shouted, shaking. He crashed into the sand, then buried his face in his hands. 'We'll all die, like the old man. Bavval, you selfless fool. I'm sorry. I still owe you.'

Across the sea, Hysh peeped from beneath the edge of the world. The first thread of its light expanded into a growing slash. Njda clenched her jaws and hobbled up. 'No. We'll live.'

Njda forced Bavval from her thoughts. He could die, but this wasn't the time for pity. Not for him, not for the others, not for herself. This was the time to remember life had never been easy. First came struggle.

'You'll watch the noajdi,' she told Valter.

He frowned, then nodded.

'You'll set up camp,' she told Heigen.

He threw the sledge rope over his shoulder.

'And you, Magga – you'll help me.'

Magga retrieved her fronded baleen sword. 'Always.'

Njda clapped. 'Come. We can't stay here. Worse things than that eel's young will smell the blood in these waters. Move.'

They lugged their sledge back up the slick stone crags. Now that it doubled as a litter for Bavval, the sledge's weight broke Njda's heart – with the noajdi, without their stores, it was far lighter than it had been. As a child Njda had grown so accustomed to Bavval's strength that in adulthood she had never grasped his frailty. But after casting his spell in the bay, he was nothing but bones and skin buried in furs and a baggy tunic. It was as if Bavval's last years had withered from his soul like the provisions he'd scattered into the sea as he chanted the amber wind's true name and pounded on his ritual drum.

In a gulleyed clearing at the top of a promontory, they built a shelter from pine boughs and wrapped Bavval in furs. Heigen coaxed a fire to life, then gathered dry wood. Njda assembled snares as Magga sharpened stakes and twisted grass fibres into cord to build more.

'How is he?' Njda asked Valter, who hunkered at Bavval's side in their shelter.

Hardship had carved Valter's plump cheeks into lean hollows. 'Look at him,' he said. 'Like a child. Time does this to us.'

'This was before his time,' she replied. Njda forced down her bitter guilt and left to scout. For a chance at saving her family, she had all but cost Bavval his life. They were on the line, now. Exhaustion panged behind her eyes as she probed the slopes and thick junipers. Brush cracked beneath her boots. She made note of the defiles and rises where her snares should be set. A glacial wall of ice caught her eye, and her lips curled into a smile.

Magga's head turned as Njda thumped back into the gulleyed clearing a short while later. 'Where'd you find that?'

'Devourer ice. South slope.' Njda hefted a half-thawed ram carcass to the ground. 'It's been here ages. All sorts of beasts caught in it. And it guards the approach, so we only need snares for the rest of the cape.'

Heigen teetered over the carrion and wrinkled his nose. 'It's unclean.'

Magga snapped Njda's knife from her belt and sawed at the dead ram's flesh. 'You should've seen sick Gumper's croft. I thought you Sigmar worshippers had fire in your belly.'

'It was the missionaries who taught us carrion is unclean,' Heigen said.

'I'm with him.' Valter emerged from the shelter and splashed meltwater out of a canteen cup. 'But unclean's better than starving. The realm takes when it takes, and gives when it gives. Can't really say no to either.'

Njda jerked Magga's dagger from her belt. Magga glared as Njda spiked a gobbet of frozen meat and cooked it over the flame until it spattered. Njda puffed as she chewed, and hot air plumed from her mouth. 'I guess things are looking up.'

Njda awoke in their shelter violently ill. She stumbled out to the treeline and back again. Valter lurked by the fire with a thousand-yard stare.

'Heigen was right.' He groaned. 'Gods and ghosts, when the realm takes, it really takes.'

Njda crouched and outstretched her hands. 'Is that you or me?'

'That's all of us. Magga's out making her contribution now. Can't decide if the reek will attract predators or scare them away.' He pulled the hems of his coat in as he settled in the fire's warmth. 'What's got you sour in the eyes?'

'A dream.' A log spat in the firepit, and spectral fire danced in its glowing grooves. Njda's ma had come again in her sleep. She'd sunk out of Njda's reach, and a burning halo had thundered closer in the deep. The undersea fire had boiled the blackness around them, too blinding to look at for long. Inside, a creature had galloped. A stag, or… a horse?

Njda shivered. Wretched creatures, horses. With their single hooves and sweaty fur and crystal, long-lashed eyes.

Valter patted his pistols. 'Powder's dry. Low, but dry.'

'Better if we don't need it.' Njda locked her arms around her belly. 'You think that a saint can kill Tjatsår Mai?'

Valter's dead eye flitted over. 'Rather not think of them at all, truth be told. You dreamt of her?'

'No. Yes. I don't know.' Njda's eyes slid shut. A blue spear blazed and vibrated behind their lids.

'I've heard your theory. Don't believe it a whit.'

'She wanted to kill Mai.'

Valter scratched his haggard cheeks. 'Folk come to market

saying they need one thing and leave with something else entirely. I think she's doing that. Chasing her tail.'

'She's not like us. She's a devil.'

Valter tossed his hand. 'My point. What drives a thing like that? I don't know. Can't see it.'

'I guess you would know.' Njda pushed hair along her shaved temple. 'She was ruthless to come to market and leave with nothing.'

Valter chugged his grating laugh. 'Sleep well. Maybe you'll be a devil too one day.'

Njda grunted and returned to the shelter. She stared at the empty furs where Bavval had lain. She hadn't noticed he was gone when she awoke.

She spun and surveyed the camp. 'Valter. Where're Bavval and Heigen?'

Snow drifted as ashes do. A faint aurora shimmered in the dun sky. Njda crunched towards a gulley within sight of the sea, where Heigen was setting a pit snare by a tree. Njda shivered. Her damp clothing gave her a chill, but if she froze to death, that couldn't be worse than eating rotten meat.

'You were right,' she called out. 'Meat was unclean.'

Heigen startled. 'They made us wash our hands for a reason, too.'

Njda ambled into the gulley and checked his snare. Magga's braided cord suspended a sharpened stake from a birch's trunk. The bark had been peeled aside; sap oozed from the timber. If something triggered the whiner, the stake would puncture the tree's soft wood. A skilled Suku finder could hear the trees' pain. The realm sang to those with the ears to listen. Or the pointed hoods.

'You're a good student,' Njda said. 'This is well done.'

Heigen fidgeted. 'Bavval's on the far side. He finally woke in the night. I told him to rest, but he insisted. You help him. I'll finish here.'

Njda straightened. She imagined a jumble of fear swimming in Heigen's head like water in his ears. She felt the same. Whenever she was unoccupied, the fear her family was dead slithered up the cracks of her. Sometimes their absence howled in her breast. Others, she was holding their weight across the realm. Worst was when the grief didn't sting, nor smart, but ached, like an ebbing emptiness. There would be no picking up and moving on if they were gone.

'I've been thinking,' Heigen said. 'At the shores, Bavval was sick. Our food was gone. We were wet.' He laughed. 'And you just stood up and told us what to do. And we did it. Now I smell your insides, granted, but we picked up our feet and moved. Ta would have wanted that for me, too.'

Njda cocked her head.

'Ta,' Heigen said. 'My Ta.'

'Oh.' Njda shifted. 'That's what we do. We fall. We raise each other up. We endure.' She cast her hand about. 'Leave a gap in your snares. Survivors might find us.'

'Suku survivors?'

'I wouldn't want any other survivors finding us.'

Birds shook the branches above. Snow pattered down, and flakes drifted between them. Pine leaves rustled like whispers in a box.

'You said we could talk if I wanted.'

Njda nodded. 'I meant it.'

'When Ta died, I couldn't imagine a world without her. I know how that sounds, because she died before my eyes. But I didn't really understand until we left her behind. She's gone. She's not coming back.'

Njda soured. 'You're trying to say something.'

Heigen gathered more whittled stakes. 'I'm saying I didn't think it would help, letting her go. But it did.'

Heat brimmed behind Njda's eyes. She gritted her jaw and marched off. 'Leave a path. They'll need it.'

Bavval dragged a snare through the frosted brush the way old finders did, as if it were an anvil. He seemed stronger, but still drained, still weak. His rheumy eyes lifted to Njda as she drew near. She eased the snare from his hands and worked it into the base of a tree. Bavval's lungs whickered, but he returned to work.

They finished just before sunset, where the devourer outcropping had colonised the ridge. Njda's ma had warned her of the predatory ice as often as she'd gone to sea. Older icebergs calved in feasting storms, and the pieces washed up as Ghur's seas raided its lands. Anything caught by devourer ice was as good as dead. In Riika-Min's ever-changing outskirts, Njda had found withered wolves and starved marauders mummified in its grip, half-alive. The ice patches had preyed on living beings' heat and nutrients for decades. In Riika-Min, Njda would have killed it with torch fire lest the ice trap a stray reindeer from their herds. But Riika-Min was a distant grave, more than a memory, less than a dream.

Njda and Bavval patrolled the ridge. Furry frost covered the devourer's milk-white crags. The rime moved magnetically, drawn to the warmth of their breath. Njda dragged her bow's tip through the packed snow to mark the boundaries of its roots, tendrils that burrowed from the glassy bulwark into the earth. Most devourer patches were small. This outcropping was massive, large enough that its bass hum tickled Njda's bones and so tall it blocked the evergreens behind it.

The tundra opened through the cage of trees. Twisters cavorted across the snowy waste, dead leaves dancing in their grip. Two wisps of light bobbed on a distant crest. Njda gasped as they blinked at her. The eyes glimmered like a snow-panther's, and then shadows swallowed the shine. Where they had stared, a granite-grey blur loped down the hill towards the closest rank of spruces. Twilight shimmered off a long fang of icy steel. The spear glowed like a needle that had been heated in coals and left to cool.

Njda unshouldered her bow. 'It's her. She's back.'

Bavval nudged down her weapon. 'That would do you no good,' he said.

Njda's gaze shot back across the tundra, but the huntress was gone.

'If she wishes to find us, she will.' Bavval tucked his arms into his furs. 'We have no say in how she does this or what happens next.'

'You know more than you've let on. You've seen her before, haven't you?' She turned and began breaking the snow to help him back to camp.

Bavval sighed. 'I know little more than you,' he said. 'The stories, like hearsay stretched into myth. A hundred years ago she killed the vargr and slew its cubs. Two centuries before that, she lost her game of riddles with Tjatsår Mai. I thought them cautionary tales, no more. Allegories that Harmony must be inviolate. I never saw her, though. I have only seen Sigmar's chosen. The Storm-cast Eternals.'

Njda's breath caught. 'So they are real.'

'Realer than most of us think.' A wan smile bled through Bavval's blue lips. 'Excelsis. A much greater city than Izalend, and much further away. I went there years ago, before your parents were born. I was a child.'

'And I thought the spirits carved you from stone.'

Bavval chuckled. 'My parents led our clan, forty of us. The Suku had no relations with Izalend then, but Izalend knew of us. A priest, bald with ink beneath his skin, asked if we would represent our people among theirs. To us, our people were our clan, so we said yes. Who else could represent us?'

He wheezed, then coughed. Njda frowned and patted his back.

'They fed us well, on a floating fortress.' Bavval cleared his throat. 'We sailed to lands so warm you could stand naked at night and still sweat like a boar. They asked us to cement an alliance between our people and theirs, in the name of their God-King.'

'And did you?'

Bavval leaned against a birch. The great tree groaned, and he shushed and stroked its trunk until it calmed. 'Understand, Njda, when I first saw them, we thought Sigramalles a lie. After we refused their demand of fealty, they sentenced us to death for heathenry. I was all the more certain, then. They were women and men of pretence and false faith.'

Njda darkened. 'Heathens? We bleed the corrupted.'

'So my uncle told them, but in us they saw only wilding nomads from lands of darkness. On the day of our execution, a bell tolled, and a white sun strode into the city plaza. He was taller than our longsled, with armour as white as the Sukuat's snows after the year's first blizzard and a voice like the call of thunder. In him, I felt... *light*. I felt it the way we hear the realm in our fairings or the song of the wind. His name was Arktaris Soul-Tithed, and ancestors watch him, he ordered us spared. That day I believed everything I had heard about Sigmar. He was doom. He was power. But too, he was right.'

'The huntress serves that god.'

'So I think, yes. Oh, Njda, stop. I see a quarrel in your eyes.'

'She left us to die,' she said. 'How is that right?'

Bavval's eyes brightened. 'But she did not. She saved us. The orruks would have killed us but for her. And she left afterwards, true. Should she have suckled us like foundlings, Njda? Or led us through the grey? She is a saint. Do not pretend to know the power in this word, for even I cannot grasp its depth. She exists above the ancestors, above even the spirits of Ghur. She *hunts* the spirits of Ghur! Who are we to demand anything from such a force? It would be like demanding from Harmony itself.'

'You defend her apathy, her inaction. Among our people those are sins. You taught me that.'

'Our own apathy and inaction have done far worse to us than Yndrasta has. She is not Suku any more than the mother kraken is. Yndrasta is like… a fell incarnation of Harmony. A lethal force, a ruthless force. But perhaps the arc of that force reaches towards good. Sometimes it helps us. Others, it harms us. But it requires no justification. It merely is. Do you praise the flame which warms you at night? Do you judge the fire which destroys your longsled? Fire is fire. We do not question it. We accept it as it is.'

Njda's teeth chattered. 'And what if she killed Brother?'

Bavval grimaced. 'Then she still is what she is. And I hope that is something good, like Arktaris, bless his soul.'

'You know she did it. I know you do. You were a finder, once. You saw Brother's wounds.'

Bavval grunted. 'I was a finder. Nothing like you, but yes, I saw. I said nothing. To protect you, I think. I hope to protect all of you, as I could not protect Riika-Min.'

The words sent a chill up Njda's scalp. She felt as Bavval must, then. Old, and tired. Wind-tossed and frigid like the lands that scorned them, the lands they loved.

'Perhaps you are right,' he said. 'Perhaps she is our enemy. Perhaps she took Heigen's wife, and your family, and my people. Perhaps the saint is the desolation in Magga's heart and the debt in Valter's pocketbook. Perhaps she is the hunger in our bellies. Or perhaps there is more to her than we see, like an iceberg prowling the waves. Flames can be good and bad. People are often both.'

'She isn't a person.'

'All spirits know the burn of suffering. Eternal, or evanescent. We have a drop of poison in us all.'

Njda pushed a bough aside. Twigs and needles scratched her face as Bavval shuffled into the clearing. The golden glow of their roaring fire haloed their camp. Magga wound more rope and belched. Valter and Heigen bantered by the fire.

Njda helped Bavval across a narrow gulley, and the campfire's spiced burn tickled her nose. The piney aroma reminded her of home, when her family had sat around their hearth flame and whiled away the nights. Her ma had often reached over the table and urged her to eat less. When Njda blushed, her ma would snatch a morsel from her plate and cackle. The delightful memory dripped away as Njda trickled back into the moment.

Her stomach grumbled. 'Bad meat.'

Bavval whickered a laugh. 'So Heigen said.' He bared his teeth in a full smile that cut twenty years off his age. 'My uncle called everything Harmony, you know. All the good days and bad, all the suffering and joy. He made no supplications to spirits or the dead. He never visited a *sieidi* monument once after marriage. He called his life a prayer to the realm. He said he would live well, and Ghur would reward him.'

'Did he?'

'He died protecting us from a roaming incarnate.' Bavval shuffled into their shelter. 'Drew it into the snows. We found him days later, torn to frigid shreds. But I swear, that night, skiing down the mountain, his laughter thundered louder than the hammer of Sigramalles Apmil himself.'

CHAPTER TEN

In fields of mist, grass drooped to mud. The snows had thawed, and stagnant water filled the fens. A ring of mountains pierced the sick sky like fangs. One of them shifted, restless, and boulders crashed down its slopes. Beyond that realm-spine, an ocean howled.

A morbid crook bent Njda's ma's neck, and water dripped from the drenched tatters of her tunic. Stagnant blood mottled her grey skin, and rotten light gleamed from her bruised eyes.

She raised her bent arm. *'Come,'* she croaked through water-logged lungs. *'Be our friend.'*

Njda trudged through the marsh, battling each step. The harder she pushed, the greater the muddy span between them grew.

A blazing glow fell across the swamp. Her ma's dead eyes widened in horror. A ring of fire appeared – a black tunnel rimmed in ruthless lightning. Thunderheads burned around it. Within, a winged horse galloped closer. Astride that pegasus, an armoured shadow sat, her eyes fierce with the perfection of hatred. They shone like needles of starlight.

Fatebutcher raised her spear towards Njda's ma. Njda opened her mouth to scream, but a mudslide spilled from her tongue instead.

Yndrasta's lips parted, and the gut-shaking voice of a god filled Njda's ears.

KILL.

Njda gasped for breath. A dream. Only a dream.

Magga's hand was clasped over her mouth. Njda panicked, then glimpsed Magga's terror. The taker's hand fell. *Quiet,* she mouthed.

Soundless, Njda rose. The wind bullied their dying campfire. Whispers rode the breeze, like a legion of iron kettles boiling a hundred miles away. The trees were screaming. The whiners had been triggered. She shrugged her coat on and drew up her hood, then gathered her arrows and bow and crept with Magga to the trees. Rock trickled into a gulley as Valter steadied himself behind a stone.

Amber light smouldered in Bavval's eyes. '*They come,*' he said. A weak baritone entwined his wheezing treble.

Valter cocked his pistol. 'Glad he's back to tell us what we all know.'

Njda counted heads. Magga, Bavval, Valter… She glanced to camp. 'Heigen?'

Magga gripped her arm and stopped her from going back. 'Bait. Like the givers do in raids.'

Njda shook her hand off. 'We're not givers. He's not bait. He's our friend.'

Bavval's shaking fingers grazed Njda's. She could have tossed the shaman's hand aside, but his gravity held her. 'Let whatever comes think Heigen sleeps alone. Our empty camp would only draw their suspicion. We will take them when their guard is lowest. Heigen will not be hurt.'

Njda knew the difference between cruelty and necessity – in the wilds she'd walked that razor's edge as often as not. This was different; Heigen was kin. Bavval's talk of Yndrasta wandered back to Njda. The ploy was callous, but it wasn't wrong.

Something thudded in the moonless night, and a bellow echoed from the woods. The treetops stirred, and saplings cracked. Valter gripped his hatchet and blew into his pistol hand. 'I need mittens.'

'Silence.' The amber in Bavval's eyes flickered, and the wind stilled. 'They are here.'

Three orruks barged into the clearing. Fickle firelight danced reluctantly upon their brutal forms. Cracked yellow fangs filled jaws that hung to their chests. Frost-rimed rags and soiled furs draped their rangy green limbs. Their knuckles dragged over the ground as they snorted lungfuls of air for prey scent. One limped, wounded by a pit snare, and wrenched a stake from the muscled mess of its wound.

'This one set all those traps?' it rumbled. 'This lone runt?'

Another banged the back of a shoddy cleaver into its palm. 'Maybe he's good sport. If he's what kilt da killaboss, he must be tough.'

'Boss Torsnout?' The third orruk scratched its peeling scalp. 'I fought Mudspleen knifed 'im.'

'That's right. This runt kilt Mudspleen. Must be real Morky to pull that off.'

The first orruk snapped its jaws. 'I still fink *she* did it. No way one humie coulda kilt Mudspleen, Morky or not.'

'She's after da world-squid,' the second orruk said. 'Long as we don't get in 'er way, she won't bovver us. Come on, louts. Can't 'ave this runt reachin' that city. They might try and stop us from makin' these lands… hospitable.'

The monsters chuckled, a noise like crushing boulders. Two orruks circled around Heigen and their pine shelter. The third lifted the straps of a ruck and shook it out. Metal and bone clanged and cracked on the scree.

Valter's face twisted. He clenched his teeth and raised his gun. Pale, Njda clawed at his arm, but he pulled free.

An orruk froze and sniffed at the air. Its ugly red eyes wandered the Suku's tracks through the thin snow. 'Boys. We ain't alone. Gut the humie. Let's go.' Its ironshod boot slammed down and crushed Valter's pillage.

Valter fired. The orruk clapped a massive hand over its bloody eye and roared.

Njda bared her teeth and stormed from the gulley. She snapped an arrow out; the fletched shaft sprouted from another orruk's chest. 'Protect Heigen! Protect him!'

The orruk grunted and tore the arrow out. Blood gouted from torn muscle as the shaft clattered to the ground. 'Lousy git.'

Njda loosed another arrow, and another. Magga surged forward. 'Get to Heigen!' Njda screamed, but Magga charged the second orruk. She slid over scree between its legs and dragged her swords' serrated fronds along its thigh and ankle. Gore weltered, and the brute collapsed to its knees.

Valter had scrambled to his ruined treasures and rifled through them. 'No, wilds, damn it!' He snatched his purse of glimmerings and marched back to the treeline to change pistols. 'You filthy things! That's everything! That's the last of it!'

An orruk wrapped its filthy paw around Heigen and squeezed. Steel flashed; flesh squelched. The orruk dropped Heigen and snarled, then yelped as Njda sent another arrow into its ribs. Heigen, still groggy, scrambled from his bivvy sack and tossed his flensing knife, which was red from piercing the orruk's hand.

Bavval shuffled forward and cast back his hood. Spell light flickered in his eyes, and a storm of crows and ravens gathered overhead. The orruk wheeled around, and the flocking birds drilled at its exposed flesh like a tornado. Three crows pecked out an eye as talons shredded its face.

Bavval stumbled into the dark forest. Shadows swallowed all but the amber fire guttering beneath his brow. 'Help the others!' he roared at a volume Njda hadn't heard from him in years. The orruk swatted a dozen crows from the air, then growled and lumbered into the brush behind him.

Magga whipped her swords into the ground and shot scree at her foe's face. The remaining orruk staggered towards Njda and punched her bow from her hands. The weapon clattered off the firepit; the string snapped.

As Njda scrabbled away, Valter, his second pistol raised, strode towards them. 'Hands up! Or I'll shoot you like that other–'

Njda pounded the dirt. 'Don't warn it! Just shoot!'

Like an ape, the orruk swept towards Valter and hacked at his feet. Valter slipped on his leather-soled boots and smashed down. His pistol discharged. Splinters exploded from a birch.

Crawling, Heigen rammed his knife into the orruk's squat thigh. The orruk snarled and booted him across the clearing. He rolled over the campfire, then squirmed as he beat coals from his coat. It caught fire.

The orruk's leg was caught in a narrow channel. Njda slid two arrows from her quiver and raced up. She shoved each shaft into the orruk's ribs. It gushed breathlessly as her darts bled the putrid breath from its lungs. The stench of offal filled the air, and Njda choked and staggered down.

Magga scaled the rangy greenskin's back. The hunched giant reached, but she dodged its clumsy grabs, then slammed a baleen sword through its shoulder. The blade snapped from its hilt as she whipped her second sword into the creature's head. The fronds caught in the orruk's jowls and ripped half its face away. Blood coursed over its desecrated skull. The orruk groaned, and the blazing ruby of its good eye died. Its leg cracked beneath its weight as it toppled and shook the hill.

Valter dropped his pistol. He kicked the orruk's head, then thumped his hatchet into its skull. 'Filth smashed my–'

Njda stormed closer. 'What was that, Valter? With the purse? What was that?' She jogged to Heigen and helped beat out the fire on his shoulder.

He slumped against the sledge and poked a finger through his coat's holes. 'I'm alive.'

'No thanks to us. Are they all dead?'

Magga circled the mountain she had slain. She examined her broken baleen sword, then tossed the jagged hilt. 'I killed two of them. I'm a taker.'

Njda quelled the tremors in her hands. 'You're lucky, not a taker. That was *luck*. And we risked–'

'Bavval.' Valter spun around, his green eye wide with panic. 'The third orruk.'

The blood drained from Magga's face. They gathered what weapons they could and sped down the slopes.

Njda's breath hissed in her ears. She bounded over gulleys and knobby roots, whipped past low branches and brittle brush. Motes of snow drifted through the darkness, like she was running through star fields.

At the devourer ice, a crowd of thin pines shot over the ridge like curious passers-by. The ice wall had expanded and caught the great orruk in its grip. Purple veins spidered through its olive leather, and furry frost blanketed its body. The foe-raider's wet breathing ceased with a sudden slurp. Its skin paled to algae green, and its shark eye stilled under verglas.

Njda pushed through the pines. 'Bavval, no.'

The old noajdi's teeth chattered. His grey eyes had frosted shut, and ice crept up his coat like white moss. The rime covered his skin and sapped the colour from his flesh. The cold had smoothed his wrinkles into doll skin. His beard crackled as he strained his head. 'Nj...'

Njda reached out, but Magga yanked her back. 'You'll get yourself killed. He made this choice. Don't take it from him.'

The cold stung Njda's dry eyes. Bavval had given everything to the ice, and the ice had answered. She cobbled together a look of false courage – the look she gave her fellow finders' children when they fell to marauders; the look she'd given her ma when she'd asked if Njda still loved Heigen, and Njda had answered *no*.

'You saved us, Bavval. We'll live. We'll reach Suodji. Go now, to the far family.'

Ice beaded in the corners of Bavval's closed eyes, then froze into cloudy gems. Steam sputtered from his nostrils. The tension bled from his fists. With a groan, the shaman stilled, and Riika-Min – the thought struck like a cold burst of lightning – was truly, finally dead.

CHAPTER ELEVEN

Powder accumulated into white drifts. Wind moaned through the trees, as if the realm itself lamented Bavval's passing. Every cold breath burned in Njda's lungs. 'We can't leave him,' she said.

A hand gripped her shoulder. Valter's dead eye met hers, as solid as stone. 'We leave. Or more orruks will find us.'

Magga tramped back through the blanket of snow. 'I say we find them first. They want death, so we give them death.'

'No. We'll not leave Bavval.'

'Then we'll join him,' Valter said.

Magga's chiselled features twisted. In the dark, her mane and wild braids made her look like another tree. 'Kill the ice, Bavval will still be dead. We may join him just for trying.'

Njda's jaw clenched. 'You. Ready to become a taker, ready to kill for your own glory and spread pain in the realm. But not willing to put a hair on the line for your own shaman – for one who gave his life to save ours.'

'You're the one who cost Bavval his strength and us our food.'

Those words stung. Njda stared at the dead shaman. 'And now I'm the one ready to atone for it.'

Flakes stuck to Valter's trimmed coat. 'What would you have us do? Make a barrow for him?'

'The old ways demand we bring him to a stone to burn.'

Valter tossed his hands. 'Then let's bring a stone and–'

'Not any stone, Valt.' Magga tamped her foot on the ungiving earth. 'A sieidi.'

Valter scoffed. 'Impossible. The nearest is the other way, at Riika. We can't.'

'We can make one.' They turned to Heigen, who crouched by a tree. 'Any place powerful with the realm's spirits can become a sieidi,' he said. 'The missionaries taught that is how we consecrated the Sukuat against Chaos. Bavval gave his life to Ghur on this hill, among these trees. We can raise a sieidi here.'

Magga sneered. 'You can pull him from the ice, too.'

'I will.' Heigen's neck was straight and hard like an arrow. 'Njda's right. Bavval married me and Ta. And he wasn't just our noajdi. He raised us all. He was with us to the end. We should be with him to the end, too. We should see him to the far family.'

Snow stuck to Magga's russet shag. Valter shrugged helplessly. Magga turned to the devourer ice, then Njda, and sighed. 'What do we do?'

They stoked brands to life from their campfire's embers, then returned to the outcropping. Magga fanned powder and foliage aside with her chipped baleen sword to reveal the devourer ice's polished roots. They picked their way around the tendrils, then thrust their brands into the ice's base.

Water trickled, and steam hissed. When the heat reached the core of the ice that had killed Bavval, cracks fissured in its glassy heart. The verglas encasing him thawed and oozed like molasses.

The mossy frost went still and dusted away. The colony's branch decayed to ordinary ice. Njda and Heigen peeled Bavval from the brittle frost.

Back at camp, they piled wood beneath his stiff corpse, then invoked a flame. Plumes of white smoke swallowed their last vision of Bavval's face. Once a year Njda had always visited the nearest sieidi with her family to give thanks to her ancestors and the realm, but she had never performed this rite. It was said when the first Izalenders had discovered the Suku, they had been shocked to learn they immolated their shamans as offerings to the realm. From the ancient stones, the noajdi's spirits could watch over their people again.

As the bonefire roared past the tops of trees, Valter paced at the edge of the gulleyed clearing. Pistols raised, he shot furtive glances towards Bavval's fire. Magga had said Valter's head and heart lay with the Izalenders, and maybe she was right. But then maybe Izalenders, too, were a people of spirit. Whatever drove Valter, Njda felt in her bones he wanted respects paid for Bavval. If he didn't help the others for what came next, he at least kept watch.

Njda guided Heigen and Magga back to the shores, to the tundra's edge. They collected rocks: smooth stones, jagged flint and gravelly clods that all but crumbled at first touch. With armfuls they trudged from the shingly beaches and howling snows back up the cape, then heaped the stones on Bavval's burning remains. As his body was consumed, let his spirit be caught in the stones' sieve, then bound to the hill. Most sieidi were monoliths of weathered rock, but they weren't tombs. The Suku's forebears – or Ghur itself, for all Njda knew – had raised the first seeing stones for communion with the spirits. Whether this makeshift monument could serve that purpose was a question Njda could not answer. But wherever Bavval's spirit was, let him see he was not forgotten.

Soon, the faint fingers of dawn clawed over the horizon. Sleepy sunlight speared through the tops of trees and warmed Njda's cheeks. Beneath the piled stones, the coals of Bavval's life still smouldered and smoked, soon to be ash. Words felt like a trivial offering beside their solemn quiet. Njda scattered leaves and tree needles and black sand on the smoking mound. Without Bavval, the world was uneven, but as much as she wanted his absence to hurt, she couldn't find the feeling in her. She was too used to this. Too used to seeing the ones she loved die.

Then Njda cocked her head and crouched. Grit at the base of Bavval's pyre began vibrating in eerie patterns, hovering and boiling away. Snow rolled over the ground in slow waves, and frost crept off like a scared slimemould. Timber creaked across the cape, and the tops of trees shook. The birches were uprooting, but Njda's hood remained perfectly still, as if the wind held its breath in fright.

Dread tingled up Njda's spine as she noticed the shadow lurking behind Valter. Six whiteless eyes stared out from the ravaged skull of a dead wolf. The monster's hunched shoulder blades rose like wicked mountains over its hanging head. Pellets of drool and blood fell from its gaping jaws. Njda's gorge rose as she saw a litter of trampled cubs in the dirt, their teething fangs shaped perfectly for mortal throats.

A fugue shook the edge of Njda's vision. Of the beast's six dead eyes, one flitted to her.

Her heart thundered like an Ironweld cannon. 'Vargr!'

The anarchy that followed trickled back to Njda in fragments and shattered images. Magga whipped her blade and screamed, then scuttled back as the wolf reared and its eyes melted. Valter raised his pistols, then yawped as they dissolved like sand. Heigen heaved towards Njda to help her to her feet, then abandoned her, his courage thwarted by raw animal fear.

Njda's mind bled back into the moment in a slow drip. She had torn her mitten off with her teeth and lay on her back. The arrow in her shivering hand clattered against her bow, but the string was limp. After an eternity, Njda conquered her mind's death. She dropped the bow, then shook her knife from its sheath.

But… the beast was gone. The tall huntress loomed in its place. Faint scars feathered her brow and shaved temples. Her glacial eyes, as distant as stars, held Njda in their grip. Frosted mail and the vargr's spiny pelt mantled her shoulders. Her spear pulsated with a force louder than Njda's pounding heart, not heard so much as felt. The flaccid wolf skull hanging from the dead pelt gurgled. Some higher level of Njda's mind urged calm, but the reptilian foundations of her skull screamed.

But for all the guttural terror fuming around Yndrasta like a stink, she was… human. Or some shadow of that. Or some blazing, blinding sun.

'Don't kill us,' Njda cried, 'I beg you.'

The huntress, the devil, the saint – her gelid attention penetrated Njda and pinned her like a sword. 'When your eyes behold me, mortal, what do they see?'

Years of hard-earned experience in the wilds ground to life in Njda's head like mill wheels. 'I wish not to say.'

'Say it.'

'The vargr. The guardian of the Druichan Forest.'

Emotion seemed beneath Yndrasta. Her face was blank ice. Still, the faintest spark of life inhabited her blistering silver eyes at the dread wolf's mention. 'That was a good kill.'

Njda tried hard not to look at the blinking, terrified eyes on the pelt's hanging head. 'Are you… her? Fatebutcher?'

'You know my name.'

Each of her words spawned distant thunder over the seas. The huntress' eyes moved to Bavval's pebbly cairn. Smoke billowed from the heaped stones. The reek of burnt pine and scorched flesh raised a war of emotion in Njda, but it was nothing before her fear.

'Your connection to this place is deep. Rich, like the soil in summer. You tap the realm's powers skilfully. I found you with difficulty. Now I smell your magic in the air like fresh blood. This ritual is powerful.'

The thunder was not from a distant storm. It was the huntress' own voice, resounding in Njda's soul. 'I loosed an arrow in Riika-Min. Forgive me, I meant you no harm. You frightened me.'

Yndrasta's implacable silver gaze all but impaled Njda. 'You think I would hurt you?'

Njda's limbs felt heavier than mountains. She scooted towards Bavval's warm sieidi, away from Yndrasta. She moved inch by inch, afraid more sudden movement might trigger the huntress' killing instinct. Her fingers bumped Valter's dropped pistols – so they hadn't dusted away.

Her hands recoiled. 'Forgive me. I do not think you came to help.'

Yndrasta's high brow remained perfectly still. 'I have only ever helped you. I have only ever fulfilled my maker-father's will.'

'Your...' Njda dredged the image of Heigen's strange gestures from her memory. Her hands formed into a hasty sign of the hammer. 'Sigramalles Apmil. Blessed be his name.'

'Do not mock me. I have no need of false faith.'

Ten years ago, a blizzard had filled Riika-Min's valley encampment to the mountains' peaks with snow. Something had knocked on their sledcroft's door in the dead of night. The croaking creature had claimed to be Gramp, cold and alone, even though he had died the season before. Gramb had brushed off her hatchet and wandered to the door and told them, *You all stay. I'll send him back.* Upon hearing Yndrasta's rebuke, Njda felt as she had then. She'd wished she were as strong as Gramb. Now she wished Gramb were here to save her again.

'Deep inside, something tells me to run from you,' Njda blurted.

'But Izalenders... revere you. Sing praise that you killed the Druichan guardian. So my shaman said.'

Yndrasta might as well have been carved in stone on this hill since the birth of time. 'If you wish to fear me, do so,' she answered. 'What I do is right.'

'But... you killed our Brother. You brought Tjatsår Mai upon my folk. These are not the acts of a friend.'

With a flick of her wrist, Yndrasta reversed her great lance. Energy sang from its shaft, and wild light gleamed in its blade. The spear's head pierced the ground. The earth juddered and groaned as stones trickled from the top of Bavval's mound to its base.

'Tjatsår Mai destroyed your city. You *revere* her. I smell it on you.'

'That's the way of her. Tjatsår Mai is a daughter of the Harmony. Her hunger is the hunger of Ghur.'

'So is mine.'

Njda's face warped. 'I know her for what she is. I can't hate her for it. But' – Njda found the precipice of her courage, then leapt over its edge – 'I do not know you. Forgive me.'

Yndrasta's lips ached into a faint but vicious scowl. 'The kraken took your mother.'

Njda could not find an answer for that.

'The kraken does not feed as any common beast might,' the huntress continued. 'She enthrals the living and the dead. Enslaves them, mind, body and soul. Your mother stands amongst that number.'

'You can't know that.'

'But I do. Your souls are entwined. The tie between your spirits sings, like the scent of prey on the wind, or blood in water. Your connection with her is strong but tainted by the kraken's touch. You must feel it. When you dream, at the very least.'

A chill ran through Njda's legs.

'For ages I have hunted this beast,' Yndrasta said. 'I have ever failed. In you, I sense... *possibility.* Many are trapped in the beast's snare. Together, we can free them all.'

Yndrasta's contralto boomed through the sky. The edgeless potential of her words opened beneath Njda like a sudden pitfall. *Possibility* – the word spiralled in Njda's heart, like the feeling of standing on mountains and gazing across her people's lands. It was dreadful. Magnificent. Nothing scared Njda more in all the universe.

'Assist me,' Yndrasta said. 'Harness your connection with your mother. Aid me in my hunt for the kraken. In exchange, I will free your mother from its thrall. I will free all whom the kraken stole. Unless the beast is slain, her many slaves will remain bound to her until the day the realms die. What say you?'

With the slow gravity of worlds crashing together, the dread huntress extended her arm. Njda stared at her frosted gauntlet. Her ma had taught her reverence for Ghur's beasts, its predators. Killing Tjatsår Mai was as close to sacrilege as existed among the Suku. Yet what was Yndrasta if not a greater beast?

Sweat poured down Njda's shaved temples. 'Will my kindred be safe with you?'

'No harm will come to you while you stand by my side. To *you,* mortal. I make this pledge for no one else.'

Every ounce of Njda's instinct shouted for her to submit to Yndrasta's will, like that of Harmony itself. Within, a mousy vestige of courage squeaked its resistance. This was not enough. It was *not enough.*

'Forgive me. Protect me or do not, but my companions must accompany us. They must be kept safe.'

Yndrasta's armour whined as her hand fell. 'The companions who abandoned you to me.'

'The very same.' Njda twitched. She would have to raise that with them.

'Impossible. They will slow us down. If this Drownharrow ends and the kraken slumbers again, your mother will be lost another century. That is the rest of your mortal life.'

Faraway mountains might have crumbled, so loud was the echo of Yndrasta's refusal. Njda bared her teeth to speak, then suppressed a whimper.

'Mortal. Do not test me.'

Njda forced her gaze away. Each pebble in Bavval's mound felt like another reason to cave before the saint's will. What had the others done for her? She had no reason to care for them – to *die* for them, should Yndrasta's patience break.

But Bavval would have. Without hesitation.

Njda fought to meet the huntress' eyes. For half a breath, the vargr loomed. Ropes of slaver dangled from its blood-encrusted jaws. Gore oozed down the rent flesh of its shaggy, mountainous shoulders. Where ghosts haunted mortals, this dread spirit had been enthralled by Yndrasta's might. Her power could have shattered kingdoms.

'The Stormcasts are said to protect the God-King's flock.'

'Everything we do is for you.'

'You left us to die in Riika-Min. Now you would leave my kin for dead again.'

Njda's defiance must have surprised Yndrasta. The barest breath of hesitation followed. 'You are not Sigmar's flock.'

'Forgive me, but you must know that is not true. We fear Sigramalles Apmil, as we fear you. You are his... saint. A slayer too, I know. But if his cause is righteous, so too must yours be.'

Yndrasta gritted her teeth, and Njda heard an avalanche rumble across the realm. The huntress snatched her spear, and its metal glinted like the sun on the sea. 'Myopic child. Prepare for the journey ahead.'

The huntress cocked her legs and blasted into the sky like a catapulted stone. A shockwave bowled Njda to the grit. She brushed snow from her face, and disbelief echoed behind her eyes. Not just because Sigmar's wingless huntress could fly – but because Njda's temerity had paid off too. And spirits bless her, Yndrasta hadn't slain her for her defiance.

Yet.

YNDRASTA

My ire rises as the Suku limp down the wooded promontory to the black shores. As they drag their feet beneath the pines, they grunt and slaver like old, wretched wolves. Whenever they cross a root or rock, all four of them heave their sledge over it, then collapse into the snow and cobble themselves back together.

As I watch, I wonder if fragility or fear defines them. They move as if haste would shatter their bones, as if they dare not give their all. They represent everything I loathe.

I am a hunter, not a warrior. Wars are frivolous enterprises. No matter how many hosts I have marched with or how many battles I have won, I have always preferred the hunt. In an army, a soldier can only be as strong as her weakest comrade. For the hunter, the truest limitation is the limitation of the self. On my hunts I require no assistance beyond the killing thrust of my spear, *logistics* becomes a meaningless abstraction, and I need no reconnaissance save what I behold soaring forty leagues up in the sky. The company of proud Stormcast warriors like Arktaris is acceptable. Despite their rare quibbles, their sword arms are as strong as mine. Yet the frailty of mortals? Intolerable.

Once, roaring laughter through his black teeth, Hamilcar Bear-Eater asked me to share cups with his auxiliaries. They were mortal veterans: one-eyed soldiers and grizzled women who shrank in my presence all. I might have joined them for Hamilcar's company alone. I am fond of the Bear-Eater. His wild mane and booms of laughter remind me of Sigmar, electrifying my breath and stirring my blood. Not Sigmar the resplendent God-King, aloof and almighty, but the ancient Unberogen barbarian, my maker-father, who looked into my eyes when I was reborn. The Sigmar who, as legend tells it, battled a heaving horde of orruks to save his kinfolk before his mortal body was obliterated and sacrifice deified his soul.

Hamilcar reminds me of this Sigmar. A Sigmar who loves – the Sigmar I crave to please.

That night braziers crackled around us and mead flowed in rivers. The Bear-Eater urged me to honour his mortal companions and accept them for what they were.

'I have, Hamilcar,' I said. 'And they are weak.'

In the present, where the wooded headlands meet the black beaches of Glacier's End, Njda's little feet crunch into the snow before me. Since our first meeting in her dead city, wheat-gold shag has started to fill in the shaved scalp around her plaited queue. She raises her pointed hood and regards her strung-out companions. Steam leaks from their cracked lips in ragged huffs and gasps.

My presence startles her. 'We are ready,' Njda says.

I stare at her companions, my ire at war with my contempt. 'You need not move cautiously. I have slain every predator within leagues. Make haste.'

Njda flinches. 'Forgive us. We are... tired.'

I flare my nostrils and suck half the sky into my lungs. 'You hunger,' I conclude after tasting their weakness in the air. 'And you ate foetid meat. Why?'

'A mistake. We lost our supplies a day ago. We were desperate.'

I might as well be at war again, marching with children and buffoons. I doubt the champions of Destruction, Death and Chaos need make time to fill the bellies of their rabble. For one blasphemous breath, I envy them.

The world warps as I pump my wings and rip into the air. If the humans require sustenance, let them have it.

It is only minutes later that I return and toss my take to the ground. The dead whale flings a wall of sand as it craters the black shore. The pungent tang of its ruptured blubber cuts the air. Cold brine and viscous blood dribble from crimson fissures in the oily mass.

Valter, the muscled glutton with the cavalier's moustache and a missing eye, strokes the whale's coiled horn. 'How much you think this is worth?' His voice, I sense, is not as gruff as he wants it to be.

Magga, whose soul-stuff reeks of a lifelong dance on the knife's edge of Chaos, props her baleen sword on her shoulder. 'No one's carrying that, Valt.'

Valter nods to their sledge. 'We can put it–'

'Eat.' I fling fat and blood from my spear. Thengavar's sacred steel purrs with my annoyance. 'Now.'

Njda snaps a claw-knife from her belt and approaches the whale's carcass with her companion, Heigen, a youth with a shorn scalp and all the realm's ages in his eyes. They glance at each other, unsure what to do. Droplets of whale gore trickle away from me like writhing maggots. The mortals' eyes grow wide and unblinking.

'Eat,' I say.

In haste they throw themselves at the dead leviathan and saw their knives into its flesh.

The mortals settle into their endeavour. They murmur amongst themselves, their whispers tested by stifled laughter. A cut tension animates their chatter, like the wires between them have been snipped, and their kinship has become a conscious choice. Perhaps strength exists in such bonds. I dispel the thought with a snort.

Valter pretends to set a watch, but I am the only danger present. He ignores me entirely. The others cajole twigs and tundra grass into flame, then take turns gobbling each piece of meat as soon as it is charred. Warmth and filled bellies improve their humours. As my eyes wander across their threadbare tunics and fur coats, my fury dissipates. They are toy people going through a doll's motions of life. But is that not the heart of mortality? The motions of life?

Envy and sonder breed in my breast, and the seed of their conspiracy bears fruit. *I would try it on for myself,* the thought goes, as it always does. I would walk among my lost kindred of the Devadatta, filling myself with their merriment and troubles. But Deva's heirs are extinct, their heritage eradicated, the last vestiges of their wild descent long ennobled by the bloodlines of Azyr. How must it feel to belong, as these Suku belong with each other? I do not, cannot know.

I am knee-deep in the surf, where Ghur's oceans gnaw at its shores. I close my eyes – and suddenly I am there. In Wrothquake Valley, on the eve of my final battle with Doombreed.

The ancient basso grudge-ballads of the Aza-Karakier echoed in my ears. The clamour of my restless host filled the hungering night. Burning torch oil tickled my nose, and the spitting and char-scent of grilled meat set my stomach rumbling.

That night, I wandered my army's great encampment. Aelf beastriders greeted me, then tossed prey-meat scraps into the jaws of their many-headed mounts. In the lightless bivouac of our vampiric allies, the Askurga Renkai's mortal bannermen opened their veins and spilt red tribute into their lieges' brass grails. The knightly vampires unravelled linen bandages taken from the embalmed mummies of their forebears to bind their vassals' wounds. Regally, the vampires bowed forty-five degrees, as if to a superior, and healed their bannermen's wounds with a black kiss. For our looming battle with Doombreed and his daemonic host, trust was imperative. Perhaps love, too. Some breed of it.

I open my eyes, and the brittle cold of Glacier's End returns. Sea breakers skirt the metal toes of my boots and seep into the sand around me. The Suku survivors have finished eating. They cut reserves of meat, wrap them in folded burlap and stow them on their sledge. Above, Hysh approaches its zenith in the crystal sky. We have lost precious daylight.

Hamilcar, he spoke true. Mortals are what they are, and that must be enough. I was once the same: stronger than most, weaker than some. The only thing that changed is that my people lived, and I died. The only thing that changed is that they are gone, and I am not.

My patience diminishes. As my ruminations evaporate like mist at sunrise, I taste smoky magic brewing in the air.

I swivel. Behind me, Heigen shrinks and makes an apology I do not heed. Beside their sledge, Valter and Magga bicker and hiss. Njda sits apart, beside the dying embers of their fire. She bangs on a ritual drum and rocks side to side as she hums a dissonant tune.

'What is she doing?'

Heigen glances over his shoulder. 'Communing with her mother. Or trying. She said you asked her to, *Rana Apmil*.'

His native honorific finds no purchase in my ego. 'What is the drum for?'

Heigen takes the ghost of a step closer but falters. His foot drops.

'The drum belonged to our shaman. Bang on it, a bead dances over the skin. It lands on certain runes. Each shows a different future. The runes give… answers. True noajdi burn incense to enter a trance and read the runes.'

'She has no incense.'

Heigen pales. 'Maybe the coals' smoke will do.'

I know better than to mock their efforts and their custom. Ghur's wild magic pools around Njda like vapour. It tingles in my wrists and the base of my skull.

'Your people are connected to these lands in the most surprising of ways.' I size Heigen up with a glance. 'Go. Tell those two to prepare for the journey ahead.'

Heigen's eyes brighten. 'We are ready. They argue. They think you…'

'Yes?'

'Forgive me. It's nothing. We'll be ready, Rana Apmil.'

Minutes pass, yet the mortal remains. 'You fear me,' I say at last.

Heigen's hooded eyes lift. 'Is it true? You feel the magic of Ghur? Is it because you serve Sigmar? I am sorry, forgive my temerity, you needn't–'

'You will not like my answers to your question. Your real question.'

He stammers. 'Are we… so obvious?'

'Nothing about mortals is obvious. Yet you stink of grief. I know how such wounds heal. Go on. Ask. I will not shield you from the truth.'

Heigen blanches but hardens. 'My people say the living and the dead are two sides of one family. Even the bonds of marriage remain unbroken by death. Are the tellings true?'

No, I think to say. His people's spirits do not watch over their lands. The great necromancer has certainly enthralled them in the Realm of Death. The afterlifes have fallen; the only links between the living and the dead are the ghosts captured by memory. But then I glimpse Heigen's sullen gaze, potent anticipation locked in his lungs like a pocket of gas. All the lonely vastness of these blinding white lands lies frozen in his chest. The truth would condemn him to inhabit that waste, alone and afraid.

The force of my own pity jars me. 'Sometimes the dead remain with you.' I think of the Nighthaunt's ghastly corteges and Tjatsår Mai's thralls. I think of how their own funeral ritual immolated their shaman's soul and incorporated its stuff into the spiritual fabric of Ghur's lands. But I say none of this. It would not bring him comfort.

A shadow of strawberry returns to Heigen's cheeks, accompanied by a spectral smile. I cannot help but wonder why I spared his feelings at all.

I frown at the taste of vacuum in the air, a sensation emptier than the void. Njda is gone.

I storm over to Magga and Valter, who still bicker amongst themselves. Thengavar's haft lashes out. The sacred steel smacks from Valter's hand the gilded pistol he has aimed at Magga's foot. The weapon cartwheels away, and Valter's awestruck eyes lift, wider than the sea's horizon.

'Where is Njda?' I ask.

When they cannot answer, rage quivers through me. My roar blasts the snow from around us, and they shrink. I thunder into the air and my wings grip the wind like sails. My gaze haunts the shoreline, then sweeps inland as I scour the snows for signs of Njda's passage.

I sail through the sky along her trail, her discarded drum an ochre dot in the tundra. When I crash into the edge of a forest, the pine canopy bristles at my landing. Snow avalanches until the evergreen branches no longer sag with its weight.

Njda breathes hard on her knees. Tears streak her eyes, which are redder than flames.

I kneel before her and raise her chin. 'What did you see?'

The electricity of my touch shivers through her. She startles, shaken from her reverie, and brushes salty gems from the recesses of her eyes. 'My mother. In the woods… in wet fields. She beckoned… wanted me to join her… I'm sorry. I'm so sorry, huntress. I don't know where Mai is. But she needs me.'

Njda's kindred caper closer over knee-high snowdrifts, their sledge bouncing behind them. Tjatsår Mai is a beast of the deep seas. How could one of her thralls commune with Njda from the inland fens?

I step back and peer at the carpet of snow around us. All in Ghur devours. Not only the realm's bestial predators, but its skies, its seas, its lands. The continents in this realm ever change, crashing into each other, feasting upon each other's bedrock.

Deep beneath the realm's crust, primordial tunnels as old as existence run the great length of each land mass. They form cavernous digestive systems, a vast darkness of burbling waters and peristaltic earthquakes. Through these waterways, devoured stone migrates from one end of each continent to the other. Such do the realm's lands grow, or shrink, or disappear altogether. Those digestive tracts connect to the oceans, too. And if the caverns are large enough, even Tjatsår Mai could transit them.

Njda gasps and covers her mouth when she beholds my sick smile. I chuckle. 'Do not be sorry, Njda. You have done as I asked.'

As I could not, no less. I, the most skilled tracker in the Mortal Realms. I, Sigmar's blessed huntress, his perfect daughter. Shaking my head, I promise myself one day I will ask Sigmar of this. And should he grin in fatherly amusement, and all this be a divine jest, I promise to comport myself with greater courage than Njda did when she saw me in the moment of my joy.

I do not care to solve the riddle of the girl's tracking prowess. Perhaps she is merely meant for greater things. But as for how the kraken has always escaped me, that mystery is finally dead. Tjatsår Mai does not slumber at sea. She slumbers in the belly of the land, in its churning gut.

CHAPTER TWELVE

Like a primordial titan that hadn't moved in aeons, Yndrasta dominated the dark boreal forest ahead. Njda almost mistook her for one of the mossy boulders in the glade. Even after twelve days, she was hardly used to it. Each time the Suku would pass her, the unmoving huntress lingered behind until the taiga's loveless embrace swallowed her unblinking visage. Then, without fail, Njda would glimpse her silhouette looming before them in the snowfall, or in the cold bowers of gloomy conifers and doleful birches, awaiting their arrival.

Njda paused as Valter limped along. 'It's not natural,' he hissed. 'She's a ghost.'

The huntress' impassive eyes watched as the Suku trudged closer. 'The path is clear.'

Njda gave a hesitant nod. Leading the huntress on their journey was different from tracking the spoor of wounded prey or navigating by the light of stars. Each step brought Njda closer to her ma. She felt it in her gut, listening to herself as she might listen to Ghur's whispers. Yndrasta had insisted Njda's heart would lead them where they needed to go. But why must that be away from everything she had ever known? Where had Mai taken her ma?

'Rest here,' Yndrasta said as the others filtered into the white glade. 'Eat.'

They took their meal in silence. Through the trees, the white seas of snow-banks deeper than lakes stretched into haze. One false step out there could have seen Njda or her kinfolk disappear with a grainy crunch, gone like pebbles in the ocean. When they finished their mirthless meal, Yndrasta beckoned for them to resume their journey.

'And Valter,' the huntress said. 'This is as good a place to die as any.'

Frozen, the Suku traded glances. Njda walked between Yndrasta and the byrkaller, who sat on a stone in bleak shock. 'You made a promise.'

'A promise I now uphold.'

Through motes of snow, Njda gazed at Valter. He had been limping for almost two days. It had seemed like mere fatigue, but…

She crashed before him and shook off his boots. 'Shut up,' she said as he objected. Beneath the worn mesh of his threadbare stockings, a rank of black toes peered out.

Horrified, Njda lifted her eyes. 'Valter.'

'I had no snow gear.' Valter gritted his teeth and brushed sweat from his brow. 'I couldn't slow us down.'

'Wilds damn you,' Njda breathed. 'You should've said something.'

'He may live.' The reverent woods quietened at Yndrasta's imperious interruption. 'If he chooses.'

Magga stormed closer and ripped into Valter's coat. He mumbled and raised his arms as she rifled through his inner pockets. She extracted a foggy phial of shining fluid and pressed it into Njda's hands.

'Queencure.' Njda shook the phial. 'How long have you had this?'

'I found it before we left. In my wine cellar. Don't ask how it got there – I don't know.' Valter's good eye crawled to Heigen, who had stiffened. 'If I'd known, I would've shared it with her. Really.'

Heigen's lips hardened. Magga snatched the phial and popped the top, then forced Valter's jaw open. 'Down the hatch, Valt. Smile now.'

He spluttered and prised her fingers from his teeth. 'I've got it.'

Magga chuckled. 'There we go. No hard feelings. You pay me to watch out for you, don't you?'

A shade of miraculous rose seeped into Valter's black toes. Njda waggled a hand, and Heigen brought Bavval's old coat. She slit strips from it and wrapped the merchant's feet, then helped cram them into his boots. In awkward quiet, the party resumed its unspirited trek.

When the others had shrunk beneath the towering trees, Njda faced Yndrasta and swallowed. 'You said you would protect us from harm.'

Frost crunched on Yndrasta's glacial brow. Verglas gleamed on her armour. Her marble-white skin looked as though truer life had never inhabited it, even as the vargr's dead eyes flickered on her shoulder. The pair of scars lacing Yndrasta's brow were the only clues she had ever been vulnerable at all. She never spoke of those old wounds; she rarely spoke at all. The saint was a riddle beyond Njda's ken. And as Yndrasta regarded Njda – just like every time she observed the Suku, perhaps unaware Njda could *feel* the fell gravity of her attention crushing them – Njda prickled with an intuition that Yndrasta felt the same about them.

'Yes.' Yndrasta's haunting contralto boomed in Njda's skull. 'And so we bleed hours twice a day, so you may restore your mortal flesh. But I cannot protect Valter from his own flaws.'

'Flaws?' Njda blinked. 'Greed. He meant to sell the queencure in Suodji, didn't he?'

'Greed, compassion. What difference does the nature of your flaws make? In the end, you are all the same. Insubstantial.' Yndrasta breathed, and leaves fell as the tops of trees danced. 'Will we continue in this direction?'

'I don't know.'

'But your heart tells you, does it not?'

Njda's face fell. 'This direction. I think.'

'Good. I cleared a glade while scouting ahead. A ram carcass awaits you there. Ripened sedges and edible lichens hide beneath the snow. Fill your bellies, and sleep well. Tomorrow, orruks hunt you.'

In a darkened copse surrounded by snowy banks, Njda and her companions gnawed meat around a roaring fire. Njda chewed lengths of rigid razorgrass as the others whispered. Yndrasta's ominous warning soured in her belly, but worse was her indifference. The huntress cared for them as she might care for her spear – even less, considering her spear's obvious divinity.

Unable to make peace with her unease, Njda took a crock of stew. The others' murmurs faded as she waddled along packed snow through brittle brush into a wider glade. A cobalt aurora shimmered overhead in a ceaseless dance. The bite of ozone burned Njda's throat.

Njda pushed branches aside and shielded the steaming crock from falling snow. At the glade's centre, Yndrasta stood vigil on a boulder. Her wolfskin mantle draped her shoulders like a dark eagle's wings. Her eyes were locked shut. Her radiant skin and armour seemed to absorb the starlight as flowers might drink the light of Hysh.

'Food,' Njda said. 'You never eat. If you do not need it, forgive me. But I thought... maybe you'd enjoy it.'

The frost on Yndrasta's eyelids cracked. Her eyes, silver knives, stabbed into Njda's.

Njda bit down. 'You could eat with us.'

A plume of white smoke gouted from Yndrasta's nostrils. 'I smell your fear. Is it me, or the orruks?'

'I fear everything,' Njda said. 'I don't know why. I don't know what's changed. I just know it's getting harder to hide.'

'Do you fear she is gone?'

Njda blinked. 'Always. But she's closer at night. It's hard to sleep sometimes. To listen to her in my dreams. She speaks… of strange things. Things beyond my reckoning.'

Yndrasta's eyes slid shut. 'I fear she is gone, too. I cornered her an age ago, and still she slipped away. But soon I shall have another chance.' The morose hint of a smile drifted over her lips. 'For an age, Tjatsår Mai has evaded my steel. You have a wild heart, to track your mother on the soul plane. Most mortals lack such spirit. I shall speak to my maker-father of you.'

'Oh.' Njda's cheeks warmed. She brushed snow from a log and sat, cradling the crock in her hands. 'That sounds like a mighty privilege. Maybe you could tell my pa, too. He said I wasted too much time as a finder.'

Scornful silence answered, and Njda's shy smile bled away. The longer she stared, the stranger Yndrasta seemed. Even if she ever dared express her displeasure with the huntress, it would have been in vain. Yndrasta was as far away as the stars she worshipped. For all Njda knew, a human's impatience meant as little to her as the impatience of mice.

Njda gasped as Yndrasta's armour caught fire with the alien glow of Sigmar's domain. Silver purity and reflected starfire simmered to life beneath each plate. The vargr's blood-emblazoned furs brightened too, until they resembled a dove's virgin pinions, as pure and white as snow. Yndrasta gleamed like the dusk-lit ocean.

To witness her felt like looking at a joint between realms, at the foundations of time.

'You speak to him now.'

'In a sense. It is beyond your understanding.'

Njda's blood raced. 'I would try.'

A hundred heartbeats passed before Yndrasta's answer shook the trees. 'Glory was a word I thought I knew. But I did not, until the God-King's lightning became my soul.' Her forlorn smile widened into a fierce shield, her canines jutting. 'Sigmar's fire is my heart. I see him now. In his long hall, upon his throne. He watches us all.'

The track of Yndrasta's closed eyes pierced the star-studded sky. Njda watched the dancing aurora. 'Even me?'

'Even you.' Yndrasta's smile fell away. 'But glory has its price. I would not curse any being with the caprices of a Stormcast's memory.'

'You remember everything?'

'The moments of my most vaunted kills. The extinctions of beasts that fed on empires. I remember those who triumphed over me. Those recollections are like carrion, spoiling in my heart. A daemon king, the father of dragon ogors, a god of earthquakes...'

Yndrasta slammed the butt of her radiant spear into the earth. Stew spilt and Njda slid off the icy log as a tremor ran through the realm. The groan of distant trees uprooting and crashing away rode the night winds to them. Moss peeled in slow curls from the boulder beneath Yndrasta, then trembled pathetically.

The huntress' eyes snapped open. 'I remember the shame of my failures. The bite of Sigmar's tongs, the heat of his crucible. The agony – the *agony*.' She gritted her teeth, and the crumble of distant hills reverberated across the taiga. 'His hammer pounds life into my broken bones. I feel it now, across the ages.'

The fire in her eyes guttered, and Njda expelled the pent fear in her lungs.

'When I have slain Tjatsår Mai,' Yndrasta said, 'I shall remember that too.'

Every ounce of Njda's being urged her to say no more. Yet fear was her close friend, and its defiance was in her nature. 'If you are Stormcast, you were once mortal. The missionaries taught me. Do you remember... your kin?'

Again, a moment stretched into minutes, but Njda waited.

'Have you ever seen a smith at work?' Yndrasta said.

'No. Forgive me. We trade our metal from Izalend. We have no smith-mages.'

'Metal remembers the shape it is given. The properties it requires, to accomplish its task. A breastplate, or a sword. A Stormcast Eternal. All metal is worked into what it must be. Purged of the flaws which would compromise its purpose.'

'You don't remember them.'

'I do not need to. I need nothing. I am not like you.'

Njda blinked, then startled. In that instant, Yndrasta had twisted around to regard her. The light had left her armour. Her shadow rose to the stars like a dark fortress.

'Return to your companions. Sleep. Dream of your mother, so we do not lose our way. Dawn is nearer than you think. The ground we cross tomorrow will be bloody.'

Again, her baffling warning. Death was Ghur's curse for those who loved it. What did it matter if orruks hunted them tomorrow? It was not they who had made the Sukuat deadly.

Njda rose. Then she steeled herself and sucked a mouthful of frigid air into her belly. She thrust out her chest and parted her lips, and with the wilful courage of a Suku taker charging into battle, she sang her favourite fairing, the one that hurt.

Njda's voice cracked, but as her song haunted the glade, it steadied. On the song's notes, a lifetime drifted back to her. She was ten, arguing with her pa about leaving Riika alone for the first time. She was five, swaddled in thick furs as her ma guided her to market with her brothers. She was twenty, and Heigen bellowed with laughter and squeezed-shut eyes as they twirled each other in a snowy court. She was twenty-one, and her ma comforted her as she wept over the shards of her broken heart.

Njda sang, and she lay in her sledcroft at night, covered in furs on her pallet. As she fell asleep, a burnished mirror over the hearth caught the tired flames and the others bedding down. Then she hunkered over a crowded table, bickering with her sisters over which of them could dredge the last of the marrow stew from the pot. She lay curled up in the driver's seat of their sledcroft, and the endless procession of Riika-Min snaked over the Sukuat's edgeless snows. Herds of reindeer bustled around them, and Njda remembered what it was like to be unafraid, the way the boazu were when they spiralled in the tundra under the tender care of her people's herdsteaders.

Njda sang, and Riika-Min's embers smouldered in her heart. She sang her mountains, her skies, her seas. She sang the water-logged timbers of their sledcroft trapped beneath the waves, then sang the memories that would outlast them. She carried them all with her, now, in the caged cradle of her heart. As jealously as she had cherished those memories, she shared their song freely with Yndrasta, and wondered if she had ever sung her own.

When the last note left her lips, Njda fell silent. Discomfort bred with relief and reddened her cheeks. 'Forgive me. I thought–'

'You need not be sorry for that.' Countless sorrows lay written in the hard lines of Yndrasta's face. She looked so old, now. So weather-worn. So tired. 'We had such a song. We chanted it before our hunts. Together, in a wild chorus, dancing around the hunts-fire. Those who felt Sigmar's touch sang the verses. And when Hysh fell and the hunt began, they led us in the chase.'

So she had always been a hunter. 'You must have sung the verses often.'

'I did. I sang them most of all.' Regret glistered in Yndrasta's spectral gaze. 'But I forgot them.'

A false smile cracked Valter's chapped lips, and a golden tooth peeked out. 'Heard you fairing. Glad nothing ate you.' He gestured at a hunk of meat. 'I can't trim ram. Or any meat, for that matter.' He jutted his chin to Heigen, who slept. 'I'd bother him, but...'

Njda removed her mittens and crouched. She slid her knife out and did what Valter could not. As she worked the stubby knife between slick muscle and yellow fat, the meat's ripping sinews made the sound of suction. She cleaned her hands with meltwater, then warmed her fingers.

Valter's dead eye flitted to the trail she had walked in the woods. 'You spoke to the huntress.'

'There is something familiar in her soul.'

'So. You trust her.'

'I do.'

'Even though she killed Brother. Even though she caused this whole mess.'

Njda's heart hammered her ribs. 'Where did you hear that?'

'From Bavval and you, that night on the promontory. Magga was pestering me for an advance, so I tracked you both down. Still know how to be quiet, when I want. Even if I didn't, old Bav spoke loud enough for the whole realm to hear.' Valter leaned forward. 'Thing is, you knew. But you didn't breathe a word to us.'

Njda took a length of bowstring Magga had wound from boar gut. Her bow creaked as she attached it. She plucked, and the string thrummed. 'I don't know what the huntress did or didn't do. I know the wounds that killed Brother were cleaner than I expected. I thought it was her, yes. But I've changed my mind.'

'Because the storm light's in your head.' Valter's arrogance rusted away. 'I remember when I first saw Izalend's cathedral. But the bricks are mortared in blood. Sigmar's servants are tough, good friends in a rough spot, but they do love their sacrifice. Don't give it to them. Don't give them what they don't pay for. Same goes for the huntress.'

Njda wrapped the crimson steaks she had cut. 'If she wanted to kill us, she wouldn't protect us. And why does this bother you now? We've been with her two weeks.'

'She told me to lie down and *die*, Njda. And even if she hadn't, I see through her. I know how people tick. I see her ticking, too.'

'You don't look at her. You hold your breath when she's near.'

Valter sneered. 'She doesn't care if we live or die. All she wants is the kraken! You're not blind. Brother kept us safe. Ate a few of us in the hard times, but that was better than this. Yndrasta killed him to bring the kraken to Riika for a chance at slaying it. She'll get us killed too, if it means another chance to bring Mai down.'

'I'd love it if the huntress killed you two.' Magga rubbed her eyes. 'Shut up and let me sleep. My head's killing me.'

Heigen rose and yawned. 'What are you both talking about?'

'About how the huntress caused this mess,' Valter said. 'About how she killed Brother. About how she'll get us killed. About how Njda knew and didn't say a thing.' He stabbed a finger at her. 'You're naive to think that if we help her, she'll help us.'

Wounded trust flashed in Magga's red eyes. 'Is that true?'

Njda raised her chin. 'We're all here with her. You could've all continued to Suodji alone, but you came with her, same as me. It's because we knew she'd protect us. It's because we trust her. Look at what she's done. That's not the work of one who would kill Brother.'

Valter raked his messy hair and scoffed. 'You don't see it! She does what she needs to get what she wants! And when she's done, she'll leave us to starve in the tundra! Like she left us for dead in Riika-Min!'

Magga beat her battered wallet from her tunic and cracked the lid. A phantom aura danced in the dilated black of her pupils. As she pushed the last shavings into the corner of the tin, omens turned in her eyes like fog.

Njda lurched over and snapped the lid shut. 'No more of that. You hear me?'

Magga yanked her shabby tin aside and glowered. 'Valt's wrong about a lot of things. But not people.'

'You knew?' Heigen's eyes flicked to Njda. 'You didn't tell us?'

Njda tossed her arms. She had cauterised bad wounds in the bush with campfire brands. She had dragged herself back to Riika-Min after mistaking good berries for bad, fighting jackals all the way. All that felt simple, now.

'I don't know,' she said. 'I thought I did, but... I know she can protect us. She can reunite us with our kin.'

Valter cackled. 'If that's not a lie, too.'

'You don't want our folk,' Magga said. 'You want your family.'

'I want us to be safe. I want things to be normal.' Njda hated the sound of her own pleading. It shouldn't have come to this. 'Bavval taught us Harmony is ours to accept, not change. What if this is Harmony, playing out before our very eyes? Tjatsår Mai is dangerous. A god-daughter of Ghur, yes, but maybe it's time she met her end. And Yndrasta didn't hurt Riika-Min. The kraken did. The orruks did. And if she did kill Brother for a chance at the kraken–'

Maybe it was for the best. The unspoken words came from a deep well within Njda. She hated them, but that didn't make them wrong.

Njda sighed. 'What I mean is we don't know what she did. All we know is she can help us now.'

Magga scoffed. 'Apmil forgot something when he was moulding your brain at creation.'

Njda loosed the words from her lips before she knew where

they'd land. 'If she left Riika-Min open to attack, how is that worse than what you all did with Heigen on the cape?'

Heigen turned berry red. 'What?'

'Our lives are suddenly gold, is what!' Magga spoke in dagger-thrust words, like she was duelling at a tavern. 'We used you the way givers do, Heigen. It was *my* idea. Thanks to you and me, we lived that night. Meanwhile, Yndrasta tells Valt he can die when he feels like it, and Njda doesn't bat an eye.'

Njda gnashed her teeth. '*I* was the only one who spoke for Valter then. But you knew about his queencure. Did he really find it before we left? Or was he just saving it for one of you two while Heigen's wife died on the floor?'

Valter swelled up and raised his voice. 'You are *not* the only one who cares about us!'

'Then why didn't you give it to his wife?'

'She passed before I found it! So I decided to save it for one of you!'

Quiet fell over the camp. They had been too loud. Njda listened for the telltale crack of a twig or the crunch of snow, but they were alone. 'What do you mean, one of us?'

'For the old man.' Valter brushed his moustache. An ornate signet ring gleamed on his thick knuckle. 'I wanted to. Maybe I should have. But I thought he'd got better that day. I didn't know the orruks would come, or that he'd call the damn amber wind and sell his life to the ice. But all that changes nothing. If this kingdom falls – and all kingdoms fall, finder – it's on you. Bavval, up in the stars or riding the wind, he'll know it when he sees it. He'll blame you from cursed Shyish, or the wilds, or wherever the hells he is.'

Njda blasted to her feet, her lips trembling. Invoking Bavval's name was a step too far. She meant to lay out Valter's faults before him, then, and pick them apart one by one. But the queencure kept orbiting in her head. Njda had seen Valter with Bavval on the cape, gripping the old man's hand as his own fingers drifted beneath his coat. Perhaps the byrkaller had thumbed the phial, eager to spill the queencure into Bavval's cracked lips. Perhaps he had even tried, and Bavval hadn't let him.

Njda raised her voice. 'Will you leave?'

'Leave? Like I would leave any of you alone with *her*.'

Magga stalked along the camp's outskirts back to the fire. 'Me neither.'

'Nor me.' Heigen pulled his furs in. 'Ta would have watched over all of you. So should I.'

Njda squeezed the rage from Valter. She felt his breath in her lungs, his pulse in her breast. He was her brother. She hadn't seen it until now.

Valter cleared his throat as she stepped back. 'I suppose... I... If you've changed your mind about marriage, the offer's still retracted.'

Njda laughed damply. She reached for Magga, who hopped out of reach then rolled up in her furs.

'I'm sleeping,' Magga said. 'And no one asked, because no one ever does, but for the record, I wouldn't marry any of you cretins.'

CHAPTER THIRTEEN

Conifers whipped by as the sledge careened downhill. Heigen yanked hard on his improvised reins, and swamp waters doused them. Njda spat damp grass from her mouth and scraped mud from her eyes. Another skirmish line of hooting orruks cranked bolt throwers in the haze ahead. '*Valter!*'

'Give me a bloody breath, I'm not a damn handgunner!' He snapped his pistol's charging tray shut, then cocked the hammer back. He perched his arm on Heigen's shoulder and squeezed shut his dead eye.

Thunder rang in Njda's ears. She choked on acrid smoke. Ahead, a squealing orruk dropped its massive bolt thrower and clapped a lumpy hand over its scarred chest. Magga hung from the skids as precariously as Njda on the other side of Heigen. She whipped her baleen sword once. As they shot past, an orruk's jag-horned helmet cartwheeled with them.

'Yes!' Njda roared. The joy trickled from her breast as she heard a splash and glimpsed Magga rolling through the fens behind them.

The sledge began keeling over with her weight. Heigen's heavy-lidded eyes stretched wide. 'Hold on!'

The sledge flipped, and Njda's stomach flew to her throat. The misty swamp spun around her. Peat squelched as she skipped along the ground. She shook off her daze and pulled grass from her hair. Nothing was broken.

Hobgrots gibbered in the fog around them. They slid chipped metal spikes from their rotted hide armour and waddled closer. Njda shrugged her bow from her shoulders and reached for her quiver, but she'd lost it when the sledge tumbled.

They were divided, unarmed. Yndrasta was still nowhere to be–

'I was delayed.'

Yndrasta towered behind Njda. Blood drenched her gauntlets. Orruk heads hung from her mailed fist by their bundled, greasy topknots. Ulcerous tongues lolled from their brick-like jaws, and red eyes rolled into the backs of their skulls.

She dropped her trophies and knee-deep swamp waters parted before her. As the sludge rippled in dread, an orruk thudded from the mist onto the mud. A bestial growl clicked in its scarred chest. The beast loped forward and raised a fleshy shield, red clay wads caked onto its face in the shape of a disgusting grin. The shield leered at Njda. Eyes blinked at her within it.

The orruk skipped forward and hammered its spiked maul at Yndrasta. The ugly iron rang and bent as Yndrasta caught it in her fist. For a blink, the orruk's malicious grin flickered on its diseased lips. Yndrasta pounded it into the mud as a child might annihilate a toad.

She straightened, and fresh gore oozed from her mail. 'Wait for me. This will not take long.'

Lightning cracked, and Yndrasta disappeared as if she were never there. Njda scrambled to gather the others and right their sledge. The abuse of metal resounded in the mists around them,

and the orruks' and hobgrots' sadistic laughter melted into porcine squeals and screams of liquid terror.

Speechless, exhausted, the Suku watched as Yndrasta's spear
glowed brighter. Their jaws fell as viscera smoked from the
lambent metal until it was pure. Rain plinked against her
armour, and she let it fall. 'She is there. Beneath the sleeping
mountains.'

Yndrasta closed her eyes and blew. A breeze whispered through
the fens and dispelled the nearest mists. Flooded fields of sopping heath expanded into the fog, peppered with pieces of the
dead. Beyond, faintly visible, a ring of mountains rose like the
realm's fangs. A veil of shrivelled pines covered their slopes. As
the stink of marsh fecundity dissipated, the unmistakable aroma
of sea spray lingered, joined by the far-off roar of waves.

The clammy air stuck to Njda's skin, like a blanket drenched in
fever sweat. She loosened her tunic and dragged a finger along
her neck, then crinkled her nose. 'This is wrong. These used to
be sedge plains.'

'Blame the orruks' swamp callers. They are dead now. All that
remains is the kraken.' Yndrasta's imperial gaze dominated the
others. Her lips hardened with purity of purpose. 'You have done
well, Njda. And all of you. I shall finish this.'

Heigen brushed his palm through his cropped hair and flung
sweat away. 'Is it safe here?'

Magga, still picking grass and mud from the fronds of her
bladed feather, scoffed. 'Not if you're driving us again it's not.'

'We're not staying.' Njda counted her arrows and slid them into
her cleaned quiver. 'We're going with the huntress.'

'No,' Yndrasta said. 'Those mountains conceal a crater filled
with dark waters. Beneath, tunnels lead to the outer seas. Fouler
creatures fill those ways. Even if the way were clear, you would

not make it through the water. Make camp where you will, and do not think of following me.'

Valter shrugged off his sopping coat and dumped mud from his pistol barrels. 'Mai's taken Izalend's galleons over the years. You think you might be able to bring something...?' His words decayed as Yndrasta's eyes pierced him. He cleared his throat. 'Valuable?'

Wind sang through the mountains, and flies buzzed in Njda's belly. She parted her lips to speak but faltered. She trusted Yndrasta.

'Do not follow me,' the huntress said. 'I will not warn you again.'

Njda gave a sharp nod. She plucked a solitary marigold from a rotten log. 'May I?'

Yndrasta's stoic ice thawed into a dour grimace, and she bent. Njda stood on the tips of her toes and slipped the flower's stem behind the saint's ear, beside the feathery lines of her scars. 'We have enough ancestors watching our lands.' Her ma had used to say that. Njda felt silly repeating the words. But maybe no one had ever said them to Yndrasta. A peculiar twitch ran through Yndrasta's brow, as if she knew.

The huntress straightened, until Njda's neck hurt looking at her. 'She would be proud of what you have done.'

'Not after I tell them what you've done,' Njda said. 'We'll be ready for them. Waiting.'

Yndrasta's blank face might as well have been carved in stone. Without another word, she thundered into the fog over the mountains. Njda craned her head up and followed, and for the barest breath, she could have sworn wings had stretched out from Yndrasta's broad back.

Scree trickled down the slopes as Njda trudged up the mountain's foot. The others were strung out behind her. Hysh sank in the sky until they reached a flat overlook on an escarpment beside the tired forest slouching on the mountain's slopes. As they unpacked their sledge, the unnatural fog that blanketed the fens below dissolved. The orruks' sick magic drained from the lands like pus. The temperature dropped until Njda could see her breath again. Flakes of snow drifted from the dun sky and stuck to gravel and clumped sedges. Diaphanous in the distance, the faint shield mountains of Suodji swelled into the crystal horizon.

Njda ventured to the swaying pines and returned with another armful of thin wood. Heigen was making camp. The wood clattered, and she tidied her wheat hair. 'Valter, where do you think you're going?'

Valter shoved a just-polished pistol into his holster. 'To keep watch. Someone's got to.'

'Just let him go.' Magga wet her hands in snow melt and kicked a pelt until it had unrolled. 'He'll only get in our way.'

Magga and Njda helped Heigen coax a fire to life. Thoughts swam and soured in Njda's head, more than just Valter's sloth. They were close to the end, but it couldn't be this easy. She was missing something. It felt like it should have been obvious.

'When she slays Mai, the ones she frees could be weak,' Heigen said.

Njda brightened. 'Then we'll need more food.'

'Forage. Herbs. Whatever we can get.'

Njda snatched her bow and stalked off onto the slopes. The orruk curse had done little to corrupt the land's bounty. She returned with six hares and fowl and found Heigen ruling a mountain of sedges and lichens he had gathered. Magga sat with Njda and helped clean the game, working her rondel dagger through the pelts and peeling feathers from birds.

'I'll cook, as I can.' Heigen tipped his head to the trees. 'We'll need bedding too. If they're sick.'

Magga and Njda traded a look, then submitted to Heigen's

guidance. They gathered pine needles and leaves and firewood. They dredged firepits from the hard earth with their bare hands. They broke the lowest spruce boughs around the trunks of trees, then tied them down. They distributed the last of their furs between the shelters and their own coats, too.

As sweat dampened the sleeves of their tunics, they took turns laying bedding. They piled spare foliage between each shelter and firepit so they could refresh the sleeping spaces where needed. They paused to admire the last embers of daylight from the escarpment, then worked hard to exorcise the cold from their limbs. By the time they were finished, the ghost of day haunted the horizon. Heigen arrayed neat piles of roasted meat, pine seeds and sedges on broad green leaves. He piled scree over a bed of coal and threw his fur over that, then sat and heated tea in Valter's canteen cup, their last cooking implement.

Magga chuckled and nibbled on a roasted lichen. 'Valt won't like that one bit. It's excellent.'

Njda chewed on the petals of a fragrant mountain flower as she watched Heigen keep busy. Her belly churned. She had been without her siida for the better part of forever. Soon they would be returned to her – at the very least, her ma. If her siblings and father weren't here, all the better. That would mean they were safe in Suodji. The horror of Hari dying in the snow spooled behind her eyes, and she blinked it away. Njda refused to consider the alternative.

'Are you ever afraid?' she asked.

Stars punctured the dimming sky. Magga placed her mittens beside her and ran her fingers through her russet shag. 'I am not.'

'Then you're brave. Braver than me. We all teased you for sword fighting with switches when we were children. Remember?'

'Of course. All you fools. Look at us now.'

Njda grimaced. 'Maybe you knew things we didn't.'

'I certainly knew things you didn't. But I'm not wise, nor brave. I needn't be either.'

'Your visions didn't calm you at the black water bay. You begged us not to go.'

'Because I didn't want you to die. For my part, I know what to fear.'

Njda's eyes dropped to the faded blue bulge in Magga's tunic. 'What have you seen?'

'My death, when I fill my eyes. It's not like how Izalenders brag, with their aelf sorcerers and collegiate wizards and their prophecies. It's a haze, and I have to fight my way through it. I only see death. It's all I look for.'

Njda's cheeks tingled. 'What happens?'

'I see wooden ships. Riika-Min's sledcrofts, I think. Fire burns in great black plumes, like that day we burned the dead. Long shadows fall over the realm – Tjatsår Mai's tentacles. And orruks, a drooling horde of them, running through the city. I see family, too. Blurs, like I'm looking at them through tears or smoke. They're dressed like me, fighting like me. When I see them, I'm not mad any more. I just miss them. Then the vision ends, and you're standing there pestering me not to fill my eyes, or getting us lost.'

'Your visions tell you you should have died in Riika-Min. But you didn't.'

'That's right. I don't fear death because it missed me. If it wants me, it'll have to catch up.'

Heigen cursed and shot to his feet. He shook out his fur as the fire in the scree smouldered back to life. Magga choked on laughter as he stood, arms akimbo, and glowered at the bed of coals. He piled more scree and dirt on it.

'I hated Harmony since I was a girl,' Magga said. 'Hated the idea. It's random and capricious. It took my parents from the realm and left you yours. It's cruel, and our people are cruel to revere it. At least I understand the glimmerings. And if they lie to me, at least the lies are sweet.'

'You're bitter, Mag. The realm's not been bitter to you.'

'You say so. But our people can be heartless at the best of times. I always wanted to be a taker to defy the teachings. Takers know. They reject Harmony when they go into exile. They fight for themselves, because no one else will. Not like the givers. The dead givers.' She chuckled grimly. 'Hari, you fool. Taught me everything I know.'

'You fought to defend us. Or was that for you, too?'

'I didn't say I don't want to protect people. I want to be a hero. The hero I never had. No one should live as I have.'

'How is that?'

'Alone.'

The parting glow of sunlight faded beneath the horizon. 'We protected you. I still would.'

'Your parents were good people.' Fragile warmth lit Magga's eyes. '*Are*. They are good people. But if you had to choose between your siida and me, we both know what you'd do. Look what brought us here. Your love for your ma. Not Yndrasta's hunt, not her protection. We came with you. You wouldn't go so far for me.'

'I would.' Njda realised the truth when she spoke it. 'Yndrasta wanted to leave you all behind so we could move faster, even if it meant losing my ma forever, but I refused. It's what she would have done, too. I care for you.'

Magga sucked in her lips. 'Yndrasta would've fit in with us, whatever she was.'

'Perhaps she was Suku.'

'I think not.' Magga tapped the empty tin at her breast. 'I wish I was like her.'

Heigen tramped over. 'Clouds overhead. The wet snow may return.'

'You cretin. It's called rain.'

Heigen held out his hands. 'The disgusting wet rain may return. Or true snow, if the realm's kind. Let's move to a shelter.'

Heigen's ebullience caught Njda off guard. She stood and helped Magga up; then brushed dirt and damp grass from her trousers. 'One of us should take up Valt's watch.'

'To brittle ice with Valt.' Magga kicked the dirt. 'If he wanted relief, he'd have come in by now. The greedy puck's right where he wants to be, mark my words.'

YNDRASTA

The pit within the mountains leads deep into the bowels of Ghur. Tunnels meander through the crust, beneath the mountains' roots, to stony depths that have never known the light of Hysh. Torchlight flickers in dank recesses as the grot clans that lurk here sense the merciless gravity of my hunt and flee. The pulsing luminescence of mushrooms shows the way.

I wade into cold currents and the crush of shadows. I battle through knee-high torrents, tossing boulders which block my way. At junctions I pause to sniff the pungent air. Where waters flood the passages, I submerge and swim through burbling currents before surfacing again. The deeper I descend, the smoother the caverns' walls. They resemble the intestinal lining of a beast.

In the greater caverns, I feel them. The kraken-god's thralls, tethered to her throbbing tentacles. They ape the motions of life, but theirs is a meaningless mimicry. They shudder and stir cauldrons which are not before them, or squeeze guts from fish as if feasting on grilled capon meat. A rout of enthralled orruks tumble in the water like feeding alligators. Glaucous-green light inhabits their dead eyes, and cave brine drenches their wasted lungs. The kraken's most ancient prisoners, a tribe of aelf-kin whose necrotic forms still reek of elder worlds, hang suspended within nests of tentacles and sway in the black waters like kelp. They heave and shiver, trapped in the maculate prisons of their flesh.

A hundred thousand thralls fill the dripping darkness. Their soul stink fills my nose – withered or fresh, chained and forlorn. A disconcerting handful are clad in the same indigo as the survivors who brought me here. I ignore them and move on.

As I creep through the dark tunnels towards the plangent drumbeat of Tjatsår Mai's earth-shaking hearts, I think of Njda. Vapid guilt stirs in me – a biteless remorse which the ages of my existence have trained me to ignore. The terrible deception I told her serves a greater good. Tjatsår Mai's elimination will further Sigmar's aims. And to say nothing of the mortals' fates, my maker-father will be pleased when I have slain this beast. Yet again I shall prove I am exactly as he made me.

But as I penetrate the tunnel shadows, a feeling I cannot recognise turns in my belly. A chill moves through the flesh beneath my silvered armour, and I spin. Behind me, a vision from beyond time seethes in the shadows. My mother.

On the night before my final battle with Doombreed, she found me. She slumped from her once mighty pegasus, its back stooped from age, then slunk into my tent. So eager was I for violence, I thought her a skaven assassin like the one the Three-Eyed King had dispatched to murder Hyndaratha. I snarled and brandished my blade in an inside guard.

She teased back her cowl, and I exhaled and lowered my sword. I returned to the pegs carrying my battered lamellar armour. 'You should not be here. No matter my queen's will, I'll not change course.'

My mother wobbled to my armour cross, then removed the first piece of lamellar. She dressed me, first smoothing the kinks in my hauberk, then pulling the cords of my vambraces tight, until soon she had laced my pauldrons to my shoulders. As she handled my battle dress, my heart thawed. What pity she decanted into my cracked heart.

As much as I craved the hunt or the kill or the dignity of slaughter – as much as I desired to protect my nation and our freedom, and to fight for Sigmar's light – I loved my mother. As Njda loves hers.

Her eyes quivered up to mine. 'You should heed your queen's will.'

Her time-abraded whisper took me aback. 'The free peoples march to sanctuary in Azyr, as she willed,' I replied. 'The Askurga Renkai promise the mortarchs guard the last realmgate to Shyish, where Nagash holds the passages to Azyr. They will live, mother. You will live. But we must fight.'

Her rheumy eyes dropped. 'Doesn't my daughter deserve to live, too? Doesn't Yndrasta deserve peace and love? You've done enough. Come with us to Azyr. Raise your daughter to be strong. Teach her, as the queen taught you.' Half a smile graced her parchment lips. 'To see my granddaughter in your arms. I would like that.'

I could not push the words I wished to say past my clenched teeth: I wanted that. I wanted to grow old with my people and teach my daughter to ride a pegasus, and to hurl a spear through an enemy's throat at fifty yards. But we had to make a stand. No one else stood between our people and our eradication, between the darkness and the light. If we all fled, Doombreed's daemonic legions would have caught up to us. They would have killed us before we reached Shyish. They would have devoured our souls.

To have not sensed this battle's inevitability – to have not realised this was my final, finest purpose – my mother was either craven or a fool. This was my duty.

She sensed the blazing fire of my ardour and sighed a bitter smile. When she finished, she took my hand and peeled back my fingers, then placed a gift in my palm. A hunter's totem – an unenchanted trinket, the merest of charms. An amber chitin shard, tied to the corded hair of a hellicore's mane.

In the caverns, the echoing darkness that surrounds me reflects the one that howls within. In a mortal soul some affliction like compassion might fill that void. After I slay Tjatsår Mai, my hunger will be abated, but it never lasts. My desire to please my maker-father will return. My remorseless desire for butchery will swell up the cracks of me, along with my sorrow.

I wish I cared, as Njda cares. I wish I felt. A paradox, this regret I lack regret. But only Sigmar's satisfaction moves me. Only my slaked thirst for the bloody moment of his foes' evisceration.

And just like that – like the rare bloom of a cactus flower, or the passage of centuries – the breath of my hesitation has passed. *I* turned my back upon my mother. *I* lied to Njda. *I* do not care.

Kill. The force of the God-King's ancient command settles in my skull like sediment. I am exactly where I wish to be.

Stalwart, I continue. The kraken's scent becomes an oozing stink that pools in the back of my throat. A sweeping subterranean cavern, an oceanic cave with no bottom, stretches before me. Aphotic darkness drowns my eyes. The rustle of captive waves fills my ears as the kraken's slow-beating hearts pound through the universe.

Thengavar's blessed steel glows silver with a lambent lust for blood. The soulless stench of Tjatsår Mai's presence fouls my humours, invigorating me. Every muscle in my body tenses, that the pent divinity which Sigmar vested in me might be channelled into my throw and Thengavar's flight. I await the kraken's movement – the crash of stone, or the subtle shift of tides as she stirs. But as the moment bleeds on, I feel nothing. I am alone.

My spear's tip falls. The rank taste of failure curls my tongue and bristles behind my eyes. Tjatsår Mai is not here. My mother is not here. And wherever Sigmar is, he is not here.

The sea in the shadows explodes, and a wet castle ensnares me. The kraken's tentacles surge from the black waters and crush me in their tectonic grip. I groan and lash, and lightning spits from my eyes. I wrench my arms out and crack the chitinous armour of her tentacles. The first of her enslaving tendrils prises at my armour collar. The ugly anemone at its end scratches uselessly against my burning flesh. My soul-wards blaze to life and sear the first of the enslavers, then another. More pound against me, immolating themselves to ash as they pull at my warplate.

I crack a hideous smile. The repulsive kraken means to enthral me. Has age dulled her instincts? Can she not sense I am beyond the reach of worms? I am no mortal chaff. I am Yndrasta, Sigmar's Celestial Spear!

A titanic shape looms from the waters like an entranced snake. Its black bulk eclipses the dim constellation of mushrooms which spider overhead. The pulsating flesh of a leviathan's empty eye socket glistens before me. Arteries of black bilge palpitate in the scarred wall of flesh, swollen and vile, as the creature lays its malign soul-gaze upon me.

Old Jasper May. Her malice is a cursed relic older than time. Her hubris, a majesty beyond defiance. I took her eye in a bygone age, but she is stronger without it.

My smile fades as my spiritual wards sputter and grow cold. The slimy fingers of her enslavers paw at my immortal flesh, and I resist a shiver. Unbidden, alien fear tingles through my bones, like a flaming arrow sailing through the sky at the beginning of a bitter siege. The kraken seeks to enthral me. What if she can?

CHAPTER FOURTEEN

The earthquakes had ended hours ago. The wretched pines had swayed like old men, and scree had trickled down the slopes and stuck in the snow. The whole realm had danced in fear, then fallen silent. Now the stillness in the cold transfixed Njda. She shivered, her own chilling fear at war with the outer quiet.

The serrated fronds of Magga's baleen sword rattled. 'If that quake was them fighting, she ought to be back by now.'

Njda stared into the woods' whispering darkness and shackled her dread. 'She will be.'

'You think Tjatsår Mai killed her?'

Heigen opened his eyes, which were red with sleep hunger. 'If either of them died, I think we'd know it in our bones.'

The weakling pines rustled as the realm's wind whispered its secrets. Njda's gaze snapped towards movement, but it was only bent grass and a breeze. Snow drifted from the night sky and thickened the white veil on the forest floor. She had hoped their bivouac would be full by now, but Riika-Min's lost joy felt further than ever.

Magga shivered to her feet. 'I'm finding Valt.'

'He hasn't been back since he left.' Heigen shifted. 'Is that like him?'

'If he thought it would benefit him, it is.' Magga loped into the darkness. 'Bastard's up to no good.'

'Stay, Heigen.' Njda collected her bow and crunched after Magga. She heard the hope in Magga's tone. The fear.

They slunk through the forbidding darkness. The trees' susurrations lifted the hairs on Njda's neck. Magga's shoulders tensed. 'There're tracks here.'

'And here.'

Magga froze. Even in the darkness, Njda glimpsed the stark fear chiselled into her face. 'Njda.' Magga raised her arm. 'Look.'

Beyond the crooked pine boughs, a hunched figure shambled closer, moving as if drunk.

Njda slipped off her mitten, tucked it in her tunic. Her heart pounded in her throat. She slid an arrow from her quiver and guided it soundlessly into place. 'Valter?'

The shape halted. The tail of a ripped hood dangled from its back, blowing in the wind. *'Njda.'*

Every one of Njda's halting breaths was a hard-won triumph. Two dark blotches sank in the silhouette's face, like the knot-holes on the tree-kin that had hunted them. Njda recognised that brow, those laughter lines, the gentle button of a nose beneath them. She tasted a scent in the air she knew well, the wet-fish stink of by-catch. Her mother had smelt much the same. Better, but the same.

'Ma. She did it. She freed you.'

The shadow shambled closer, and her eerie movements unsettled Njda. Njda's eyes dropped to the shadow's feet. They were bent in, as if her legs had been cobbled. Her tattered clothing was frozen stiff. By starlight, torn flesh glistened in her midriff. *'Njda.'*

Njda's eyes ran along the ripped hood. A long rope ran beneath it back up the mountainside, buried in the unsettling figure's nape. The slithering snake palpitated as if swallowing an egg.

Panic surged through Njda's head. She backed away, and a pair of clouded eyes stared at her from a shrivelled, scabby face. The grey scales of her ma's skin fell away like mountain granite as she shuffled closer. 'Njda. Will you be our friend?'

A gnarled hand shot out and clamped around Njda's throat. Her bow and arrow clattered, and her feet dangled. The eyes staring at her, craving her, were not her ma's. They weren't there at all. It was only starlight catching in empty sockets. Her ma's eyes had rotted away, and the naked flesh gleamed.

Like a siege-ram, Magga tackled Njda's ma. Njda collapsed and wheezed. Magga and the shade of her ma wrestled for her baleen sword. Magga groaned as Njda's ma twisted her arm behind her, far enough to force a sympathetic grimace onto Njda's face.

She scrambled for her bow. 'Ma, stop!'

A grey-skinned revenant – a diminutive grot, shambling like a wight – burst from the snow and leaves. Njda hammered her heel into its chest, then whipped her knife from its sheath. She hacked until the tentacle plugged into the grot's broken skull split. Viscous fluid sprayed, and the thrall slackened and toppled. The tentacle snapped up the mountainside like a taut rope suddenly clipped.

Njda's ma had shoved her foul fingers into Magga's jaws. Tears welled in Magga's eyes as she pulled. 'Magga. Come for dinner. We're so lonely.'

Njda loosed an arrow. The dart went awry. Magga's scream decomposed into a wet gurgle. Like a feeding jackal disturbed, her ma's gaze shot up. 'Njda. Wash up. Our friend's coming over.'

Her ma's heinous smile fell open. In the pit of her throat, the orchid-like petals of an anemone writhed.

Hot with anger, Njda screamed. She snapped an arrow through

her ma's mouth. The barb and shaft erupted from the back of her skull. Bloodless chunks of flesh peppered the snow. A dead breath rattled from her frost-crisp lungs, and torn eyelids closed over empty sockets. She crumpled.

Njda's breathing slowed. The skewered orchid stilled before the tentacle burst from her ma's skull like a triggered snare. Njda stared through her ma's corpse, through Ghur itself. The realm was empty at its heart, in its gut. The tundras, the oceans, the skies – they held nothing. Njda had feared those expanses because she knew what they meant. All the love and warmth in the universe couldn't fill Ghur's belly. Njda tumbled in it.

She reached for her ma, but Magga seized her. More shadows shambled down the slopes ahead, snapping frail branches and staggering through the scree with a duck-legged shuffle. The vague shapes of orruks and duardin, humans and aelves marched among them. There were too many to count. The forest had come alive.

'Valter,' Njda slurred. 'Where's Valter?'

Magga flexed the ache from her jaw and whipped her blade, then crushed the tears in her eyes. 'Move.'

They stopped twice to fight their way clear. Njda gained ground as Magga slashed in wild arcs. Each time her sword's fronds snagged on a thrall's ratty armour and snapped off its spine, she swung harder to compensate. Saliva strung from her teeth as she hacked down another assailant. 'My sword's losing its cut!'

Njda's bowstring thrummed. Three arrows stitched a revenant to a tree. She swivelled and snapped a dart into the skull of a thrall that had seized Magga.

Magga pushed free and pointed. 'Njda!'

Bloated grey fingers curled around Njda's arm and squeezed. She grunted and stabbed an arrow from her quiver into a dead aelf's eye. The revenant staggered, and she yanked at the fleshy cable buried in its skull. The aelf-thrall tumbled drunkenly into the snow.

Magga whipped her baleen blade through the aelf's abominable beauty. 'Faster, Njda, faster.'

They ran. Wracked trees and thin brush whipped by. Ahead, Heigen's shelter loomed. He pushed the pine boughs aside and joined their race to the overlook. 'Where's Valter?'

'Shut up.' Magga dragged her sleeves across her eyes. The first thought to tumble through Njda's head was that she needed glimmerings, but the tears on her cheeks told another tale.

The campfire burned on the overlook. Beyond, the Sukuat expanded into forever: taiga studded with snow-meadows and bouldered glades and defiles, and boreal trees that seemed to jealously guard the tundra's hinterlands. The night aurora painted the vastness green and gold, and Suodji's distant mountain shield weighed down the horizon like midnight's shadows. Njda raised her hand and caught a mote of snow drifting like a falling star. She felt foolish enjoying that moment in the midst of such horror. But yes, why not? She was a fool, and her ma was dead.

Magga paced around the fire. Shrieking thralls shambled closer.

Njda nocked another arrow. 'I'm down to three.'

Magga shrugged her quiver to Njda's feet. She flung scraps of damp flesh from the gaps between her blade's fronds. '*Alro jeknja die!*'

'What's happening?' Heigen said, his thin flensing knife shaking in his hand. His hooded eyes smoothed as more shadows seethed from the pathetic spruces. Revenants shambled closer. '*Sigramalles…*' Courage flared in his eyes. He shook two brands from the fire and raced up the slope, slipping Njda's frantic fingers.

'Heigen!' she yelled after him.

Heigen sprinted along the camp perimeter. Fresh, he moved

faster than the kraken's thralls. He thrust his brands into the shelters, firepits and bedding. Damp wood hissed and spat. Snow thawed and steamed away as smoke billowed from each pile, then glowed copper with flame. Njda watched as he barrelled through the snow from one shelter to another, dodging the clumsy revenants that clawed at him. One clenched the hem of his tunic in its bone-thin fingers and tore the fabric. Heigen jerked free, then hurdled the tentacles in the mountain scree. The repulsive worms thrashed, and from the overlook, they reminded Njda of a weaver's thrumming handloom.

Heigen tripped and crashed to the ground. As he scrambled from the snow, one of the kraken's slaves shuffled closer. Njda loosed, and her dart thudded into the back of the thrall's skull. By the time the creature keeled over, Heigen had already dashed away.

Panting, he shuffled back to the fire. The mountainside was aflame. Fire scorched the tentacles ensnaring the mortal thralls. The heavy snowfall shielded many of them, but most – still not enough – released their slaves and snapped back up the slopes. The abandoned thralls teetered stiffly and smacked into crackling needlebeds as fire sputtered and devoured them. The remaining revenants, too many, stumbled in around the campfire.

The Suku backed to the overlook's edge. The night was on fire; the flaming slopes painted the sky bronze. Njda read the letters of their fate in that blazing curtain. She saw–

Snow crept before them, and a gap opened in the dirt. The scree and hard rock crushed itself into a growing crater, as if a subterranean sorcerer were collapsing the mountainside in on itself. But nothing was digging its way up – the earth was crawling out of something's path, as if bracing itself. Tongues of static lightning licked up from the crumbling soil in fervent greeting. The whole realm moaned in submission.

Yndrasta appeared in a flash of silent light. In that weightless moment, sound bled from the realm. Njda's lungs wheezed in her ears as light strobed. The huntress flickered from one place to another, through the revenants, silent and scornful. A shining sword in her hand carved through the night air. The immaculate sword twitched, and a dozen revenants toppled to the snow. The glint of starlight caught on its long edge, and a dozen more were bisected. In the wake of the blade's movements, stars gleamed in the nether, as if each slash opened seams between realms.

Sound roared back into Njda's ears as a third rank of thralls thudded in the scree. Their legless torsos clawed closer. Fire spilled from Yndrasta's eyes. She slid her armoured hand down the length of her blade's hilt.

The spear, the blazing spear, materialised in its place. As the impossible polearm screamed with starfire, Njda covered her ears. For one blistering breath, she squeezed her eyes shut, but she couldn't unsee the blinding white wings outstretched from the huntress' back. Her battered armour gleamed on the insides of Njda's eyelids. Electricity crackled in her nimbus, accompanied by the cold howl of burning oxygen.

Yndrasta's spear slammed into the mountainside. Blue fire blazed from the contact, and gas boiled from stone. Boulders avalanched from distant cliffs as four rocky arms split from one of the colossal peaks. The realm rocked as it howled and tromped away. Without warning, the huntress rammed her open palm into her spear's haft. The metal god-fang rang and carved out in a wide circle around the revenants. Brilliant white flame surged in its trail as it severed the tentacles connected to the thralls. They crumpled, and the sundered remnants of their enslavers cracked up the mountainside. A horrifying, bellicose noise gripped the mountains like the horn of the fabled end times. Another mountain uprooted; another earthquake shook in Njda's bones.

Before her weapon had finished its scything path, Yndrasta

slammed another miraculous spear – the same spear – into the rock. Again her palm clanged into its haft, and again the spear carved in a crescent path around the revenants. The weapon's roaring movements drilled migraines through Njda's skull. She couldn't make sense of it, of any of this. Yndrasta and her hellish weapon existed in many places at once, as if her merest presence wrinkled the warp and weft of the realm.

As the last thrall twitched, the starfire faded and the base glow of burning trees returned. Yndrasta was herself again, whatever that was. The vargr's lifeless pelt hung from her shoulders. Her breast heaved with her bellows-breaths. Compared to the silence that had nearly broken Njda's mind, the crackle of the mountain flames was a reassuring whisper. Thick smoke scratched at the back of her throat and eased her into the moment. 'Yndrasta.'

The world wheeled around Yndrasta, and the Suku staggered with its momentum. She hadn't turned to face them; the realm had spun on its axis around her. Blazing blood oozed from a gash in her brow. Grisly light caked the fractures in her armour. A dissonant glow flared from her wounds, as if the stuff of divinity leaked from the cracks of her.

Yndrasta parted her lips, and thunder sang through Njda's soul.

WHICH OF YOU FOOLS DID IT?

WHICH OF YOU FOOLS WARNED THE BEAST?

CHAPTER FIFTEEN

Everyone in Riika-Min had known not to stare at shadows. When Njda was a girl, decades had passed since Old Widow Ulgu had last screeched from the darkness or left straw dolls in place of the children she stole, but they remembered.

Once, Magga had bragged to Njda that she'd stared at the sun. Desperate not to be outdone, Njda had marched into the pastures and glared at Hysh's blinding white orb for three seconds. Then she had gasped and squeezed her eyelids shut and shook her head. Through tears she had reassured Magga, who was pale despite her calm, that everything was fine. She never told Magga about the old man without eyelids in the burning light. His ancient visage had been smooth, too smooth. His eyes had been lecherous with the hunger for all knowledge. And when Njda had stared at him, he had stared back.

What Njda saw now was almost as bright as that had been. Through the rifts in Yndrasta's armour and flesh poured out the blinding substance of her soulfire. In that white furnace, the truth of the entity called *Yndrasta* shone through. It glowed as lightning limned thunderheads.

Saints were not human. A pair of argent wings blossomed from the huntress' back, forged in endless starlight. The silver of her armour made Ghur's growling beast moon look like a lump of sullied lead. A familiar face peered through the brilliant glare – the high cheekbones, the shaved temples, the feather-light scars...

But that was only one of her faces. On the thousand sides of the saint's head, the harsh grimaces of slain monsters leered. Daemons beyond description, and jowled troggoth kings, and finned, gilled titans. The thousand crowns of Yndrasta's divinity were trophies hacked from the dead – manticores, chimaera-kin, elementals of old – and branded into her soul.

Heigen convulsed on the ground and covered his eyes. Magga staggered drunkenly to a knee, rose tears streaming down her cheeks. Behind Yndrasta's burning presence, the forest inferno bloomed on the mountainside. Above it, fixed in the night sky, Njda glimpsed the foundations of the universe. Star fields without end, and the negative space between them like heavenly black tundra. Seen from afar, the stars coalesced into a throne of gold and virginal light that towered in the void.

The shadow of Sigramalles Apmil crushed the universe. Njda craned her head so far she stumbled back, but she couldn't comprehend the sweeping scale of his form. Only the ageless penumbra of Sigmar's presence bared itself to her, as if all the suns in all the realms struggled to cast his shadow.

This was divinity. This was Harmony, and infinite awe and wrath, channelled through the needlepoint of Yndrasta's existence. Faced with Sigmar's majesty – with his saint's bottomless, wrathful apotheosis – Njda felt an impulse to prostrate herself, to beg for mercy. But against that dread storm, a mouse's voice whispered. It was hers.

She was one of us. Njda repeated the alien concept like a mantra. *Stormcast, once human, almost family. And...* Njda almost feared to think it... *And she's hurt.*

The awesome spectacle faded. Bronze flame and black smoke crowded the night. Battered armour and the torn mantle of wolf fur remained, and Yndrasta leaned on her glowing spear like a staff. Blood redder than roses trickled from the seams of her armour. She cradled her side.

Invisible force repelled Njda. 'Yndrasta. My ma–'

'Is dead.' Yndrasta's voice struck like thunder. 'Your mother is dead. The kraken is–'

GONE

Tears blinded Njda. She struggled to stand. 'You said you'd save her. You promised.'

A lungful of air reinvigorated Yndrasta. As if in fear, the mountain fires dimmed. 'Foolish girl. *Stupid* girl. Look around you. Mortals enthralled by the kraken cannot be freed. They can only be slain.'

Njda's face wrenched. 'You didn't tell us.'

'Tell you?' The butt of Yndrasta's spear shook the realm, and the Suku stumbled. On the ground, Heigen started and hacked for air. 'Why need I tell you anything? Why must I bargain for a mortal's help? You should have seen what was at stake. Tjatsår Mai destroyed your city. But you tossed aside the nobility of vengeance, and for what? If the kraken is left alive, what she has done to your nation will be repeated to a thousand more, as it has been for the past age. The kraken's death is all. Your mother's fate is nothing.'

'There has to be a way to save them. My ma...' Njda's final encounter with her ma swelled in her eyes. Her mother's empty sockets, the writhing thing in her skull. 'My ma.'

'You *absurdity.* Tjatsår Mai is a sponge. Her being is the sum total of all the beings she has enslaved. Once in a hundred years, she collects prey for her long hibernation as an ogor butchers meat for the Everwinter. She feeds upon them, mind, body, soul. The only liberation for the kraken's thralls is the liberation of death. She is the most dangerous predator I have hunted in this half of Ghur.'

Njda's face twisted. 'You lied to me. To us.'

'You would return these wretches to the halls of life?' Yndrasta crushed a dead revenant's skull beneath the hammer of her heel. 'Do not blame your wilful ignorance on me. The truth was written in your city's extinction. Your people are gone. Dead in the kraken's thrall, or at the orruks' hands, or in the wastes of Ghur. Death is the fate of you all.'

Snow and scree crunched, and Yndrasta spun. Valter lurked at the edge of their camp, aghast. He clutched a speckled stone, heavy enough he couldn't lift it with a straight back. 'Bad time?'

The realm slid like a duardin conveyor beneath Yndrasta. As the others tumbled with the world's movement, the huntress towered over Valter. She snatched his prize and sent him reeling.

Yndrasta brandished the smooth stone. 'Mortals. You question my deceit. See now why it is necessary.' Her fingers plunged through brittle shell, and a dead creature slopped from the strange geode. A withered squid.

'Worm.' Yndrasta's merciless attention fell across Valter like the shadow of an eclipse. 'Your greed has cost me everything. Perhaps the time is come to correct the winter's error. You should be dead.'

Valter clambered up, coughed. Unthinkably, pride rusted through the wall of his fear. 'I should be, because of you. I'm sick of this. You did this all. You killed Brother to bring old Mai to Riika-Min. You got our kindred taken and made exiles of us on our own lands. You broke our city, you stole my wealth. Now I'm poor, and we're at the edge of the world, on the verge of death. You! All of this is on you!'

'Valt's... right,' Magga slurred. 'An idiot for trying to plunder a kraken's lair, but… right. We did everything we were supposed to. If *she* couldn't kill Tjatsår Mai, that's on her. No warrior blames another for her failings.'

Yndrasta's arrogant indifference towards Magga's words made Njda's blood boil. Her lips hardened into a merciless line. Her ma was dead. What did Yndrasta's quest matter?

'Blame me for your frailties,' Yndrasta said. 'Your weakness is not my fault. What glory would there be in slaying your city's pathetic guardian? The orruks did that. To lure the kraken to you, then slurp you from your city's broken bones.'

'But you knew,' Njda said. 'And you didn't stop them. You let Tjatsår Mai take our kin. You let the orruks gut us for sport. You lied. And for what? Honour and glory? A shot at Tjatsår Mai?'

Yndrasta's snarl sucked the courage from Njda's bones. 'I could have intervened. I could have saved your city for another century or two, to die in this millennium or the next. But the realms darken, child. New threats from every pit of creation have thrown nature and order into disarray. Those orruks you faced nearly slew this very realm. I have seen their poisonous touch in the ashes of a hundred kingdoms, and not all they contrive to kill is so easily replaced as you. Tjatsår Mai is worse – a fell force that may come to enslave gods and end the cycle if left alive for another age. But you? You are mortals. Doom is your fate. If some good may be had from your deaths, at least the realms can be safer for it. Your purpose is to live, then die. Mine is to–'

KILL

The word rumbled in the sky, and the growling beast moon fell silent and shrank. Njda's eyes wrinkled with the sting of their own insignificance. 'The God-King was said to protect mortals. All I hear in your words is the thirst for vainglory. The Izalenders preach Sigmar cares for humanity, but you don't. Why? What do you have to prove?'

'I need not defend my purpose to you. What I do, I was made to do. If you benefit from it, all the better. You are Sigmar's domain. Mine is different.'

Njda's face fell. 'What are we to you?'

Yndrasta's silence was more telling an answer than any words she could have spoken. On the mountainside, wretched trees creaked and screeched as they died. Ash billowed where they crashed, and fire roared as it spread afield.

The gash in Yndrasta's brow knitted itself closed. Her spilt blood seeped up her armour back into her skin, absorbed like quicksilver. 'You journeyed to a city when I found you...'

TELL ME ITS NAME

The thought exploded in Njda's skull. Beside her, Heigen's eyes rolled up. 'Suodji. It's Suodji.'

Magga rammed her sword hilt into Heigen's side, and he grunted. Valter grimaced and scampered over the smoking remains of Tjatsår Mai's offspring towards Heigen. 'Easy, there, easy.'

Magga raised her shaking blade. 'What's our kin-city to you?'

'I shall replicate the only strategy that has worked with the kraken. I shall bring Tjatsår Mai to Suodji and slay her once and for all. One day, perhaps your progeny will pray to me in gratitude for it. But I will not hold my breath.'

Njda's brow smoothed. 'She wants the Faceless Hunter.'

Yndrasta's silver eyes narrowed. 'An incarnate protects Suodji?'

WHERE IS IT?

Njda bit her tongue until it bled, fighting the fugue in her head. One shallow breath at a time, she cobbled herself together. 'You're the same as them. Just like the orruks.'

'The orruks sought to kill *you*. I seek a more impressive prize.'

'Slay the Faceless Hunter, you condemn Suodji to death. Mai will take them all.'

'If not the kraken, then the orruks. If not the orruks, then another. Now, before the end of time. It does not matter when your doom comes. Not in the grand scheme of Sigmar's designs.'

Anger teased words from Njda's tongue she wouldn't have dared speaking before. 'You're obsessed. Cruel. You don't even care if we die for this. You don't care.'

Disdain and wrath burned in Yndrasta's blank expression. 'I have only ever cared. I care for my maker-father's satisfaction, for the golden thread of his kingdom's sacred existence. Do not ask me to care for you, too. I do not.'

'We *endure*. Whatever happens, we endure, together. Abandon this vain hunt. Help us. You called yourself Stormcast. I've heard the ancient ballads. Of good Steel Soul, and tall Hammerhand. You're the chosen, the best of us, made to protect us. We're your own kind.'

Genuine puzzlement warped Yndrasta's brow. 'I am not your kind. I have as much in common with you as I do with ants. Why would I abandon my maker-father's sacred task for... you?'

Njda opened her mouth, but a forceless croak rolled from her tongue. Suddenly Yndrasta's spear seemed longer, more menacing, a shadow reaching towards her. The huntress had skewered the orruk in the threshold of Valter's sledmanse. Njda imagined herself impaled on that merciless tooth, dangling. For all she knew, it would have felt the same to Yndrasta.

Yndrasta advanced. Wind howled through the vastness beyond the overlook. 'The guardian of Suodji. Where?'

Njda's gaze crawled over the others. They trembled as she did, but valour was rarely a proud display. When she was certain none would answer, she locked a breath in her lungs. 'You've lost.' Her legs shook as she nocked one of Magga's arrows. Magga cleared the final snags in her sword's fronds. Valter brushed his moustache and reached for a pistol, then took aim.

It was the same as it had been at the red house. Yndrasta, looming before them, her eyes aglow like a panther's. The Suku, defying her, together. The mountain fires limned Yndrasta's dreadful silhouette. 'You dare resist me?'

'You won't do to Suodji what you did to us.' Njda lifted her chin. 'And sure as snow falls, we won't help you.'

Yndrasta's scarred brow twitched. She straightened and gripped her purring spear, then thundered into the burning sky. Snow spiralled in her wake before floating lazily to the burnt scree. The mounded walls of the crater she had stood in crumbled.

Stars twinkled in the scornful void, faint through the pall of smoke. Njda exhaled her pent breath. They were all ragged and sooty, tired and broken. But together. Still together.

Valter uncocked his pistol as Heigen rubbed his temples and moaned. Magga's shoulders slumped. 'That could have gone better.'

Njda nodded. The mountain flames still roared, but they had done their worst. On the horizon, the ghost of the God-King's visitation haunted the stars. His endless throne, his realm-wide shadow... But it was just the fog of an unfamiliar nebula. On the faint line where the land joined the sky, reindeer roamed the tundra. Now that the orruks' curse had been dispelled, the swamplands hardened back into sedge plains. Wild boazu had returned to graze.

'Gather what you can.' Njda's eyes drifted to the soft mountains on the coast. 'The journey to Suodji's long. We must warn them. Before Yndrasta and Mai destroy them.'

Valter shoved his pistol into his belt and kicked a plank in their sledge's debris. 'We'll never get there before her. Not like this.'

Dawn burned below the horizon. If any of what Yndrasta had said was true, she'd at least been wrong about them. Doom was never inevitable. Not if they stuck together. Not if they fought. Njda parted her lips and sang a fairing from her belly, one she'd never heard. The others picked up her haunting melody, as they could.

The reindeer in the far fields wandered closer. One stag, tiny in the distance, lifted its crowned head. It brayed, and the sound was like the song of the Sukuat's snows and the burn of betrayal; the song of hope against all odds, and the song of help when it was needed.

YNDRASTA

I was a fool. A fool to think the Suku would be useful. Mortals' lives are too paltry for them to understand the utter scale of Sigmar's plans, or the all-encompassing necessity of my hunt. They have not seen the forces which would extinguish the guttering flame of order in the realms. They have not faced down the end of reason and raised shield and hammer knowing nothing else could save them. They were not there at the beginning of time, when Sigmar set into grand motion the relentless clockwork of his designs. They have not felt the ruthless strike of his hammer, nor heard the timeless echo of his voice.

Mortals do not know what must be sacrificed for the greater good. Not until they have sacrificed it themselves. Their callow wishes are irrelevant. I must be the daughter my maker-father forged.

Finding Suodji is simple. Seated on the jagged coast of Glacier's End, the stone city swells up through the clouds. Unlike Riika-Min, Suodji is no sprawl of wandering sleds. I swoop lower and glimpse

205

piled stone houses roofed in sod. Scorch marks from ancient battles mar the most venerable edifices, which are anchored upon the bluffs surrounding a deep bay. Fjords stab out from the water into the rocky surrounds. Patched Izalender merchantmen fill the deep harbour, many moored at low quays at the bottom of a tiered port. The bright ensigns of Izalend sag from their masts, stitched many times over to repair old battle damage. In the bay's surf, falcons hunt fish in reefs formed from old shipwrecks.

Tree-scattered plains surround Suodji's highland fastness. Fresh snowfall blankets the anchorite lands in virgin white. Faraway shield mountains girdle the rolling fields, similar to the crater mountains where I found Tjatsår Mai. This place was once a gateway into the bowels of Ghur, but war and the feasting of time have spilt its guts into Glacier's End. A mortal city blossomed on its bones, rejuvenated time and again by the blaze of war and the new growth which follows.

I soar over the outer mountains. Steep defiles lead into the inner snow plain, then onward to Suodji. Suku longsleds file through gorges towards the city's spectacular heights. Magnificent reindeer drag them from the defiles into the plain. Somewhere in these shield mountains, Suodji's guardian lurks. The Faceless Hunter, Njda called it. Rarely have I slain incarnates of Ghur, and the ancient Suku were canny to have beguiled such a beast into their service. Njda had been just as skilled. I weigh her prowess against her infuriating compassion and scoff. Perhaps one paradox breeds another.

As the sky whips past, I sniff for the elemental's spoor but detect nothing. My hunter's eye haunts the mountains' ravines. The Suku of Suodji must assuage their guardian's hunger with offerings to prevent it from prowling their inner plains. I wheel around in search of where such sacrifices might be made. Soon I crash into virgin snows on a wooded plateau.

Trees loom overhead, and young moss carpets their amber bark. A megalith covered in smooth verglas and a dusting of snow rises in the glade's centre. The ages have weathered the stone monument. A fine seam divides the megalith from the plinth below it. Birch bark and twigs protrude from the seam where they were stuffed in. Other offerings surround the monolith's base: juniper berries, reindeer meat, frozen solid. If this tribute was intended for Suodji's Faceless Hunter, it has not been collected for days.

I pace around the heavy stone. In its shape I almost glimpse a weeping woman bent over a lesser lump, perhaps meant to depict her child, or her aged mother. Maybe the Suku carved this. Maybe Ghur spat it from the earth. Or maybe the image is not there at all, and I only glimpse what my heart will show me. The way we perceive clouds – the way mortals perceive me.

Nearby, the musk of death commingles with the burn of cold air. Snowfall from a recent blizzard has crushed a Suku shelter. I carve a path through. Snow sticks to my vambraces and stings my fingers. I peel back a wall of pine boughs bent down around a towering goldwood. The bent boughs form a roof and wall bound with fibrous rope.

From the nest of shadows within, the fragrance of pine attenuates the fester of forgotten death. What I behold does not surprise me. Live one thousand years and one will harden her heart to the realms. Another thousand, and she will eradicate her pity altogether.

Dead fill the shelter. Twenty-seven mortals frozen in their final clasp for warmth. The cold has desiccated their skin. Starvation has shrivelled their faces, hollowing their cheeks until their lips and eyelids peel in a grotesque parody of shock. A snowstorm must have trapped them before they expended their provisions and starved. Empty sleeping mats lay scattered about; a bold few must have departed in search of help. I do not bother searching for them. I smelt their snow-buried mummies from the sky.

My eyes slash through the dark. A trifold shrine carved from shingles of lacquered goldwood catches my eye. For a sliver of a breath, my immortal heart thaws. My maker-father adorns the central panel. But his visage is too compassionate, too saccharine. Where is the wrath? Where is the dignity of his hate?

On the left panel marches a Stormcast legion wreathed in lightning. They are carved in an elegant but crude tribal style, full of movement. Each warrior in the faceless host is one and the same. If Sigmar's depiction is wrong, these are at least passing.

Then, in the right panel, a terrible monster hovers over a broken kingdom scorched by its passage. Fascinated, I trawl its form with my eyes. I cannot recognise its place in the realms' cosmology, nor in my arched trophy halls above Sigmaron. One of the beast's clawed hands is raised in a prayerful gesture, suggesting an affiliation with Chaos or a primordial curse-god. But then a filigreed nimbus gleams around those carved talons, and another filigreed halo encircles its blackened head. Both are gilded with Sigmar's gold.

My smile bleeds from my lips when I glimpse the creature's spined wings, the stylised depiction of the vargr fleeing in the background. Her other hand grips a mighty spear over her bestial head, the blade painted to resemble a fierce sun. Her expression is the death of pity in the realms. It is perfect.

I turn to leave. I *killed* the vargr, and my wings are *feathered*. If these dead wretches thought their invocations would persuade Sigmar to send me or the Stormcasts to come save them, mortals are more naive than I thought. And I am *not* a monster.

Before I go, my gaze drifts. A band of light from the entrance illuminates a pair of dead mortals. They lie in each other's arms, and their heads are buried in each other's shoulders. My eyes trace the wicked lines of their rake-thin faces. Even after death, I recognise their final affection. Love alone survived them. Inhabited by such force, perhaps even humans are immortal.

I crouch, then prise apart the cage of clasped fingers. I pluck out the totem within: an engraved bead on a twine cord. My eyes fall to my vambrace. Sigmar's gift – the last token of my mother's grace – dangles on its cord.

I fly from that place and do not look back. My wings punish the air, but as fast as they carry me, my ruthless reflections overtake us. In the gulf in my breast, the sight of those two mortals and their love blazes like foreign fire. In the cold clockwork of my head, the gheists of that useless flame haunt me.

In another life, lovers stirred beneath my furs on cold mornings as we hid our faces from the wintry air. Suddenly those lost comrades lie before me in repose, slain on deadly hunts. The funeral fire swallowed the last visions of their faces, and bitterly I turned away.

Then I laughed as I raced my kindred-cavaliers through blood-red skies. Then Lauka Vai's self-effacing pleasure rippled beneath her sylph-like iron countenance when I gifted her an aether-mirror, and she glimpsed her reflection for the first time.

Beloved Ruladaha chased me through the training paddock. She was a foal as young as I, and she had sniffed cubes of Glymm death sugar in my small hands, a treat from my mother to seal our sacred bond. I had giggled as she chased me. Looking on from the end of the paddock, my queen and my mother had smiled.

I, too, was loved. All these memories from that useless affliction, all lost to time. The pain bristles, but I cannot bring myself to tears. That font has long since gone dry.

On the eve of battle in Wrothquake Valley, no part of me had wished to leave. But knowing what awaited me, I had hoped my mother would *witness* me. I had hoped she would be there to nod in vicious satisfaction, just as she had so many years before as Tarrabaster rammed his spear through the chimaera's heart and ripped out its viscera.

Above the frosted peaks of Suodji, my wings cease their labour. Wind whistles past my ears. I crack into a mountainside and skid through rock like a fallen star. A prescient goldwood lurches up and tramps from my path. Others flatten like toppling towers.

I rise and stare at my knees. I was wrong, I have always been wrong. I did not resist Chaos for duty or faith. I did not slay Doombreed to protect my people, nor to satisfy my craving for glory. When I disobeyed Hyndaratha's order to lead our people to sanctuary so I could battle the daemon king, it had been to protect my queen and mother. For the same reason, she had ordered me not to fight.

I cannot fathom it. I cannot *fathom* it. In the red temple of my heart, I crave obliteration – I worship it like a divine sickness. Alone in the entire universe, only Holy Sigmar ever saw this in me and accepted it. How could I have ever been so frail?

A desolate wind howls through the mountains and me. My eyes travel to the totem on my wrist. Long ago, before the curse of Chaos fell upon my realm, my mother had slain the last of the hellicores in the mountains of the Devadatta. She had fashioned this trophy from her final kill and bestowed it to me.

Hyndaratha. My mother, my queen.

Sigmar returned her meaningless charm to me after my Reforging. Why? He had perfected my fragile mortal soul into immutable Stormcast flesh. He had purged all my frailty, all my weakness, and I was ready to serve his divine plan. Why risk his master-crafted perfection with the corrosive touch of extinct sentiment?

I recall my mother's final embrace and the mortals who loved me, who fought for me. For me they gave their life against

Doombreed, and for each other. Sigmar had been right to see the good in what I was. Just so, he must be right to see the good in mortals and their affections.

In my breast, a wretched shade scrabbles at the walls of its Stormcast prison. I wonder what my mother's life was like after my fall. Perhaps she led our people to new prosperity in Azyr's starlit cities. Perhaps the Devadatta restored their lost glory, toiling beneath Sigmar's midnight-blue skies. But deprived of her daughter, Hyndaratha must have died as I now live – as Njda, too, will be doomed to live, if no one protects her kin.

My fingers clench around Thengavar's haft. The spear burns white-hot in my grip. It sears my palms, igniting in my heart. My wings hammer the air until they enthral Ghur's winds. Njda did not understand the fathomless scale of what I work to accomplish, but neither was she wrong. All kills must serve a greater purpose.

My nose twitches as the soul-spoor of Suodji's guardian turns in my belly like a pang of spiritual hunger. I swivel, a fresh grin mutilating my face. Thengavar howls in fury.

The long-limbed titan lays sprawled behind me, a croak caught in its lungs. Amber fire smoulders in the black orbits of its antlered skull. A hoarse groan of undiminishable hunger rattles from its throat. Dozens of dead orruks surround the enormous incarnate. In the place where they wounded the dread spirit, dark tendrils betray the unnatural poisons infiltrating its veins.

With an impotent hiss, the amber flames in the Faceless Hunter's skull gutter out. Its lungs empty, and it flattens, twitching. What a wasted kill.

The fungal reek of orruks pollutes the mountain winds. The Kruleboyz have come to Suodji, as they once came to Riika-Min and Amberstone Watch. Tjatsår Mai flickers across my mind. I banish the thought of her and take to the winds.

CHAPTER SIXTEEN

The reindeer grunted and threw back its crowned head. Njda stirred from her restless sleep, and a white wall of light abraded the backs of her eyes. Suodji's shield mountains towered over the blistering-bright snows. The boazu had brought them there.

Njda groaned, every inch of her resisting her movement. Her joints creaked. If she removed her boots, the crumbs of her toes might rattle out like dew-ice shaken off canvas. 'Hey. Wake.'

The words came out in a ragged wheeze. Njda slumped from the reindeer and toppled. The gentle boazu prodded her temple with its moist snout. The warm kiss of life bloomed into her breast and limbs as it snorted and licked.

Njda staggered up and yanked the others' sleeves. 'Wake.'

A shock of matted hair fell into Valter's eyes. 'Wilds. I was having the most lovely dream.'

'Suodji.' Magga blinked the sleep from her eyes and shook Heigen. He started and slashed wildly with his knife, but Magga caught his wrist. 'We're here.'

Longsleds dotted the last stretch of tundra below the mountains. Proud peaks bulged overhead. The sheer scale of their gulleys and gorges, their cliffs and forests, took Njda's breath away. *Possibility* – the word had once filled her with hope. Now it was *possibility* she had come to slay: the possibility Yndrasta would murder Suodji's guardian, the possibility Tjatsår Mai would swallow the city as snakes gulp down eggs.

The reindeer stag's crystal eyes met Njda's, and the noble creature threw back its crown and keened. Its herd trotted in and joined its song, and Njda, an animal as much as they, sniffled, then did the same.

The itinerant herdsteader lifted his cap and loured. His stubbled lips were fixed into a jaded scowl. He shook his reins and kicked the running board. 'In the back. With the pelts.'

The herdsteader's longsled was no more than a skidded cart with eight draught reindeer. Njda and Heigen helped Magga and Valter up beside them. Six children and their mother ogled them like they were vagabonds, and the longsled trundled into the ravine.

Oppressive crags and imperious trees towered overhead as they passed by. The siida had already made its ritual offerings at the mountain's sieidi. More longsleds ground through the defile behind them. Reindeer with tracks in their ears snorted and trotted alongside shaggy dogs. Three-toed hooves and beaten skids packed snow and earth into deep runnels.

Njda's pa had described Suodji to her many times, but the sight of it still sucked the air from her lungs. The city's grey bluffs resembled the collapsed rim of a volcano. Her pa's eyes had sparkled as he'd told her of how those craggy headlands soared over a cobalt bay and branching fjords like blue gashes in the realm. Rope bridges soared over the inlets, and a bustling port filled the city's inner rim. The latter was tiered into shelves as if a god had pressed a mould over its bluffs to force them into a more civilised shape.

In the outer bivouacs, the trade fair had already begun. Merchants haggled and shouted, then shook out strange currencies that chinkled, jiggled, slopped and flowed. Rival bands of takers had set up posts in the outskirts to practise fighting. Magga's eyes glittered as trios of them danced in mock combat, some kind of tournament. Behind a nomad's pavilion, a taker-chieftain with a hauberk of painted metal chewed salted fish and smoked greasy resin between mouthfuls of scalding tea. The siida came by land, but the warbands came by sea. They returned from mercenary wars abroad, and over the weeks they would spend their riches and mingle with kindred, then return to their martial exile. As far as Njda knew, Magga had not padded her eyelids with glimmerings, but her eyes still turned at the sight of them.

When they stopped, Njda bumbled from the grumpy herdsteader's longsled without breathing a word of thanks. The city's disorienting grey cliffs reared into the sky. Suku longsleds filled the slushy bivouac, and a scaffolded clock tower rose from the anarchy. The tang of grilling meat and boiling tea taunted her nose. The earthy whiff of dung and a dill fragrance warred in the air.

Valter, Magga and Heigen straggled as Njda hustled through the shifting outskirts towards the grey bluffs. Their heels thumped over plankwalks. Magga and Heigen craned their heads around in silent wonder, but Valter only drank in Suodji's bustle with tired eyes.

'Have you seen…?' The Suku whose sleeve Njda had grabbed shook her off and scowled. Njda rushed around a staked canvas flap to a collapsible stall and banged the table. 'Could you tell me–'

'No handouts!' the woman barked. 'To any of you!'

Magga slammed the hilt of her dagger to the table and growled, but Valter wrapped his arms around them and eased them away. 'This isn't how you do things here.'

'How you *do* things?' Njda felt like she was back in Riika-Min, but that was no blessing. This was the joy before the doom, the calm before the blizzard, like the morning Tjatsår Mai had come. That morning everything had been fine when she prowled through the palisade sleds into the wilds. And so quickly, everything had gone wrong.

Heigen drifted in the crowd pulling on strangers' coats. A tall man with a queue hanging to his knees shouted him down. Njda stormed over and prodded the stranger off with a scowl and an arrow.

'It's like folk here speak a different language,' Magga said when they shuffled back.

Valter spat. His bad eye flickered about like a weasel's. 'I reckon we should split up. We'll get more done.'

'I reckon not,' Njda said. 'We have one thing to do. We've come this far together. We finish this together, too. Must I explain? Suodji's elders–'

'Not elders.' Valt waggled a finger. 'Aldermen.'

Njda glared. 'Look at us. Rags and bones with sunburnt skin. They'll doubt one of us as a rambling fool. They can't doubt us all. Our tidings are stronger if we bear them together.' She looked up, where switchback stone ramps and timber stairs criss-crossed the sheer cliffs and grey crags to Suodji's heights. 'I don't even know where to begin. No one will show us the way.'

Valter thumbed his hatchet. Agitation glistened in his good eye, and his scarred eye seemed more vulnerable than fearsome. 'We're in a different realm. Don't take these merchants for kin. The byrkaller here couldn't even tell you the name of their mother's siida.'

'You know them?'

'Unfortunately. What's worse, I owe them. My presence won't help our cause. They'll think I want out of my debt. I'm better off checking my accounts with the merchants in from Ereham and Skythane. Guinmark will have someone here, too. I made promises about Riika-Min. The brotherhood can be forgiving, when they want to be, but I'll have to tell them what's happened sooner than later.' He winked his good eye. 'Unless I want to lose this, too.'

Njda's demeanour softened. 'Can they reach Suodji's leaders?'

'Maybe the takers can.' Magga's eyes were sunken in her chiselled face. Her tone was as flat as her haggard lips. 'I trained with those who came to Riika-Min in the thaws. If the elders here–'

'Aldermen.'

'–don't help us' – Magga stared venom – 'the takers might. Their help will be better than nothing when the time comes.'

'Takers don't fight for free,' Njda said.

Magga's braids shook as she rubbed her eyes. 'I'll talk to them. Maybe they'll see.'

Valter frowned at Magga. 'Come with me.'

She lifted her head. 'Why?'

'I owe you back pay. I'll borrow against credit with Excelsis' clothiers. You look terrible. And I'd like to retain your services, when all this is done.'

The glint in Magga's gaze faded. 'My services.'

'We can find the takers together afterwards.'

Njda's eyes narrowed. They seemed to be having two conversations at once, one hidden beneath the other like meltwater coursing beneath a river's thin ice.

'When all this is done...' Magga blinked blearily. 'It's already done. I'm done being a tool, done with the glimmerings. All my life I've run towards futures I don't believe in, from a past I hate. I'll find you when I'm done, Njda. But don't come looking for me, and don't wait for me, either.'

When Magga was gone, Valter champed at the ends of his moustache. 'To my people then.' Njda reached after him, but he shook her off. 'Same as Mag. Don't wait up.'

As Valter stalked away, his tarnished spurs clinked at his heels. He disappeared into the sea of roiling indigo and dark furs. The clamour buffeted Njda's ears like a sea storm's roar. 'They're gone. They won't come back.'

Heigen's hooded eyes fell to the curled toes of his worn boots. Snow drifted and stuck to the dirt. 'I don't know. Maybe.'

Njda gazed at the sinuous paths climbing Suodji's heights. Stone buildings with arched frames and sod roofs jutted at the top like ambushers. 'Let's go. We find the elders.' She started off, then stopped. Ice filled her belly. 'Heigen. Come, please.'

'My wife's siida is in Suodji. My duty's to them. Please understand.'

'Fine. I'll go with you. Then we find the elders together.'

Heigen held her at arm's length, shook his head. Stunned, Njda peered at his hand. It was the same way he'd ended their betrothal.

'Ta's relatives know you. I can't bring you to them. It'd be an insult. Same as Mag and Valt, I'll find you. Don't wait up.'

'Heigen, *lives* are at stake. People like your Ta, and my ma.' Njda gritted her teeth. 'We can't bide time. How much time do we really have?'

Heigen backed into the crowd and raised his hands. 'This is something I have to do. Forgive me.' The throngs swallowed him whole.

Then, like the day doom had come for Riika-Min, Njda was alone.

Passers-by in Azyrite livery and ursine furs burst into laughter, then fell silent as Njda ambled by. She waved for their attention, then slouched onward to the bluffs, where children chased wagon-wheels with switches, giggling. The rich burn of smoked meat and crushed dill made Njda want to retch. Once she thought she saw Magga waiting in the crowd, and her heart lightened. But the girl's temples were shaved, and her hooded tunic bright blue. Soon her husband sauntered up and took her hand, stupid smiles pasted to their faces. They didn't know what was coming. They hadn't seen the end of the world lurking in the sea like a citadel, or a yellow-nailed monster lapping mouthfuls of Hari's gore from his steaming ribcage.

Njda pulled tight her ragged coat and hiked up the cliffs. 'Is there a governor here?' she asked. 'A conclave?' No one answered.

Breathless, she crested Suodji's heights. Her legs throbbed. She ignored others' gasps and squatted by the crags to rest. Across the city's whistling plains, the shield mountains arced up. Njda wondered where Suodji's guardian lurked out there – in a cave, as Brother had, or perhaps at the top of a tall, saw-tooth summit. Yndrasta might have already slain it; Tjatsår Mai might be out there now, shifting seas, reaching through the snow...

Njda ignored the screaming muscles in her legs and lurched into the city. Suodji's piled stone buildings reared over narrow alleys. Here the roof of one structure connected to the walkways of another. The fitted timber frames prickled Njda's skin; each strange edifice had the craft and spirit of far-off lands. A century ago, the Izalenders and Suku had raised the city's first structures as a permanent meeting place for the nomadic herdsteaders. The merchants of Izalend had a different name for Suodji. *Coldhearth,* her pa had said.

Richly dressed servants glided past with baskets sampling Suku crafts, or with carts of Izalend's steel, scrolls and tools. The Suku traded the Sukuat's endless bounty to Sigmar's cities for their treasures and secrets. Suodji's year-rounders were mostly byrkaller or their household servitors. Watching the servants lift their nose at her, Njda wasn't sure what to expect from any of them, or where they were even from.

On the city's highest promontory, two chattering dignitaries in fine robes swept from a door between four sentinels. Njda shuffled up the stairs onto the raised plaza of cut stone to a looming timber palace. The entire cliff looked like a mountain that had been saddled.

At the palace's colonnaded entrance, an armoured sentinel lifted his gaze at her approach. 'You got a death wish, bringing arms to the Aldermen's Hall?'

Njda gathered him in her eyes. 'What do you know of death?'

The sentinel's lips drooped. He puffed out his chest. 'Name and business.'

For one glacial moment, Njda's face became stone. 'Njda Inda Nisu,' she said. 'I come from Riika-Min.'

On a straight-backed chair, Njda squirmed. She hadn't liked the way Suodji's watch sergeant had grown suddenly reverent and smirked. She hadn't liked how he'd spoken to her with honorifics and assured her she could present her case to the aldermen *as an equal*. He'd guided her through the palace's doors, and the others had chuckled.

Tall stanchions rose to the arched roof. Light streamed through high windows to the rugs on the floor. Njda's eyes lifted as a girl in a long maid's skirt froze before her. The servant curtsied and fed logs to a crackling fire, then hurried away. This was the second time she had come. The first had been an hour ago.

A chuckling merchant cracked the door and slid from the aldermen's chamber. His heels clicked over the brushed stone and padded over heavy carpet. He avoided Njda's eyes, and her worn tunic and weathered furs suddenly felt heavy. She looked like a wind-blown vagrant, not a Suku kinswoman. She leaned forward and caught a glimpse of an empty table in the aldermen's chamber. Before the door slammed, she heard laughter.

Njda shot to her feet and burst through the doors. She halted in the threshold. Her eyes wrinkled, and her fists quivered in her shabby mittens. 'So this is how the elders of Suodji receive kinsfolk.'

Three merchants bantered in the space before a sweeping crescent table of teak. They wore no furs, only colourful robes of foreign dye trimmed in mink. They smelt like old wildflowers cured in alkali and hung on the wall. They shared steaming ceramic mugs and picked at a platter of dried fruit, roasted nuts and seasoned lichen. Braziers roared around the council chamber, a hall that Njda doubted had ever known winter's breath. Tapestries and ridiculous oil paintings hung from seamed stone walls. Clerestory windows at the second level admitted the day's dying light. The whole place was novel and false, like the councillors within it. Even now, they hardly noticed her.

'Elders.' Njda grimaced and slammed the door. The merchants' startled faces almost made her smile. 'Hear me.'

A woman with flowing robes and combed bronze curls raised her brow. 'Elders do not govern Suodji, dear. Those with *sense* administer Coldhearth. I am Lady Mervelle of the merchant aldermen. Who are you?'

Another alderman in a brass breastplate and a manicured jet beard clapped his mug down. 'It's the girl from Riika-Min.'

They had known Njda was here and avoided her. She searched for malice, for some insult to throw at them, but settled on hateful silence.

Lady Mervelle brushed crumbs from her fingers. 'Times must be hard in Riika-Min, Catur. Look at her.'

Njda winced. 'Have you not heard?'

Mervelle glanced at Catur. 'Did the guards tell you anything?'

'Only that she... You know.' Catur whistled and drew a finger in circles by his ear.

Njda stomped, and felt that much more like a child for it. Her voice broke. '*Hear* me!'

The third merchant, a fat man in a fur cap and a charcoal double-breasted coat, jiggled with amusement. 'Adorable, she can't even conduct business.'

Lady Mervelle clucked and simpered. 'Stop it, Jobial. We're the businessmen, after all. They're the reindeer-loving rustics.'

Painted wooden teeth crowded Lord Jobial's displeasing smile. 'I love the reindeer, too! This season grazing fees for the bump-kins made up most of my rents!'

They all gave a dainty laugh.

Mail chinkled as the sentinel sergeant marched into the chamber. His gloved fingers dug into Njda's shoulder. 'The girl from Riika-Min, your lordships. Forgive me, she didn't–'

Njda twisted his arm around and thrust him back. Caught off balance, he toppled. His shame evaporated, and red anger coursed into his cheeks. He rose and gripped his dagger.

Lady Mervelle rolled her eyes. 'Not more of this. You rustics always do this. If you must be heard, we listen. Let us finish this before the night's festivities begin, shall we? What tidings bring our dear cousins of the fabled sled-city? I notice you've sent none of your clans to this season's fair.'

The sergeant released his dagger. Njda massaged her shoulder and glowered. 'Riika-Min is fallen.'

The force of her words rippled through the councillors.

'Fallen?' Catur stroked his jet beard. He passed a curious smile to Jobial, who drained his mug and burped.

Jobial's fat eyes creased, yellow pouches of flesh hanging beneath them. 'Fallen.'

Mervelle sucked on her lips and narrowed her eyes. 'Fallen.'

Njda's heart quickened. 'Tjatsår Mai came. And with her, the biro jeknja. They killed ev–'

'Tjatsår what?' Jobial blurted.

'Old Jasper May.' Catur glanced at his nails. 'The leviathan. No idea what biro are, though.'

'Orruks,' Mervelle said. 'Those junk pirates the conclave warned us of.'

'Orruks!' Catur snapped. 'I fought a war with them once. A wonderful investment. The returns were incredible, even after factoring in the losses.'

Jobial turned. 'Would you recommend–'

'*Cruel-boys* slaughtered our kin for sport.' Njda dredged up Bavval's word for them. If only he was here to make the councillors listen. 'They gutted us like fish. Cut pieces from us for sport, dragged others away like that. They'll come here, too. Just like the kraken.' She whimpered and then faltered. None of this was coming out right.

Lord Catur scoffed. In his gleaming brass cuirass, he reminded Njda of a useless reindeer bell. 'Old Jasper May hasn't returned to Coldhearth since she slipped from Fatebutcher's hands in this very harbour. Today it would be impossible. That wretched incarnate claims these lands.'

'The Faceless Hunter.' Lady Mervelle nodded. 'I sent a handful of pious retainers to leave our oldest stores of offal at its shrine last week, enough to placate it. Jasper May wouldn't dare.'

The fat lord Jobial bore down on Njda. 'None dare encroach upon our guardian's territory. Not if they wish to live. We needn't even guard the mountain forts any more. We are safe.'

Njda canted her head at Jobial's attempt at intimidation. For a delicious moment, he writhed. 'Your Faceless Hunter is at risk. Sigmar's huntress has come to slay her. To lure Tjatsår Mai here, then slay her too. You must lead your people to safety. Immediately.'

Catur's eyes twisted. 'Who?'

'Fatebutcher, from the old legends.' Njda's eyes moistened. 'She is called Yndrasta. Sigmar's saint. His devil. His huntress.'

The merchant lords fell silent. Jobial and Mervelle exchanged grave looks.

'I've never heard of her,' Catur said. 'Does she hunt boar, or stags?'

'Is a saint like a Stormcast?' Jobial asked. 'Why would Storm-casts hunt if they needn't eat?'

'My thoughts precisely.' Mervelle poured steaming fluid from a pot into her mug. 'Sigmar's mercy, I forgot how it all goes. I haven't been to chapel in ages.' She lowered the pot and strode closer, then crouched. She cradled her mug in ring-encrusted fingers and looked down at Njda from the raised council floor. 'So. Your city is this desperate.'

Njda stared.

'Don't play us for fools, dear. The Ten Thousand sledcrofts have been losing ground in our trade war for decades. Each fair season your kin come to poach our market contacts. You find them to trade your inferior wares directly, like your thin pelts. But as they say, all snows lead to Coldhearth. Better to let the traders find you than chase them.'

Lord Catur grunted in his cup. 'Looks like they've learned.'

'Indeed.' Mervelle sipped.

'You don't believe me,' Njda said.

'I'm only surprised at how bad your ruse was.'

Jobial grunted and gnawed on a string of dried fish. 'Can we get more of this, someone?'

The maid from outside glided in and collected their platter. She offered Njda a sympathetic frown and left.

'Here's the problem, dear...' Mervelle rose. 'What is your name?'

'Njda Inda Nisu.' Njda's family names blistered her tongue. She hadn't protected her clan. She couldn't protect Suodji, either. Not from these vultures.

'Dear Njda.' Lady Mervelle's raiment billowed as she began to walk. 'Here's the problem with your ruse. You backward herdsteaders still don't understand Sigmar. You try to cram the God-King's great truths into your obsolete traditions. You believe him a force of… oh, what is it, Equilibrium?'

Tears stung Njda's eyes. 'Harmony.'

Mervelle twirled her dainty fingers as the maid returned with another heaping platter of fruit and fragrant nuts. 'The God-King would never do evil upon his subjects. Neither would a servant like this huntress. But that assumes she even exists, or you crossed her path. Chilling though it is, Fatebutcher is a children's story. This Yndrasta, she does serve the God-King, no?'

'I'm not lying. You must leave. Your lives are at stake.'

'Of course. Darkness comes in many forms, but Coldhearth stands against all odds.' Mervelle's pupils sharpened into pitiless black pinpricks. 'Riika-Min knows the dangers of this realm as well as we. But the kraken-god? Or Sigmar's so-called saint? I laugh, dear. Return to your wretched shamans. Tell them your ploy has failed. When your clans finally wish to enrich themselves in earnest, we've a place for those who come first. But if you think fear-mongering will frighten off our merchants or scare us into ending our fair, you'll need to do better. Much, much better.'

'I want to help you. We're one people.'

Mervelle tossed her hand. 'We were, once. But now we are as different as snow and rain. Guard, remove her. And book her a bath at the Hightown on my account. We don't want her returning to her people the way she came, like a pauper. Not from Coldhearth.'

CHAPTER SEVENTEEN

At the base of the stone stair that led to the Aldermen's Hall, Njda buried her face in her hands. A mother led her family into an ancient, battle-scarred building that smelt of hot bread. The children laughed until one pushed another, then broke into tears as if by agreement. The mother shushed them and shot Njda an irritated smile. Njda couldn't even bring herself to warn them. Why scare them? Let them enjoy this. Soon it would end.

A pair of torn boots scuffed to a stop before her. Njda's eyes rose. 'Heigen?'

Heigen blushed a shy smile. He offered Njda a folded tunic that smelt of lavender. 'I was wrong. Ta's family asked why I didn't bring you or the others. Here. A gift.'

Njda crushed the tunic between them as she squeezed Heigen to death. 'I didn't think you'd return.'

He patted her shoulder. 'You said you were still my friend. I was so hurt, I couldn't see I needed that. Or that you needed that. I'm sorry, Njda. I was a poor betrothed, and a worse friend.' They parted, and his lips firmed. 'Ta always admired your strength. Me too. Whatever we were, you're my sister of Riika-Min. I won't lose another of us. I won't lose you.'

Magga called out and clawed her way onto the sod roof of an adjacent building, then panted and scowled. 'Wilds take me, I knew there were stairs.'

Njda stood as three chuckling Suku takers stalked up the steps to the landing. Scars lined their leather faces. Each wore thick reindeer furs over mail hauberks. Steel poniards were stuck in their belts. Baleen swords and long spears were propped on their shoulders, and arrows jostled in their quivers.

Magga held Njda at arm's length as Njda tried to embrace her. 'Not that again. Look. Once again I've found what I'm guessing you couldn't. Help.'

The takers' leader, a muscular man with eyes like a statue's and bowl-cut hair, glared. 'Name's Ramas. Magga told us what's coming. The exiles stand ready to protect Suodji. My warband campaigned with Heaven's Claw in the Amber Steppes. Most takers here have seen Sigmar's chosen on the fields of death. The Stormcasts do not place their confidence in mortals lightly. If Sigmar's slayer fought for you, Njda of Riika-Min, so shall we.'

Njda looked Ramas up and down. A peaked iron helmet hung from his belt, and a buckler with a dented boss was strapped to his shoulder. 'I'm honoured. But she didn't–'

'A hand here?' Valter shouted. A ponderous wooden box clunked up the stone stairs behind him. Two Izalenders marched with him: a soldier in a tabard and brimmed helmet, an arbalest propped on her shoulder; and another Njda assumed was a merchant captain, with a great feather in his cap and a serge coat beneath his robes. The clutched dagger etched into his brooch seemed familiar. Other acquaintances of Valter's who had passed through Riika-Min had worn it.

'Didn't think you'd be back.' Magga crossed her arms.

'I didn't plan on coming back.' Valter dragged his box closer. 'Meant to settle my debts, buy passage to Izalend. Then word slipped out as to why I might want such a thing, and I had more ears than I wanted. Turns out nobody wants to let Suodji go down without a fight.'

The merchant captain cackled, a sound like axes being sharpened on a wheel. 'The reluctant-hero act, I see. Dost Riika all but begged for our help.'

As Njda grinned, Valter raised his hands. 'Maybe I missed you wretches. Got you something, Mag.' He kicked the box's lid off. 'Consider it thanks. For all you've been to me.'

'Valt, these are blackbone.' Magga's hands whispered over the twin baleen swords. 'How much were they?'

'Practically nothing, when I reminded Ereham's arms merchant what she owed me. I figure, if you won't take glimmerings, maybe these'll do.'

Magga tested the blades' balance. The fronded swords whooshed through the air. Naked envy burned in Ramas' stony eyes.

Then Valter heaved a quiver of arrows from the box to Njda's feet. 'Might be a smidge heavy for your ranger bow, but they'll do damage.'

Carefully, Njda slid a war arrow out. It was steel-tipped, helically fletched. Her lips ached with a smile. 'Valter. Thank you.'

The arbalester tipped the metal brim of her helmet. 'You must be Njda, then. I'm Iaterria. From what the one-eye spoke of you, you're brave. My grandfather, bless his soul, served with the Auric Lions at Amberstone Watch. Sigmar praise them, our family wouldn't be here but for them. We hang up the huntress' sigil once each year, on Prowlers' Night. If she chose you to defend this city, I'd be honoured to fight beside you.'

'Friends,' Njda said. 'I thank you. But she didn't choose us. She...'

She betrayed us.

'No.' Ramas' voice was gravel monotone. 'I have made the pilgrimage to Wrothquake. Nearly died for it, but I lived. And in the long nights, the Stormcasts of Heaven's Claw sang songs of the fell huntress' glory. If she chose this city to make her hunt, Sigmar praise her, this is where we must be. Where all of us must be.'

Iaterria grunted. 'We're ready to fight.'

The ship captain with the brooch barged past Valter. His face was stuck in a scowl, from greed and hard living. 'I represent certain interests in Coldhearth. My organisation has far too many investments here to give the city away for nothing. We've sway with the merchant crews that come this way. And we agreed – I made them agree – we'll pull together to defend this city.' He sneered at the takers. 'But I want assurances you Suku will *fight*. Everyone in Izalend's heard how you people run and hide.'

Ramas' eyes flattened. 'Exiles don't run from fights. We run towards them.'

Valter beamed a mouthful of yellow teeth. 'Njda, you convince those vultures up on the mount to prepare?'

Moments ago Njda had felt hopeless and alone. But as always, the seeds of friendship planted in warmer seasons had survived the snows and bloomed. She turned her grave gaze to the wooden palace. A pair of armed sentinels gazed down at them from the plaza. They murmured and pointed, then waved for help.

Njda's fingers clenched. 'Not yet. We'll do it together.'

On the raised plaza, a line of Suodji's sentinels faced off with Njda and those who had hearkened to her companions' warnings. Snow danced from the grey heavens and blanketed the stone, thawing and refreezing into slicks around the plaza braziers. The cold air burned Njda's throat. The dun sky over the glimmering seas reminded her of a pall over the realm.

Suodji's laughing councillors burst from the Aldermen's Hall. As they bantered of the evening's merriments, they absentmindedly glanced up and froze. Lady Mervelle was first to react, pushing through the sentinels. The thick hems of her robes piled at her feet as she stood and faced the Suku. She lifted a pale finger. 'I assume you've come to settle your debts?'

Valter gripped Njda's arm so hard she felt his rings through her coat. 'No, Merv. I'm here to tell you to listen to this finder before it's too late.'

'A finder?' Alarm flashed across Lord Jobial's fat face. 'Doesn't that city need its finders to stay alive?'

'They're that desperate.' Lord Catur squared his shoulders and made a show of gripping his ornate cutlass. 'But we knew that. Hells, they even roped Valter dost Riika into this.'

Lady Mervelle clucked, rolled her eyes. 'Valter's not the man he used to be. Once the one-eye would have sold his mother's sled-croft out from under her feet for a profit. But last I heard, he was in Riika-Min buying up his neighbours' debt with Izalend, then forgiving them. You've spent too many nights cooped up with the reindeer, Valter. Or maybe your heart was always with the rustics.'

Njda reached for Valter's hand, but he released her. She hardened and marched forward. Like a dangerous incantation, the words she had been rehearsing swirled in her head. She straightened to cast that spell, and the Izalender mercenaries and Suku takers teemed behind her with a breed of courage and respect. Suodji's smallfolk crowded the stair leading to the councillors' hall. Word of brewing trouble must have spread.

Lady Mervelle muttered to her watch sergeant. The man's gravel bark echoed. From either side of the Aldermen's Hall, lines of spearmen marched at double time into the plaza. They closed ranks between Njda and Mervelle, then slammed their kite shields and lowered their spears.

Njda fingered an arrow's fletching and eyed them. Drawing kin-blood to save kin-lives was a savage irony. But if the city's leaders wouldn't hearken to her call, she had no choice. It was them or everyone. It was what Yndrasta would have done.

'I have tried to be reasonable.' Mervelle's jaws clamped. 'I have tried–'

Her watch sergeant staggered. 'My lady!'

Heads lifted, and flakes of falling snow slowed, then floated. The powder drifted upward in lazy spirals and spun into helixes. Above, a second sun drew closer, painting the stone plaza the shade of dusk on fire.

Yndrasta descended on wings as wide as a sledcroft. Faint runes burned in her blistering nimbus, difficult to behold for long. Each sigil summoned the inexpressible name of a dead beast in the base of Njda's skull, and she shuddered. A halo of electrum fire orbited the huntress' crown. One hand was extended in a gesture of perfect piety. The other gripped her magnificent spear.

The sun dimmed, and Yndrasta's armoured heels boomed against the stone. Her beautiful pinions fluttered as her wings retracted. More snake-like runes danced on the face of her flawless battleplate. Njda shielded her eyes, and behind her, she heard her supporters thump to the ground and groan. Suodji's councillors retreated, and the armoured sentinels bent their knees. Njda refused to look away. She had spent too much time doing that already. For better or worse, Yndrasta was not human. For better or worse, Yndrasta was the only one who could help them.

The huntress met her eyes, and the golden radiance in the plaza faded into a warm electrum glow. From elsewhere across the city, marvelled visitors and resident traders crowded up the city's heights. The longsleds had ceased moving in the outskirts, and timber cracked as two ships in port crashed together, their pilots distracted by the blaze on the promontory.

Yndrasta offered Njda her hand. Helical runes spiralled around her fingers and made Njda nauseous.

COME

Njda obeyed. The huntress clasped her shoulder, and electricity tickled Njda's bones.

Yndrasta turned her lance-like gaze against Lady Mervelle. Her voice, velvet bass, thundered in Njda's heart. 'Njda of Riika-Min warned you. You did not listen. Ignore her no longer. You will not ignore me.'

Lord Jobial pushed through the walls of sentinels and fell to his knees, his double-breasted coat fit to burst. 'We would never, my lady... We paint you in our shrines! We know you! We could never forget!'

Yndrasta's gut-shaking attention robbed Jobial of his courage, and he ceased his lies. When she spoke again, her voice was a grave murmur on the wind. 'Stand, human. Meet your doom on your feet.'

Like a spirit of invincible supremacy, Yndrasta spoke of what she had found in the shield mountains.

'You are fat with easy triumph,' she said. 'Spoilt with prosperity. You abandoned your ancestors' ways and ceased making offerings to your guardian. You forced this burden on the wandering clans that have enriched your city. Your own folk.'

No scorn marred the huntress' tone, nor accusations. She spoke with the rectitude of one who had seen all right and wrong.

'For your sloth, for your avarice, the Faceless Hunter is slain at the hands of orruks. After I found the incarnate, I tracked them. To distant tundra, beyond the outer mountains. A great horde gathers to corrupt your ancestors' lands. They seek to break Suodji with the help of Tjatsår Mai, who has set her fell eye on your city.'

Mervelle's fearful eyes flitted to Njda. The blood had drained from her face. 'How could you know this?' she whispered.

'*I* was at Riika-Min. I saw what the kraken did there – what it will do here. The greenskins will eviscerate those not enthralled by Tjatsår Mai.'

Lady Mervelle's eyes fell in shame. Below, a child's strident sobs shattered the calm. Fearful murmurs filled the plaza.

Yndrasta drank in their despair, then slammed her spear's heel into the stone. 'Unless you fight.'

'Fight?' Catur pushed past his guards and Lady Mervelle to Lord Jobial's side. He tore off his belt and hurled his cutlass to the stone. 'We cannot fight, huntress! I've financed wars against orruks. Do you know what the casualty rates were? Of Old Jasper May, we've all heard the mariners' tales. We're traders, milady. Merchants!'

The lord turned to face the assembly. 'The exiles are dispersed to the eight winds, to contracts we have signed! The mountain forts are in disrepair, abandoned since the Faceless Hunter came. Fight? How can we fight?' Fear had maddened the coward. He shook his hands before Yndrasta. 'Call upon the God-King! Call the Stormcasts! Don't leave us to this doom! You'll kill us, huntress! You'll be the death of–'

The butt of a sword thwacked into Catur's skull. He collapsed and stroked his jet hair, then wrenched at the hem of his robes and sobbed.

The watch sergeant lowered his sheathed sword and made the sign of the hammer. Fifty sentinels' spears slammed into the flagstone, a salute to the huntress. 'My lady, my huntress. We stand at your disposal. To brittle ice with the council.'

The crowd roared assent. Lord Jobial raised his hands in supplication. 'Any who know me know of my steadfast, unshakeable faith. But Lord Catur spoke truth. Coldhearth's garrison is minuscule. We require the God-King's succour. Stormcasts, milady – call the Stormcasts!'

Njda held her breath. Snow blew from the saint's path as she advanced. Her armour's soft glow warmed those present, and their eyes brightened.

Yndrasta stopped before Jobial. 'In the seasons of life, every word and deed has its day. The time comes when our fears must be faced. This city is strong, even if it has forgotten its strength. The day to defend it has come. The realm's monsters have underestimated you. What a piteous mistake. I see in this city two nations which would defy all the cold cruelty of this realm. Two nations which, side by side, have carved out an impossible existence in ruthless lands. As long as those who would call this city home stand ready to live or die in its defence, Suodji will never fall.'

Heads lifted. Eyes gleamed. Yndrasta's was a subtler look, an uncanny blankness which conjured icy fear as much as hope's fire. That flame burned in Njda's breast, too.

Yndrasta's lips cracked into an unsettling smirk. 'Stormcast Eternals... If any here await Sigmar's Stormhosts, know they shall not come. With warriors such as we, you have no need of them.' Her resonant chuckle disturbed Njda as much as it reassured her. 'I have fought terrible foes, in hopeless wars. What I say now, I say in earnest. You *can* win, men and women of Suodji. We *will* win.'

At the thunder of the crowd's approval, Yndrasta met Njda's gaze. The union was electric. Njda shuffled back and stroked her brow. 'You returned.'

A glum look twisted Yndrasta's icy features. 'Yes. And no matter what, I will not leave before this is done.'

CHAPTER EIGHTEEN

'I would rather swallow raw, rotten fish' – Ramas propped his foot on the snowy terrain display – 'than stand and be gutted beside you stinking pigs.' Behind him, his overturned war-sled – the word was as strange to Njda as the concept – provided cover from the elements. Distantly, a blizzard howled in from the mountains, a wall of cloud. Almost as if the orruks had summoned it.

'And as much as I'd love to watch you run from another fight,' said Iaterria, 'that's not how we do things. We move in formation.' She leaned against her arbalest and thrust her chin to the miniature battlefield before her, which the takers and soldiers had moulded from snow and earth. Dirt mounds reared over packed snow, gathered pebbles and stacked twigs that depicted Suodji and its shield mountains.

Other soldiers and takers mumbled as they sipped stew from their helms and gnawed on bread, or grunted assent.

Njda stepped into the snow model. 'This has to be a jest. You've agreed on the hard things. Where to stow the ships at port, where the elderly and frail will hide. Herdsteaders are breaking down

237

their sleds to build snares as we speak, and Suodji's wealthy have opened their doors to the siida. Now you can't agree how to fight?'

Ramas and Iaterria turned away. 'That's right,' Ramas said.

Njda had thought her own kindred had been hard-headed. 'The huntress wanted your battle plans by nightfall.' Her hand stabbed at the grey sky. 'That time's come and passed, and I need to tell her something. Ramas – you and yours do what you do best. Fight in the snows, hit and run. That way the Izalenders can watch you prance away from the orruks to their heart's content. And don't you grin, Iaterria – you'll defend the city like you wanted, and Ramas and his takers won't have to smell you.' She tamped her foot in the snow. 'Or, you could both set your differences aside and work out an actual battle plan, and we can win.'

Ramas' gaze snapped to Iaterria like a magnet. 'Her plan could work.'

Iaterria shoved off her arbalest and crouched. She gestured. 'The snow-banks are deepening. We could cover you here, and here. Our spears could guard the approaches. How much time do you dancers need to prepare positions?'

'We'll have ambush hides ready. You Izalender pigs build barricades for the ramps.' Ramas' stony gaze turned to Njda. 'General. Bring word to the huntress we'll be ready.'

General. Captain. Champion. The words rolled like marbles in Njda's head. She had been ready to act as Yndrasta's herald, but after the episode at the Aldermen's Hall, the people saw her as more than that.

'Apologies!' a Suku runner shouted as she hurtled past. In her wake, a train of herdsteaders and seamstresses bumbled along with hot food in cauldrons and salvaged supplies, heading to the city from the outer bivouacs.

Njda returned to the sledcroft, one of the few yet to be

disassembled. Heigen supervised a clutch of children as they built snares on the porch. 'You teach them as well as I taught you,' she said. 'Impressive. These are dangerous compared to whiners.'

'We have you to thank.' Heigen smiled. 'Nimble in hand and mind, these little ones.'

'Ramas told me he didn't want you fighting with them. What happened?'

'I told him the truth. I'm no warrior.' Heigen tapped his flensing knife. 'I'll help the infirm and old. Protect them, if it comes to it.'

A pair of children swatted at each other with cord and laughed. Njda frowned. Not because they were wasting time – that was the point of childhood – but because soon they might not have any more time to waste. Soon it might all end.

Heigen shushed and urged them back to work, then helped a girl with the tension in her trap. 'You ever wonder what it would've been like?' he asked.

'Children?' Njda shoved her hands into her pockets. 'There'll still be time for that. As long as we do this right.'

Quiet followed, broken by the tensive whispers of children, the clatter of wood and creak of cord. Beyond the low-hanging timber eaves, snow danced on a wicked wind. The whiteout rolling in from the mountains billowed like cliffs of charging smoke.

'There's no guarantee we'll live,' Heigen said.

'Nothing was ever guaranteed us. Everything we have, we took from Ghur's teeth.' Njda lifted her gaze to the rocky mouth of the harbour and straightened. 'Who let them do that?'

Heigen stepped out into the snow and cupped a hand over his hooded eyes. 'A ship. Someone's leaving.'

A rime of cold sweat coated Njda's brow by the time she pounded onto the trading caravel's deck. Relief blushed down her neck. 'Valter. You're here. Did you send them off?'

Valter stood beside his companion, the merchant captain, who patted his back and barked orders to another mariner. 'That I did,' Valter said.

Before the city had set about preparing its defences, they had agreed no one would flee – Suodji needed every living soul to protect it. Njda opened her mouth to question Valter's decision, then paused. 'And you didn't go with them?'

Valter trumpeted a grating laugh. 'I would have. Even volunteered. Someone's got to get help from Izalend. But I'm the best hope these merchants and mariners have at communicating with the Suku. They've lashed together the ships to keep the smallfolk safe here, away from the kraken. If Yndrasta slays old Mai, they can set to sea. Orruks won't harm them there.'

Njda planted her hands on the gunwale and narrowed her eyes. The waves had grown choppier, and briny mist chilled her knuckles. On the forecastle, mariners cast an oiled tarpaulin over a ballista. They'd removed the ships' cannons, but the ballistae and catapults were bolted to their hulls. 'Who'd you send?'

'Catur. Mervelle.' Valter picked at his molars with a grubby finger. 'Sent them on Trow's ship, fastest in the fleet. If anyone could convince Izalend's conclave to send help, it'd be those cowards. Their wealth is tied up in Suodji's port.'

'As yours was in Riika-Min.' Njda sat on the deck's balustrade. 'You are shrewd. It's the best use for them. I didn't even think of that.'

Valter snorted. 'Out in the bush, things are simpler. No messy business, no people. But when you deal with folks, sometimes you have to do wrong to do right, like sending those cowards off. It's not always honest, but that's the way of integrity. As long as you remember who you are, you can do good with bad. My wisdom impress you yet?'

Njda grinned a mouthful of chattering teeth. Her sweat-dampened tunic gave her chills. 'Yes.'

'Good. I still won't marry you.' Valter hefted two bundles of arrows from a barrel. 'Mag sent word the taker hides need these. Can you run them to her?'

Njda heaved the bundles up. She had a thousand things to do already, and Yndrasta was still waiting for her, but they were on the line. 'I'll see you on the cliffs before the battle?'

Valter's moustache wriggled on his lips. He touched his pistols, and his eyes sparkled with tested nerve. 'Right. I'll be with you, Njda. As always.'

Njda trotted back to the snow plain with needles in her lungs. She had crossed Suodji's winding alleys and hiked its switchback crags more times than anyone else this evening. The prospect of her meeting with the huntress hatched flies in her belly, but Njda had to go. Everyone else was doing their part to defend the city. So must she.

The blizzard's thrash dimmed the auroral brilliance in the sky. Squalls whipped shards of ice into the air, forcing those crossing the snow plain to shield their eyes. Njda found Ramas perched beneath a wretched tree, his stony eyes peering out at her from beneath his pointed helm.

He stood. 'General. Those for us?'

Njda's arrows clattered at Ramas' feet. She crouched to shrink her profile in the whipping wind, then nodded.

Ramas' stony eyes fixed on her. He grimaced, and a deep scar danced along his cheek and chin. Once, Bavval had told Njda most takers would have been finders, if they could have cut it. Perhaps Ramas was the same.

'Have you told the huntress our battle plan?' he asked.

Njda's gaze shot to Suodji. A steepled bell-tower rose on a solitary crest. Torchlight flickered through the heavy haze. 'Not yet. Soon.'

'Just as well. There's been a change. On the morrow I'll be on the heights with you and Iaterria. Reserves.'

The way Ramas spat the word told Njda he didn't much care for it. 'You'll fight together? With the Freeguild mercenaries?'

'We must. Some of us, at least. Your kin-sister, Magga, helped me see reason. More takers in Suodji than those pigs.' He gestured to the hillocks and dips and rises in the endless white. 'If we crowd these snows, the orruks will have the advantage. Better if our triplets can strike and displace and leave them guessing at every inch. It will be an honour to fight beside you. An honour to know the God-King, at last, chose us.'

Ramas' observation sent a turbulent wave through Njda's breast. It was real. *This* was real. She huffed in a lungful of blistering air. 'Is Magga near?'

'At the old outworks nearer the mountains. The sleds should be back soon. She is a fine warrior, general. One of the finest I've ever met.'

'She can fight, yes. I wouldn't stake much on her thinking.'

A laugh whiffled from Ramas' flat lips. 'Warriors must think. All battles are won or lost in the head before a blade's ever drawn. Clear thinking makes the difference between warriors and pasture brawlers.'

Njda's experience had taught her the opposite, from the time she held frothing Gumper down for Bavval's knife, to the fight with her ma and Mai's thralls on the mountainside. Even the shadows of those memories jellied her legs and liquefied her bowels. Njda was at her best when her mind was silent – when her body could simply react. 'How do you mean?' she asked.

'Four seasons ago I fought alongside Black Ark aelves against an Iron Jawz clan. Those greenskins gravitate towards the biggest foes they can find. Skilled captains corral them this way, to control the flow of battle. Magga told us these orruks are different. They like unfair fights. They do their worst with a hobgrot to back them up, to knife their opponents in the knees. They only attack when they think they have the advantage, and they approach differently depending on how they weigh you up.'

'Magga notices things I missed.'

Steam jetted from Ramas' nostrils. 'She spoke the same of you.'

Ahead, takers crunched out into the snow plain in twos and threes, some armed with bows, others with flintlocks. A formation of exiles gathered around old women ladling stew from cauldrons. The Suku tipped their hoods to Njda, and when the women were done, children helped them lug their pots back to Suodji's heights. The city loomed in the snow's haze like a rearing bear, sleepy but vicious when roused.

Njda scanned the haze for Magga. 'I'm sure the glimmerings don't hurt.'

Another whiffle of laughter. 'Spoken like an addict. Glimmerings slow warriors down more than anything. Even so, Magga's better than most of my swordsmen. I asked her to join my party in Thondia when the next thaw breaks the far seas.'

Njda tensed. 'Did she accept?'

'She said she didn't want to leave her siida. You and those others, I'm guessing.'

The weight of those words settled in Njda's skull, and her brow smoothed. Bells rang as grunting reindeer galloped closer dragging two war-sleds with shields on their hulls.

Magga plopped over the edge and crunched closer, her braids swaying with each step. 'Njda? I bet you were looking for me. Wilds, you're really not as–'

Njda swelled forward and threw her arms around Magga. 'I know. I'm not as good as they say.'

Hesitant, Magga patted Njda's shoulders, then kissed her cheek. 'Not a good finder. But as far as sisters go, suppose you're the best I ever had.'

Suodji's dilapidated chapel leaned with the wild winds. Below, blurry through the whiteout, antlike lines ferried supplies from the scrapyard of dismantled longsleds up the city's switchbacks. Tongues of faint fire glowed beneath the eaves of sod-roofed buildings where soldiers, merchants and militia grabbed a wink before battle, or sipped on bowls of hot broth. Lookouts with hunters' horns patrolled the city's bluffs. They monitored the far-off shield peaks for signals from their lookouts in the ancient outworks.

Njda mastered her nerves and crept to the chapel's door. In the wide seam, she glimpsed Yndrasta hovering before a faded fresco. The painted plaster had begun to crumble in the age of the chapel's disuse, but Sigmar's divine certainty was still unmistakable. The dusty wooden pews and altar looked as if they had been hacked from the wreck of a fisher's dinghy.

Decrepit though the church was, Yndrasta's presence completed it. A warmth filled the shabby nave, a glow that blurred the edges of Njda's vision like a fugue. The building was like a tuning fork singing in perfect harmony with Yndrasta. In the fresco, the words SIGRAMALLES APMIL blazed with golden filigree...

'Njda.'

Njda blinked. She was on her knees, in the chapel. Yndrasta's wings flexed and flickered like the canopy of a white tree in a breeze. Her thrumming spear floated above her haloed head. Wisps of dancing light hissed from its steel.

Njda scrambled up. 'How did I get here?'

'I summoned you, and you entered. Though you may stand in the snow if you wish. I am fond of the sound of your beating heart, but I hear it here, there or three miles away. Where you stand makes no difference.'

Njda shivered. She craned her head at Sigmar's fresco. 'So this is him.'

'No. This is a mural. Sigmar is *Glory*. When the Tempest first came to these lands, the crusaders who relit Izalend's Everflame never revealed the full truth of my maker-father to your people. They feared scaring your naive forebears. They told your shamans Sigmar was an aspect of Ghur's sky. You flattened the God-King's majesty into your understanding of the realm. But you must see the truth by now.'

'I think if Sigmar sent you, he's better than I thought.'

Yndrasta's eerie nimbus diminished. Her glacial eyes fell to a token hanging from her wrist. 'Perhaps.'

Njda glanced around the chapel, then lowered her hood and removed her mittens. 'Are you… communing with him?'

'I am wondering why we keep secrets from the ones we love.'

On the other side of the chapel's shabby doors, Lord Jobial raised his voice so his prayers could be heard over the blizzard's howl. No one else had been ready to lead prayers before battle, so now Jobial pleaded for Sigmar's protection. Mostly, Njda felt, for himself.

Njda cleared her throat. 'I bear tidings. Preparations go slowly but steadily. People are scared, but we'll be ready when the orruks come at dawn. I have details on the battle plan, if you still wish to hear it. You can help us improve it. If it pleases you.'

Yndrasta's wings twitched and retracted, and her heels rammed the ground. 'Suodji shall fall in seven days.'

The huntress' flat words struck Njda like a hammer. 'We can't win?'

'I wish I could change your city's fate. I wish I could change many things. But I am not all-powerful. I am doing all I can to stave off the end. As I ever have.'

Njda backed into a pew. 'You never meant to protect us. This was all to lure the kraken. Did *you* kill…?'

'No, Njda. The orruks were cunning enough to slay your Faceless Hunter as they did your Brother Bear. But had they not, *yes,*

I would have slain it. Think me cruel. I do not care. But I would not have let Tjatsår Mai harm your kin-city. I would have made her rue the day she tried.'

'Then why can't we change our fate? Why will we be defeated?'

'The days when your people's hosts carved the Sukuat from the dread grip of Chaos are long past. I have seen the orruk horde which musters, and they are beyond your ability to defeat. I am no longer even certain I can defeat the kraken by my own strength, let alone the orruks. But tonight, I shall do what I can, as you must.'

This wasn't right, Njda's mind insisted. There had to be another way. 'What of the Stormcasts?'

'Njda. This city does not warrant such intervention. Across the Mortal Realms, in the great universe beyond your reckoning, Sigmar's Stormhosts are sorely tried. Suodji is nothing in the grand scheme of my maker-father's plan.'

A resistless scowl throbbed on Njda's lips. Her breath raced. She wrested arrows from her quiver and smashed them against a pew. She groaned and bared her teeth and slammed, again and again, until the arrows were all cracked and splintered. She tossed the broken shafts and kicked an arrowhead that had flown from its fitting.

She slumped to the ground. 'I'm a fool. I needed those. I needed you.'

The blessed metal of Yndrasta's greave shone so brightly it polished the dusty floor as she knelt. She was utterly unmoved. 'Many lifetimes ago, I would have done all in my power to save my people. I would have saved everyone, if I could. That is behind me, far and away, but I understand your mortal heart. And though you may never understand me, I hope one day you do. Do you know what the God-King fears most?'

A futile tear dripped down Njda's cheek. She returned Yndrasta's statuesque look – a blank slab, a hulk of marble.

'He fears he will fail you. It is the fear that haunts him most. Ask him, he will never say it, but it is there, like a shark in the waves. When he forged me, he gave me a task he hoped I could never fail, so I would never share in his burden. But I know what it means to carry that weight. I will risk failure to do all I can for you, Njda. Whatever is in my power.'

Yndrasta's massive fingers snapped her token from her wrist. The charm dangled in her massive palm.

Njda blinked. 'For me?'

'From my own mother. A woman I loved more than all the realms. I am sorry for what happened on the mountainside. I am sorry for my part in your grief. And though I have learned to temper my hope, I sincerely pray that one day you are reunited with those you seek, and that this meeting is happier than was ours in Riika-Min.'

Njda squeezed the charm, that some shred of magic might seep into her hands and empower her, but it was only looped cord and cracked chitin. A memento. Of what, Njda had no idea.

She dared to lift her gaze. Yndrasta's brilliant features were so much brighter than that day in the doorway. Still, she might as well have been on the mural with her god. She was not a person, nor human – only a picture of one, as harsh and unfeeling as a statue. Perhaps there was nothing behind that facade, or perhaps it concealed something worse. A cold killer who couldn't stand the whiff of her own hypocrisy; a psychopath who would do anything so her father's subjects thought as highly of him as she did. But even if Yndrasta scared Njda, Njda trusted her. Yndrasta trusted Njda, too. Njda could feel it.

The deep wail of hunters' horns filled the night. The knell of the clock tower in the bivouac rang across the city.

Njda's head snapped to the cracked glass window. 'No. It's too soon.'

In a single movement of inexorable purpose, Yndrasta's hand rose. Her blessed spear clanged into her open palm. The metal flared.

'Thengavar,' the huntress whispered. 'Let orruks' flesh do for now, little one. You will eat of our quarry's meat soon enough.'

Yndrasta marched to the doors, and they exploded from their hinges. Lord Jobial shrieked and tottered from her warpath. The Suku and Izalenders who had prayed with him already rushed down the slopes to the defences.

Njda raced to keep up with Yndrasta's monstrous stride. Blizzard snows whipped and stung her cheeks. 'Our barricades aren't ready! Our fighters aren't in place!'

A flash of distant lightning showed Yndrasta's crazed eyes devouring the snow-veiled expanse. A wicked arch bent her brow, and a diabolical grin possessed her lips. Sea wind filled her feathered sails and lifted her into the sky.

Eyes wide, Njda toppled to the rugged rock and scrambled. The red pleasure in Yndrasta's twisted face was the same as that orruk's as Hari's gore had dribbled down its wolf jaws. Hers was a barely shackled sanity, a shark's frenzy at the taste of chummed waters.

'*Your will be done!*' the saint rumbled through her rictus, and thunder answered. Her laughter shook the skies. Sigmar's slayer jetted towards the mountains, and Njda felt a pang of pity for the orruks. They had no idea what was coming.

YNDRASTA

As Njda dashes to her place in the city's defences, I wing through the clouds. Suodji's jagged bluffs shrink below. In the gauze of snowfall obscuring Suodji's plain, the orruks emerge. Hundreds of them lope closer, then ravenous thousands, their skin coloured the tainted shades of regurgitated meat left to dry. The largest specimens ride shaggy-furred monsters, icicles of frozen slaver hardened into the beards hanging from their jaws.

In Suodji, cannons crack, and spinning shot whistles beneath me. Ranks of shouting arbalesters line the bluffs and make ready. Spearmen brace themselves behind half-built barricades on their city's crags. The Suku takers are more difficult to find. They lurk in concealed hides in the snow plain, or prowl the wrecks of abandoned longsleds beneath Suodji's heights.

As the mortals await their moment of truth, I wonder if they glimpse the flensed hides of Riika-Min's Suku on the orruks' banners, or if they hear the sniggering hordes of grots that shamble behind their masters. Hobgrot swarms drag knotted nets and meat hooks on chinkling, rusty chains.

Briefly, I lament Arktaris' absence. If he were here to witness these grisly horrors, the flame of his righteous indignation would blaze that much hotter. The mortals will only grow fearful. They will think of their loved ones, aching to spend their final moments with them. In terror they will flock to fill Suodji's chapel on the bluffs, as if prayer to Sigmar is not best made through war. A precious few might swing their blades harder in the coming slaughter – Heigen and Magga come to mind. But most mortals are broken when death's inevitability is finally laid bare before them.

I know where each of us goes when we die. I know exactly what happens, and where. Death's dreadful mystique is long dispelled for me, and with it the fear. For the Stormcast Eternal, the promise of annihilation is nothing more than that – a promise. After it is kept, we return to the cycle of war.

I circle in the sky, striking where I sense my assistance will be most precious. With my bare hands, I rip orruks' heads away and smash their frangible skulls in my fists. I crush grots beneath my boots and rip entrails from shaggy behemoths as Thengavar whistles in merciless laps around me. For every crimson mural splattered into Suodji's sterile snows by my spear or Suodji's cannonades, hundreds more rangy greenskins advance from Suodji's mountainous passes. I had hoped the plain's snowdrifts – twenty feet deep, and a blizzard piling them higher each minute – would delay the horde. But crude snow-shoes sheathe the orruks' ape-like feet. The pig-nosed greenskins are not native to these boreal wastes. They must have learned that trick from the Suku whose scalps hang from their belts.

Barely visible through the blizzards' gauze, the first orruks fall into the Suku's pit snares. Then, like snowstorms themselves, Suku takers blast from their hides. They sweep forward, flaying orruks with baleen swords, or skewering them with hunting spears. The mortal takers fight as if possessed. Others of their kindred flit arrow after arrow into the greenskin rabble. As the archers loose, the front-line takers retreat to more snow-banks and barricades further back. The archers empty their quivers, then retreat to prepared positions in the city's outskirts.

The incensed orruks roar and give pursuit; more snares and staged resistance extract their bitter toll. When they are within range, a thousand arbalests scream from Suodji's cliffs, and clouds of bolts thud into white snow and green flesh. The splendid display makes me question my earlier doubt for the mortals' valour. The Suku takers fight as the Kruleboyz would, were they in their own stinking fens.

Visions from another horrific battle swim into my eyes. I was there, on Ruladaha's back above Wrothquake Valley, surveying a terrible slaughter. The silver-and-crimson thread of my legion lay stitched across the valley's foothills, through flame-shrivelled trees smouldering with war's fire. Askurga Renkai knights stood side by side with ancient aelf swordmasters whose soul-stuff and blade instincts were older than the Mortal Realms. Against these champions flowed a scarlet tide of Khornate bloodletters, serpent-tongued daemons that swung pitted swords longer than they were tall.

Battered by this red tide, my battle-line bent. Regiments of the Aza-Karakier filled in our gaps. Reinforced, my allies held the front. Every strike of their hammers, every sweep of their blades, purchased us precious moments.

A roar of violence filled the realm. From the north, where the red sun assailed the horizon, twelve of the Amber Steppes' legendary great worms blasted through the mountains. Clouds of earthfire and igneous stone exploded into the upper atmosphere as the titans carved into the valley. Hosts of human warriors crowded howdah-platforms staked into the worms' tectonic flanks. They hurled javelins and snapped ballistae bolts into the daemonic horde, their great leviathans like the war elephants of humbler kingdoms.

As my ploy bore fruit, I resisted the smile on my lips. My pegasus-riders cheered. Victory was at hand – but our jubilation was premature.

Doombreed had come. I had thought the rumours of the daemon king's size to be an exaggeration, but years of unresisted slaughter had made him mightier than mountains. The horned demigod erupted over the horizon, a living volcano, and his shadow eclipsed the sun. With a world-ending axe, Doombreed chopped one of the great worms in two. Another he scooped from the ground, then crushed in his mountainous fist. He tossed the ruined carcass back to Ghur. The worm's hulk blazed through the atmosphere, and where it landed, Ghur's crust cracked. Newborn basalt mountains jutted from the rock. Rivers of earthfire cascaded down their slopes.

Entire regiments were annihilated. The battle had turned against us. The Aza-Karakier transformed into stone as their potent but treacherous grudge magic punished them for their now inevitable failure to avenge their lost karaks. Amidst that serried duardin statuary, a living tsunami of daemons swamped my aelf beastriders. The Askurga Renkai who had not yet fallen transformed into grotesque bats, then beat their leathery wings and fled. The greatest of the worm-cities, Shu'gohl, shifted the realm's spin as it writhed from the valley. Mountains crumbled in its wake.

Clouds of Chaos furies darkened the skies around me. Their spine-toothed jaws and hammering black wings disoriented me. Through that ghastly storm, I met the dark sun of Doombreed's eye. The daemon king's oceanic gaze showed no pity, no pleasure, no purpose. This was the nature of his existence. Carnage, for no cause other than his blood god's obsession.

I knew we were broken, then. Broken in the soul, broken by battle. In those hopeless heartbeats I thought of my mother. I wished I had one more moment to cherish with her, to embrace her a final time. Up to that point my faith in Sigmar had always been a matter of course. But staring at the end of my world, I decided if Sigmar would protect my people, I would fight for him. I would kill for him.

Thunder roared through greying skies. Rain plinked at my lamellar armour. I reined in Ruladaha and we plummeted through the cloud of furies to the magmatic canyon at Doombreed's breast. Heat boiled the rain away, scalding my face. I prayed that if I should have no mother, no lands, no people – no trophies, no lovers, no hope – then I would at least have this final, glorious kill. As my mother Hyndaratha had once slain the last of the hellicores, I would carve out Doombreed's blasted heart to hang over the throne of my annihilation.

The daemon king slashed at me. Its worldwide claw swept through the skies with the inevitability of falling mountains. I screamed and reined Ruladaha up, but Doombreed's blow smashed her out from under me, tearing off my legs with her.

I howled with agony and futile hatred. I tumbled into the burning cavity of Doombreed's chest. The momentum of a life spent craving this moment carried me onward.

In the breath before my collision, my skin tingled. My gore-dampened hair stood on end. Bright lightning crackled around the red hellfire blazing before my eyes. For one perilous breath, the realm went migraine white and fell silent. Then thunder screamed, and Sigmar uttered my name.

YNDRASTA

The God-King cast a Great Bolt across the cosmic void that day –
not at Doombreed, but at *me*. I conducted his strike home, my
lance a lightning rod for his power. Together – *together*, and not
alone – we smote the thrice-damned heart of the daemon king.

The deafening physicality of Doombreed's roar ripped the last
shreds of life from my corpse's cells. The violence of that thrilling
moment branded itself into my soul. An age later, after distilling
my eternal purpose from my final mortal desire, Sigmar leaned
over his anvil and answered my whispered question with the only
command he knew I would obey.

The lightning fades, and I soar again over Suodji's snows. The
Suku have retreated to the barricades. The Izalenders re-form
their lines to hold the cliffside approaches leading up the city's
bluffs. In the wet scarlet sludge of Suodji's snow plain, the cunning orruks linger and regroup.

For a blink, I wonder why Sigmar withheld the memories of my
mortal past. Perhaps only my final faith and bloodlust survived

my fall. Or perhaps, when the unworked metal of my soul lay piping on his anvil, my maker-father cast aside all my frailty, all my love and hurt, to prepare me for the eternity which awaited me.

Or… perhaps he had not meant to. Perhaps he had returned my mother's gifted totem hoping the heroine he had salvaged from Wrothquake Valley would rediscover the qualities which had made her strong.

My spear's metal purrs in my hands. The riddle's answer does not matter; only my sacred task remains. I offer a thought of gratitude to my maker-father. I am everything he made me. I am more.

Through the whiteout, six gargants with corpse-grey skin stagger towards the city. Scaffolds in the abandoned sled encampment collapse from the force of their tread. Suku and Izalenders flee up Suodji's switchbacks. Packs of snickering hobgrots on the gargants' shoulders cast stones at the mortals and brace themselves to disembark from their living siege towers. More greenskins surge up Suodji's crags, blades clamped in their teeth. The porcine beasts scale the cliffs and bypass the defenders' barricades entirely.

I cock my arm to invoke Thengavar's wrath against the closest gargant. But as I do, a deep horn sounds from the sea. My grin falls from my lips as I wheel around to face the violent storm-swells of Glacier's End. Beyond the turbulent waves, a tsunami rolls towards the harbour.

Tjatsår Mai. If she senses my presence here, it has only emboldened her. Our previous encounter has erased the kraken's fear of me. Likewise it has spawned a tingle in my belly, a twitch in my hands.

I count to three and slay the seed of this fear. Next is the kraken.

The wind bears me from Suodji's terraced port to war with my chosen quarry. This battle was preordained. Mai's death is what I was forged for. I make no apology for who I am.

So of all things, I am surprised to find myself praying Njda will understand.

CHAPTER NINETEEN

As the crack of Yndrasta's war cry in the storm skies faded, the cannons on Suodji's crags thundered one final song. Light flared within a wall of smoke. A gunner's grizzled shout banished the ringing in Njda's ears. 'Cut the carriages, lads! Roll 'em off the deck!'

Njda prepped an arrow for the unseen orruks scaling the heights. Their piggish squeals echoed as plummeting cannons smashed them from the crags. Njda's brow wrinkled – why were Suodji's defenders ditching their powerful guns?

A shadow resolved from the haze in the snow plain. Ramas and Iaterria shouted across the city's anarchic heights. Fighters threw themselves behind low walls or into Suodji's winding alleys and made ready.

Njda's eyes flickered across the chaotic plateau. '*Valter!*'

Magga hurled her baleen blades' covers and backed towards Njda. 'I'd worry about us.'

A gargant stumbled from the blizzard – a cannibal stallo freak.

Two dim-witted eyes stuffed the sinking grey sockets beneath its caveman brow. A jumble of crooked teeth jutted from its half-moon mouth like cemetery headstones.

The air thrummed as a cloud of arbalest quarrels thudded into the hobgrots thronging on the gargant's shoulders. Grots tumbled and screeched, and crossbows ratcheted as they were cranked and reloaded. '*Make ready!*'

Njda strummed her bowstring. Her arrow lanced into the gargant's crusty eye. The brute moaned, and its eyelid thudded shut. Its massive fingers crashed into Suodji's bluffs; stone screamed as the city's edge crumbled. All Suodji seemed to lean with the gargant's weight.

Gibbering hobgrots skipped and scuttled from the giant's arms onto the cliffside. Magga and the takers forged a loose skirmish line, then thrashed the snivelling grot-kin as peasants might scythe down grass. Njda loosed arrow after arrow, ten for every arbalest's bolt, until her quiver emptied. She snapped the arrows from Magga's belt and tossed them to her feet.

The gargant snatched a silent taker from the city's heights. Stoically, the taker hacked at its filthy thumb until she was tossed into its dark gorge. The cloying reek that rose from the stallo's throat made Njda retch.

Ramas hurled a lance. Without waiting to see if he'd hit his mark, he hurdled a low-hanging wall and two dying men. He leapt into the creature's putrid mouth. His hide boots stamped into the gargant's mossy tongue, and the taker slid down the monster's gullet into foetid darkness. His blade fronds dragged bloody gobbets of mucosa from its throat all the way down.

The gargant choked, its spluttering coughs a noisome gale, then keeled into the snow plain. Grots and hobgrots were flung from its shoulders as the realm shook with its fall.

Njda helped dispatch the remaining grot-kin. Iaterria leaned over the cliffside. 'You takers. That was something else.' She gritted her jaw. 'Idiot gargant smashed the orruks on the crags. Let us hope the city's other bluffs should be so lucky.'

Njda narrowed her eyes. Down the length of Suodji's spectacular heights, more titans loomed. Red-eyed orruks with greasy topknots poured up the city's sheer crags.

With a ripping squelch, Magga wrenched her blade from a hobgrot's skull. 'We can't win like this. Where's Yndrasta?'

'Busy,' Njda said bitterly. Beyond Suodji's harbour a storm ravaged Glacier's End. In the fjord below, the packed merchant fleet rolled over the waves. The ships' hulls cracked into each other; the crowded fjord resembled a floating city.

Magga followed Njda's eyes to the covered ballistae. 'I doubt we can hit the gargants from there. The city's in the way.'

Njda gripped Magga's shoulder. 'I was a finder, daughter of a herdsteader. You were a taker.'

'And today, what? We're heroes?'

Njda shook her head. 'Today we slay the gargants, or the city falls.'

The city's last cannonade echoed as Njda and Magga reached the slick stone stairs overlooking the fjord. Wounded takers pleaded for slit-throat comrades drowning in their own blood not to die. Surgeons treated screaming warriors impaled by orruk bolts. Njda launched an arrow up; a dead hobgrot tumbled from a sod roof and its cleavers clattered. An old woman urged her grandchildren indoors and brandished a boat hook as she barred the door shut.

On a landing close to the port's highest tier, Heigen ushered a pack of children up to the Aldermen's Hall. City sentinels lined the stairs that led to the timber palace, spears propped on their kite shields, eyes locked ahead.

'Heigen, here!' Njda slashed her arm in the air. 'Help with the ships' ballistae!'

'Go. Let me do what I couldn't for Ta. I can protect them.'

Magga yanked Njda onward. 'We all have our parts. Come on!'

Heigen shrank behind them, shepherding his charges up the stair. The snow swallowed him, and Njda left.

Deserted esplanades separated each port tier overlooking the fjord. Warehouses, ramshackle hovels and mortared granaries crowded each level. Apish orruks carved through defenders throughout the port sprawl. The battle had bled deep into the city. The port quays and moored merchant fleet lay within shouting distance of the bloodshed.

Ghost crews worked to free their ships and take to sea. Lightning flashed over raging ocean, and a great shadow spidered in the storm. Tjatsår Mai's arrival had spawned cyclones in Glacier's End. A blazing gold meteor stabbed through the storm and screamed.

'The ballistae!' Njda yelled. 'The gargants!'

A bemused breath rippled through each mariner before they leapt into action. A hard-eyed girl pounded beat-to-quarters on a signal drum. Greased tarpaulins were torn from the nearest ballista, and the command spread to the other ships, whose crews soon joined in. Magga and Njda hurtled below decks to shuttle ballistae bolts from the carrack's hold.

In a damp corner between stacked barrels, Valter and Jobial hissed. They fought over a woollen blanket and stabbed their jewel-encrusted fingers at each other.

'Valter!' Njda smiled in relief, then scowled. 'Are you cowering?'

Valter looked up. Jobial ripped the blanket from him and wiggled into the corner, then cast it over his head and whimpered.

Valter's stubbly cheeks blushed. 'Are *you* cowering?'

Magga pushed past with an armful of bolts. Amber fluid sloshed in phials tied to their heads. 'People don't change, Njda. No matter how bad you want them to.' She skewered Valter with a poison look and huffed. 'Let's go. We've gargants to slay.'

Valter's head bent in shame. Njda seized arrows from a chest and trotted after Magga above decks.

On the forecastle, a mariner guided a bolt onto the ballista's track. Another adjusted the cradle, fine-tuning elevation and deflection. 'Good news!' he barked. 'The angle's good to–'

Gore sprayed Njda's face. A savage length of wood had erupted from the gunner's breastplate. The orruk bolt's momentum tossed him over the gunwale. Down the quay, orruks reloaded their own bolt throwers alongside a riot of scuttling hobgrots. They had broken through the port's defences. Blood-red shark eyes sent a nauseous chill through Njda's belly.

'Wilds, damn!' Magga whipped her baleen swords. 'Make this count! I'll hold them off!' She rocked to the gangplank and scowled. 'Get back below decks, you filth. Live, live like you always wanted.'

Valter's rough hands coaxed Njda from the ballista. 'Let me do this. There only need be one of us.'

Njda resisted. 'We'll do it together.'

Valter cranked the ballista's winch. 'I crewed a merchantman before. You've never done this. Go. A dinghy's aft. Tell Suodji the port's lost – they need to hold the heights. Tell them *she's* with them. The daft fools will like hearing that from you.' He cupped his hand over his mouth. '*Mag!* If we make it out of this, you marry me, you understand?'

Magga paced on the quay before the gangplank. A hobgrot came at her; she slashed through its ratty jerkin and kicked the squealing imp into the grey waters. 'No! Are you mad?'

'Yes!' A crimson craze lit up Valter's eyes. '*Yes!*'

Njda's stomach caught in her throat as the dinghy plummeted and smacked the water. She banged her knees and groaned, then rowed between barnacled hulls. Once her creaking boat had cleared the ships' nest into the fjord, Valter's shouts echoed. A volley of bolts whistled into the city's jagged heights. Three lanced into the chest of a towering gargant and exploded. Red flame and black plumes spilled from the wounds. The gargant's death croak thundered as its broken ribcage smouldered. The giant keeled from sight, and the bay's waters rippled after a resounding boom.

A mariner roared out aiming corrections, and the ballistae repeated. Other gargants groaning over the city were taken by the next volleys, or ducked away as their brethren fell.

Valter's pistols cracked, and after thirty seconds, they barked again. Njda held her breath – and again, another pistol cracked. Telltale rage echoed in Magga's frothing scream on the quay. A final pistol shot followed, trailed by silence. Loping orruks and hobgrots flooded the ships' decks. Hunched mariners drew cutlasses as their drum tempo picked up and the battle-lines crashed.

Njda's oars sliced through the water. She pumped her dinghy towards another quay. To brittle ice with Valter's entreaty – she had to send them help. But above, smoke billowed from the palace on the crest. The Aldermen's Hall was aflame. Scattered sentries resisted a horde on the steep approach. More orruks gushed up the bluffs surrounding them.

Njda's shallow breathing filled her ears. The harbour's grey waters lapped against her dinghy's hull, louder than the noise of Suodji's death. Across the city's heights, throughout its tiered port, a heartless wind scattered gouts of oily smoke. A lucky schooner peeled from the floating mass of moored ships, which was now aglow with flame. She collapsed and kicked an oar into the bay. A curse died on her tongue, unspoken. Magga, Valter, Heigen – they would all die. The people of Suodji, too. Her kin.

Njda's shoulders slackened. She finally saw her kinfolk how Yndrasta must have seen them. Even if they had defended Suodji today, would the final hour of their fall not have come? Njda had grown closer to the Sukuat's beautiful cruelty this past month than in the two miserable decades of her life. All became ash – this year, or in ten thousand. That span of time must mean nothing to an immortal.

Still, Yndrasta had tried to help. From the turbulent sea, the huntress' perturbing battle cries echoed. Lightning limned the kraken's terrible mass – the citadel of its bulk, the towers and minarets of its thrashing tentacles. The storm of their combat echoed like the steps of walking mountains. In it, Njda heard a song. Like a fairing, or a mega-orca's musical keen. The aching notes whispered the terrible shape of mortal life. Yndrasta had been mortal, once. She could have been like Njda, no different. *Valters* could have enraged her and made her smile; *Maggas* might have made her rake her hair or giggle. *Heigens* had broken her heart, and *Bavvals* had been strong for her, then frail. Yndrasta's cruelty was no anomaly; it was a well-healed scar, a logical progression. Ten thousand *Suodjis* and *Riika-Mins* had burned before her weary eyes. A thousand *Tjatsår Mais* had died at the jaded end of her smoking spear.

Too, Njda could have been as Yndrasta had been, no different from the million mortals across creation. The *Haris* and *Mas,* the *Gumpers* and *Grambs.* They had all suffered as much as Njda had suffered. For most, there was still hope. What did the puny thread of Njda's existence mean in the marvellous tapestry of creation? If all the gold she had ever known should be lost and forgotten that the kraken might be slain and others preserved, was there not Harmony in that? Was it not *right?*

Njda seized her last oar. The dinghy carved through the choppy waters. A hateful wind and frigid mist knifed through her garments, but the cold gave her iron. She tossed back her pointed hood, let the sea drench her braided plait. The hunger winds screamed, but she didn't heed them. Predators and monsters were all she'd ever known. They had raised Njda, as much as Bavval, or her ma. She was done running from them.

CHAPTER TWENTY

Yndrasta's war with Tjatsår Mai glowed in the storm. Lightning flashed, and an arrowhead mountain thrust from the sea. Wyrms of jointed chitin erupted from its titanic bulk. A glowing orb flitted like a sparrow in the gloom between the tyrant's scaly tentacles. Yndrasta's brilliant spear lanced out, and thunder split the skies.

Waves rolled through the ocean, and Njda held her breath trying to balance herself. A drifting iceberg emerged in the grey breakers ahead, and she rowed closer. Her boat rammed the ice, and she scrambled up the cold crags on hands and knees. Ice stung her bones as Njda reached the crest and squinted, then nocked an arrow. Only Yndrasta could end this, only by slaying Tjatsår Mai.

Lightning flashed, and for one liquid moment, Tjatsår Mai's horrifying hulk burst through the darkness. Her fatty flesh writhed and glistened the colour of drowned men. Barnacle-scabbed chitin encrusted her, and water sluiced down the gnarled plates. Her main arms cracked on their joints as they turned; once those legs had crashed like the fingers of gods into Riika-Min. Soft tentacles uncoiled from slits in their sides like parasitic worms. The lecherous vines thrummed after Yndrasta and turned Njda's stomach.

Beneath the foamy churn, the kraken's dark shape loomed. Her lurking mass reminded Njda of the gargant-eel, a malice forged in hunger. Njda had nearly got herself killed, there. She was doing it again. She could do no good out here. This was beyond her.

Yndrasta's bloody howl pealed through the sky. She cast her spear, and again lightning exploded. Torrents of brine frothed around rings of razored teeth as Mai's maw emerged from the water. A vortex swirled around her – her stomachs could have drained the sea.

In the seams of Mai's mountainous mass, a translucent eyelid slid back like a crocodile's. A veined socket pulsed within. Njda readied her bow, but her feet were stuck. Ice crawled up her boots, onto her trousers. A devourer, same as the colony that had taken Bavval. The feeling left Njda's toes, and she imagined her leaden feet frozen through, like Azyrite marble.

Shivering, Njda twisted and drew her arrow back. Her bowstring creaked with the storm's abuse. To brittle ice with the spirits and gods and her ancestors, to brittle ice with Harmony! Njda prayed to a god who would change things, a god who would *fight* for her. She prayed to Yndrasta, his murderous saint.

Her bowstring slapped her cheek, and her arrow flew into the storm. A gust carried the dart home as verglas crackled on Njda's waist and shackled her.

The kraken's roar crushed Njda like a horn of apocalypse. A deafening baritone shook the snow and mist in the air, and warm fluid trickled from her ears. At the iceberg's base, mindless thralls seethed from the waves. The ravenous ice devoured them, and others piled over their frozen friends. The corded mass of Tjatsår Mai's enslaver tentacles writhed in the water like eels.

Yndrasta's vicious ululations split the skies. A flaming meteor plunged and dragged a sword of starlight across the thralls' tentacles. White fire raked the iceberg's base, and the revenants toppled into the sea as Thengavar struck in a hundred lightning strikes at once.

In the storm, before the kraken could react – before she could *scream*, from *fear* – Yndrasta cocked her arm and hurled her howling spear. Gore weltered from the kraken's horrific eye, and Yndrasta's laughter boomed like thunder. She pounced through the sea spray onto the kraken's mountainous bulk, and her momentum dragged the kraken in its vortex.

With bare fingers, Yndrasta ripped red trenches into Mai's flesh. Bilious gore erupted where she gripped the kraken's tentacles and twisted until the joints broke. The more blood drenched the saint, the brighter she grew, as if slaughter fuelled the dread fire of her hunger. As Yndrasta batted Mai's helpless tentacles aside, a snarl warped the blank marble of her face – wicked pleasure arched her brow, a frothing grimace split her lips, rapture peeled open her eyes. A lion's growl clicked in Yndrasta's chest, more head-splitting than the beast moon's roar when it was full.

The kraken-god's furious horn decayed into a morbid croak. Like a digging dog, Yndrasta gouged out handfuls of fell flesh. Blood dripped from each gobbet, reddening her teeth and brightening the moonlight of her plate.

Tjatsår Mai's death throes tossed the sea like a hurricane. The iceberg rocked beneath Njda as spuming grey waters swallowed the saint and her quarry. Njda's neck stiffened, and sensation bled from her cheeks. The devourer iceberg calved, and unnatural warmth migrated down her legs. The cold was killing her. As the iceberg capsized, torrents of ocean burbled. Mai's horrid mass dissolved into aphotic blackness below. For one heartbeat, the starfire that punished the kraken's carcass glared up in vicious gratitude. Those eyes were unfeeling. Those eyes were *alive*.

Njda reached out in the gelid waters. Behind her eyelids, she saw the huntress in the doorway one final time. Death gripped the edges of her soul, and bitter satisfaction spidered in her skull. She wouldn't drown. The water couldn't fill her lungs, because she had already stopped breathing.

CHAPTER TWENTY-ONE

'Never heard of anyone surviving devourer ice,' a man said, in a gravel monotone Njda knew. 'Never heard of anyone surviving a leap down a gargant's gullet either. I guess we're both miracles.'

Njda's eyelids slid open. A Suku taker with bowl-cut hair and a burnt brow stared at her. Gore and dried mucus caked the links in his mail hauberk.

'Ramas?' Njda's voice cracked from disuse. 'You look like reindeer pie.'

'You should see the gargant.' Ramas lifted his bandaged hand. 'Broke my wrist and swords cutting myself free.'

Glistering spires clawed into the crystal sky over a far port. Njda had seen those towers from afar, but this was the first time she'd been so close. Izalend, the city of Sigmar. A great ring of fire glistened in the distance.

She sat up, rubbed her eyes. A hangover thudded in her skull. Furs were piled on her shoulders. The raised flap of a hide tent was staked up around a crackling fire. Shivering Suku refugees filled a scattered camp. Reindeer pawed at the ground and snorted. They must have been in the snow tracts between Izalend and Skythane. The Gryphspine Mountains clawed up over a wedge of far-off green, where the green kings of Druichan Forest held their jealous reign.

Painted longsleds and sledcrofts towered over the closest tents. Survivors, from Tjatsår Mai's first attack – Njda would have known those sleds anywhere. In the meadows beyond, green from an early thaw, a great herd of reindeer spiralled in trampling circles, driven by Suku with switches and playful, panting dogs. The herd's pounding shook the taiga's loam and vibrated up Njda's bones.

Suodji flooded back to her. The flames, the smoke, the cracks of Valter's pistols, Magga's farewell scream. The waves' grey tumult, and the hideous kraken sinking beneath them. Yndrasta's blood-stricken eyes, stretched open in vicious pleasure. Her gauntlets flashed as she ripped into Tjatsår Mai and howled the secret names of annihilation.

Njda gripped her temples. 'Suodji.'

'Fallen, but its people live. Iaterria died holding the orruks off. On the sixth day, two aldermen returned from Izalend with reinforcements. A wolf-fleet, and a host of Freeguilds. They say even the junk fleets cleared the way for them. Even greenskins hold grudges, it seems. The *cruel-boys* are gone.'

'Magga?' Njda blinked. 'Valter? Heigen?'

Ramas lowered his eyes. 'Many lived. But not them.'

Njda exhaled. She tried to make sense of that.

'Njda?'

A hunched, willowy man with laughter lines sprouting from his eyes shuffled closer. Behind him, Wulf limped on his peg leg, and a tired smile graced his lips. Freid and Varga milled behind him, and little Millie. Njda's heart stopped when she realised that was all that remained of her family. Five survivors from her siida, and herself.

She shrugged off her furs and stumbled into the patchy snow. She looped an arm around her pa's neck, and Wulf's. She squeezed as hard as she could, then exhaled from exhaustion.

'Njda. I didn't think you'd made it.' Her pa patted her back, his tears damp on her neck. 'I thought...'

A sob robbed him of his words, and Njda's shoulders pulsed as she wept with him. Their remaining family piled into their embrace. So much death, for so hard a life. Njda's ma rotted on a mountainside. Bavval's ashes lay crushed beneath the monument that was raised for him. Heigen, Magga and Valter. Hari, and Gramb – *yes*, Gramb too. So many hundreds more. So many thousands. Gone, wherever the dead sang their fairings. And Yndrasta, wherever triumph and sated bloodlust had taken her.

Njda's memories with her friends flashed behind her eyes, too many to stop. They washed away the horrible memories of Yndrasta in the doorway, of red-eyed orruks looming in the fog. All the hard times, the good and bad. The bitter love she'd shared with them, and the hurt. Njda carried them alone now, in the caged cradle of her heart. And what hurt most was knowing that once their absences had healed, she would only be stronger.

POSTLUDE

SAINT

There is a story in Izalend, of a girl who helped Sigmar's huntress in her moment of need.

After the battle at Suodji, Tjatsår Mai's eviscerated corpse was found bobbing in distant ocean. Gulls pecked at its flesh, and plate-toothed sharks ripped chunks from its shredded carcass. In the place where the beast's horrific eye had been, only a crater of flesh remained, carved out as if with a sword, perhaps as a trophy.

The divine huntress who had slain the kraken was not seen again, but the girl who had helped her was found half-frozen to death on a dead devourer iceberg in the harbour. Witnesses claimed they had seen the mighty vargr drag her from the grey waters, then shed its own pelt to keep her warm. The mythic wolf, skinless and silver, disappeared afterwards. If not for the beast's peculiar compassion, the girl would have died. So the story went.

In an Izalend cloister, beside a fire stoked by priests, the girl told her story. Monks with quills crafted from the hollowed spines of wolf-walruses recorded her tremulous words in unerring script.

Blind nuns illuminated this heavy tome before they enshrined it within Izalend's cathedral. Njda's ragged clothing and the bow she had used to assist Sigmar's saint were set in glass reliquaries to be displayed once a year on the huntress' new feasting day.

So ended the story of the maiden, slayer and beast, and another began. Decades passed, and portents of a new monster haunted Glacier's End. Not Tjatsår Mai, but one of her brood – a lesser kraken that had grown cunning and strong enthralling the last remnants of the now extinct Kruleboyz of the Sukuat.

This fell monster, they said, was worse than its mother. Malicious and spiteful, with a thirst for vengeance only Izalend's destruction could slake. A new Drownharrow loomed. The Suku, now guardians of the sanctuary snows within the Everflame's boundaries, knew the beast must be slain.

On the darkest night, Njda of Riika-Min, greatest of her people's noajdi, invoked a potent rite. She cast powdered amberbone cut with the crushed essence of Azyrite celestium into a seeing fire. She inhaled the vapours and pounded on a ritual drum, then burned an ancient token gifted from an ancient friend. The bonefire's roaring flames flared blinding white, like starfire. Alone among the Izalenders and Suku present, ancient Njda looked into the flames and whispered a name.

Yndrasta, huntress. We need you, now. We need you again.

As the shamaness beseeched the huntress' assistance, the sad glint in her rheumy eyes betrayed the truth: she did not know if the huntress would come.

But in the hardened metal of her soul, in the furnace of her hope, she knew I would always do what was right.

Her face stares at me through the flames. A wizened woman whose wrinkles remind me of the canyons rippling through the Ghurish heartlands when seen from many leagues above.

Her back is bent with age, and her memory teases at the edges of my mind.

The crash of sigmarite warplate upon stone tells me Arktaris Soul-Tithed kneels beside me. 'My lady huntress,' the Lord-Celestant intones after a breath of pause. 'Dharth and his Broken Blood Annihilators are destroyed. Our allies among the Hallowed Knights hunt down their mortal servants, to redeem those they can.'

'Yet the sorceress escaped.' I clasp my hands. The metal in my gauntlets squeaks. 'Will you purge them?'

'Those who resist.' Arktaris breathes deeply. 'I must thank you, my lady huntress. Your assistance was instrumental. Dharth was a glorious kill but no substitute for the sorceress or her secrets. My chamber stands ready to resume your hunt for Doombreed's shards.'

We are in Wrothquake Valley, a landscape I hardly recognise. The pulverised flesh of the great worms Doombreed slaughtered have petrified into shattered stone hills. Water has filled the dead daemon king's footprints into lakes. Lush forest carpets the valley, peppered with mysterious duardin statues which stand eternal vigil.

Arktaris' armour creaks as he glances to the burning tree. Smoke and flame billow from a knot in its trunk. 'What do you see in the flames?'

'Sigmar's faithful. They are in dire need.'

'As they ever are.' Arktaris rises and salutes, his heavy white gauntlet clanging against his breastplate. 'Speak the word. We shall follow. The Ruthless Tithe awaits your command.'

As the Lord-Celestant departs, I return my gaze to the face of winter's woman in the scrying flames. She must know my soul-fire deeply, to reach out from as far as Izalend. She must sense the very substance of my being. I can continue my fruitless quest for Doombreed's shards and see duty done, or return to Izalend to slaughter Tjatsår Mai's heir and offer those mortals the succour they seek.

I recall my God-King's command at the moment of my first rebirth. Then I accept Thengavar's whickering metal into my hands and rise. My gaze falls to the naked sigmarite vambrace upon my wrist, a force of habit I cannot explain. A story is there – a story I cannot recall.

But what are stories? Only the echoes of ancient deeds. Compared to those who stand above us, below us, beside us, stories are nothing. Fool I was, to once think that in the woe-times, mortals looked to their stories for solace.

They look to each other. And I look to them.

'Arktaris,' I say. 'Prepare your chamber.'

ABOUT THE AUTHOR

Noah Van Nguyen is a freelance writer who lives in the U.S. with his wife. His tales set in the Mortal Realms include the novels *Godeater's Son* and *Yndrasta: The Celestial Spear* and the novella *Nadir* from the Warhammer Underworlds anthology *Harrowdeep*. He has also written several stories set in the grim darkness of the 41st millennium, including 'The Last Crucible', and the Warhammer Crime stories 'No Third Chance' and 'Carrion Call'. When he's not writing, Noah enjoys studying foreign languages and exploring far-off lands.

YOUR
NEXT READ

GODEATER'S SON
by Noah Van Nguyen

Heldanarr Fall just wants to be left in peace in Aqshy, but the gleaming golden warriors of Sigmar won't let him be. So he fights back – and draws upon a more primal power…

An extract from
Godeater's Son
by Noah Van Nguyen

Sometimes, when I look out over my world, I want it to end.

This time, the shadow of a sailing mountain drew my cold eyes to the burning flats. In its shade a woman staggered, her patent screams drifting up the way mirages do.

My spite warred with my pity. My soul groaned from the weight of my false indifference. Because I couldn't not care. This was a priestess of Sigmar. Her Azyrite shrieks betrayed her, as did her ragged raiment and the worthless relics she carried.

The human in me wanted to help. Everything else screamed not to. Whatever the Azyrites claimed, they'd made beggars of us all. And I had not come here to save anybody. My conscience commanded me only to my sister's word.

My eyes traced the priestess' discarded baggage. Along that dotted thread, three figures gave chase. They were microscopic in the distance, yet lean and strong, accustomed to Aqshy's heat. I saw it in their lanky swagger. I felt it in the glimmer of their sand-iron.

They were warborn of the Ushara, one of the Beltoll tribes. Centuries ago the Beltollers had submitted to Cardand and Bharat: the empires of my mothers and fathers, ruled by the great Yrdun houses and clans. That was a time of balance. Of restraint.

But this was the Age of Sigmar, and the old balance was gone. The Azyrites had destroyed the old order for the sake of their own. We were their prey, now. We were each other's.

So I didn't move. Let the priestess revel in the fires her people had kindled. Her tiny figure, swathed in bright clothes, stumbled. If her pursuers didn't claim her, exhaustion would. If not that, then thirst.

If I didn't help her, she would die.

And Varry would be disappointed.

My jaw hardened. I gulped a lungful of hot air. All I'd ever wanted was to make Varry happy. I'd seen her joy in guarded moments, in the dead of night. Twinkling in her smile, fading like cinderflies. But her joy was so rare. She took care of me, and I knew the toll those efforts extracted.

Always tired, Varry. Always bleak and forlorn. If I helped the priestess, I might see Varry smile. Something in that pleased me. Something covetous, something earnest. Most of all, something true.

Were this priestess sitting in my place, on the lee of this ridge – and were I in her place, in the shadow of leering mountains – she would not have helped me. Azyrites took everything and gave nothing in return. They'd never helped us. Not when we were rag-thin and roaming, nor when we built our home on the broken hill, digging our well into the rock until our hands bled.

But the Azyrites had never had what I had. Varry was all I lived for, the only mortal in blazing creation I would have died for.

Killing a handful of warborn for her would be nothing, nothing at all.

* * *

Dust billowed in the Ushara's tracks. The nomads' coal-black flesh gleamed beneath their Idoneth-dyed shawls, which whipped in the wind. The Ushara resembled serpent-dancers in Cardand's night markets. Those dancers would gyrate like spinning tops, then plunge and roll to their feet. The warborn's movements were similar, economic but showy. But when they fought they would be savage and merciless.

The priestess scrambled through the brimstone sands. She huffed prayers for protection to her god who didn't care, who didn't listen. She clutched a handful of precious jewel boxes in quill-thin fingers and ebony hands.

'Please,' she rasped. Her plea went unheeded, gobbled by the sounds of her scrabbling.

As I watched, I sneered. The priestess was a mewling child in the manicured flesh of a woman whose life had known only privilege. I loathed her – but it was not for her I had come.

Rising, I drew my javelin. Yolk-yellow sands dusted from my arms in sheets as I quit my concealment.

The warborn halted. *'Yrdunko!'* one barked.

I whipped my arm forward. The javelin flew. My throwing thong slapped my wrist as the lead-weighted shaft speared the closest nomad's eye. He snapped down headlong, blood misting the space where he had stood, then blossoming into a pool around him.

I drew my long dirks, both Hammerhal-forged. They were gifts from Jujjar, an old friend. Before this I had only appreciated their utility in cutting cord or slitting the throats of rustled cattle. Never in battle.

Immediately the nomads were upon me. The two remaining warborn expended as little energy as possible, exposing themselves not at all, cautious the way predators are. I fended off probing strikes. The Ushara's serpentine fighting style was lethal, not a display I'd ever hoped to witness at blade's length. At least, not without a rank of Yrdun Ashstalkers beside me.

Those days were gone. But before our Freeguild Ashstalkers had been disbanded, we had trained against warborn mercenaries. I knew this foe. The Ushara fought high and far, lofty in body and spirit, so I stayed low and tight.

They circled, thrusting their sand-iron, their falchions clanging off my dirks. If they attacked from both sides, they'd finish this. I had to stay calm, maintain control.

Then tremors ran beneath my feet. My eyes flickered down. A lavamander tunnelled through earthfire beneath the sands, sacred and massive and precious. Just what I hunted for – just when I wanted it least.

The second nomad barked and struck. Impulse had mastered her sense. She spent herself in a wild flurry, and when the time was right, I lashed out and swept my feet. She toppled; I finished her with a perfunctory thrust.

Sweat ran down my tarred brow. I had to focus on the third warborn, but fighting as a lavamander migrated only made this harder. Its moving mass shivered up my bones. The beasts were as quickly lost as they were found. To have followed this one's movement now would mean losing sight of my foe. Even for a moment, distraction meant death.

Control. All I needed was control.

He thrashed forward. I parried a frenzy of blows from his sand-iron falchion, until a dirk slipped my grip. Survival in the Ashwilds required endurance, agility, tenacity. This foe possessed all three, in greater abundance than I. But rage ran in his veins like a curse. Fury had robbed him of reason. His breathing warbled as he panted hoarse oaths for the lives I had stolen. He had not mastered Aqshy's heat; it had mastered him.

He was off balance, out of control. I could best him like that.

I feinted, then disarmed him. He gritted his teeth and shoved through my guard, tackling me.

Our blades thumped to the sand. His lithe fingers locked around my throat. With iron strength, his eyes cobalt fire, he squeezed the life from me.

I couldn't breathe, couldn't prise his stone hands from my neck. The world went red, then silver at the edges. I groped through hot sand until my fingers grazed a dirk's edge. I seized the blade. Pain sang in my hand as its edge sliced through my palm and fingers. I jolted the dirk into the warborn's arm, then twisted until sinews crunched.

He screamed, spraying me with spittle, drenching us both in blood. He crumbled and nursed his mangled arm.

I shuddered at the sight of his suffering. I would have closed my eyes if I dared. I finished him kindly, quickly. Not with pride, nor vim – just a breed of patience and remorse.

I sputtered, clearing the beetle in my throat, the throbbing in my head. Sand moistened by blood had infiltrated my wraps. This gory clay abraded my flesh and painted me rust. The stench of death hung in the air.

The mountains passing overhead reminded me where I was, and I scanned for more opponents. No Beltollers remained – only I and the mewling priestess, her eyes willow-green. Her thirst-gnarled lips hung awry, like the fixed rictus of my father's death mask, a grimace that could frighten the dead.

The priestess hissed, half-mad. 'Boy! Where did you come from?'

I raised a bleeding finger to my lips, then tucked my dirks into my sash. I padded after the tremors I had sensed. Here and there I paused to listen, holding my breath. Aqshy's heat ebbed into my heels, running up my bones. My blood was hot; I fought to make it cool.

Then, beneath a shifting blur of heat, fissures split the earth. An animal's coal-rough muzzle pushed up from beneath the ash-stricken sand. The lavamander.

I went prone as the black behemoth emerged. Ranks of thick legs carried its char-scabbed trunk from the ground, shedding crumbs of earthfire like slag. The blind creature sniffed the air, and I dared not breathe. The cracks in its tough hide glowed orange with the heat of its blood, which boiled mine.

A male, a juvenile. He bleated, then groaned. His call was all bass and glottalisation, like a knotted cord pulled through my head. He dragged his outsize mass onwards, seeking out a fresh vein of magma. The lavamander nosed into the hard earth and burrowed the way dogs play in sand.

I hugged the ground, still not breathing. When the earthen crush had ceased, I lifted my head. He was gone.

Varry had once told me our father uttered special words for lavamanders. Invocations to Sigmar, the god he worshipped, in Yrdo, the tongue of our people. In the past I thought that seemed right and well. But all things seem right to children.

I tugged a scrap of fire-resistant hide from my carrying sash and clambered into the cooling crater the lavamander had left behind. Magnure resembled crackling embers, smouldering and snapping with forever heat. Even through the enchanted hide it seared my hands and roused my heart. I kept the ice in me cold, counting my breaths, fighting the scalding heat with everything I had.

I wrapped the magnure, sashed it, then emerged from the crater.

'What was that?' the priestess croaked.

I regarded her. A priestess of Sigmar, yes, but not one of *those* priests. No shaven scalp, no scar-stitched face. No platemail or hammer or storm-swell voice, holy books chained to her war-heart breast. I glanced along the trail of treasures she had dropped during her flight. The warborn must have thought her a gift from the gods; perhaps she thought as much herself. To have carried so much so far, she must have been strong. But I couldn't understand why she'd bothered.

'You come from Capilaria,' I said, in the Azyrite tongue. 'From that damn city, Hammerhal.'

She furrowed her brow. 'Yes, yes. That damn city. My damn city, damn you!'

I stared.

'Are you alone?' she asked. 'I don't care if you are, but please say you aren't. You're from Candip? You must be. Where are your spears? Your vassals? Or… your liege?'

My eyes wrinkled. 'What's a liege?'

She huffed. 'What's a liege… Well, yes. At least I'm alive. There's always that.'

I followed her gaze into the wastes, where ash danced over blistered sands.

'We brought something,' she murmured absently. '*Izmenili* of Chamon. Precious gems. Gems… shiny rocks.' She made shapes with her hands, as if to qualify the shininess of rocks. 'You'll need to go back for them with whomever's accompanied you. It's too dangerous to go alone. Beastkin overtook us at dusk. They killed my party, tore them apart.' She shuddered. 'They'll be back. Won't they? Or… perhaps you *can* go alone?'

I planted my foot on an Ushara's skull. Brains squelched as I yanked my javelin free. 'They'll be back. Eventide. Just wait.' I wiped the javelin clean, checked its shaft for cracks. 'How'd you survive?'

She exhaled. 'I don't know. Hiding beneath the wagons. I ran when I could, but they chased. Damned things they are, but they're vicious. I ran and ran through the night. Somewhy, they gave me up at dawn. Then, those…' She glanced at the corpses around us. 'Them. They came.'

'Ushara. Warborn.'

'Yes. Them.' She peered at the jewel boxes in her arms, as if all her suffering were nothing compared to their value. She held at least a dozen. More were tied into her clothes.

Then she sighed. 'I shall wait here, beneath the metaliths' shade. The flying mountain, metaliths are flying mountains. Bring water when you can. You know these lands? Look at you, of course you do. You'll have no problem, you and whomever you've brought. Yes? So. What're you waiting for? Go on.'

I peered at the ridgeline. Part of me had hoped Varry would see all this. I had saved this woman for my sister, not for charity. The priestess was not some motherless infant I would elevate to adulthood and teach my ways. She was a grown woman, strong enough to carry many things, then drop them. Thanks to me, she was still alive. She required nothing else.

The priestess grimaced. I thought she saw me for the first time, then. The flesh of my face like a nightmare's, painted in sun-daub tar mixed from stolen scrivener's ink and crushed charcoal. My matted, unbound hair. The heat shawl and wrappings I had drenched in blood to save her life, already crusty and scabbed.

Or...

Did she see a man? A mortal like her, with mortal wants and mortal needs? I had dreams, once. As she must have had – as all children had. Once my eyes were delinquent with wishes. As a child, I had possessed hope and faith.

But I don't think she saw any of that.

'You're not going to help,' she said.

I pointed to the wasteland horizon. 'The beasts are Smoulder-hooves. They move when Hysh sinks below the hills and the sky's fires dim.' Then I pointed to the ridge. More drifting mountains – more metaliths – peppered the sky beyond. 'Smoulderhooves are scarce beyond these bluffs. That way lies the Burning Valley, Cardand. And within it, Candip.' I hawked, spat. 'Your city.'

She grew flustered. 'I need help, not waypoints. I need *your* help. I need the other Izmenili.'

I palmed sand over my hand until my cuts clotted, then brushed the dried filth off. 'I did help.'

'The warborn? That was *duty*, not help. We're both children of Sigmar. *Kindred*.'

I chuckled. 'You're no kin of mine.'

She narrowed her eyes. 'What's wrong with you? Why this indecency?'

Enough was enough. My head pounded, my blood blazed, and the magnure's heat burned in my veins like a hillfire. I sipped from my waterskin and departed.

Her feet crunched into the sand behind me. 'You ingrate. You animal! You're an ashfoot, aren't you? A Paler, an Yrdun native. I've heard of you Yrdun. Miscreants and reprobates, charging extra for those who speak Sigmar's tongue! After all we did for you! After everything we *gave* you!'

Ashfoot. My shoulders tensed, but I walked on. Perhaps I need not share the events of this day with Varry.

'We raised aqueducts in Candip!' the priestess said. 'We walled your city, our armies patrol its reaches! We contain foes who would ravage your lands, you know that? *Ra-vage!* You'd be gheists but for us. You'd be thralls to the Dark Gods! This is how you repay us?'

I stopped and turned. 'Repay who?'

'Us! The God-King!'

My finger jolted out at her. 'You did nothing when the beasts came for my family. Nothing when me and my sister were alone, except hire us to fight your wars. I'm not thankful for *nothing*. I don't repay *nothing*.'

'Civilising the Reclaimed is not nothing!'

I marched onwards. 'Hail Sigmar.'

Blissful quiet followed, broken only by the rustle of wind. Then, a sizzling reached my ears. The air suddenly stank of brimstone and baking pottery.

I glowered and turned. The priestess made the old signs with her fragile fingers, trying to cast some spell. Cuneiform runes perforated the air, disturbing to behold for long.

'Put your hands down.' When she didn't, I drew a dirk and lurched out. 'I said, *put them down*.'

The priestess blanched, her skin going the shade of dusk. Her fingers danced faster. But she tugged the wrong threads of magic, and her sleeves ignited. The rune's cinders caught aflame. Her eyes widened.

I ducked just as the spell exploded. Heat washed across me. Then I straightened and stormed over, swatting away the embers of magic. I seized the coughing priestess by her ragged raiment collar – she stank of sickly perfume. I hurled her down, then pushed my blade to her neck to silence her puling.

Breathless with terror and forceless indignation, she spoke. 'What are you doing?'

I twitched, my knuckles digging into her soft neck. Soft, from a soft life of creams and silk and touching soft things. To a creature so soft, I must be jagged and ungiving.

Then the thought struck me. She thought *I* was the bad one.

For a moment, I wondered what she might have thought if we had met in Candip and not here. In the crevasse-city her people had stolen from mine, sitting on one of her priesthood's heavy palanquins as it was borne upon the stooped shoulders of my impoverished kindred. Men like Jujjar, or women like Varry. Varry believed the Azyrites deserved reverence for the salvation they brought to Bodshe. *Salvation.*